Light Weaver

Carol Anne Strange

RED ARC

First published in Great Britain 2012
by Strange Publications (UK)
An imprint of RED ARC

ISBN 1-899561-04-8
ISBN 978-1-899561-04-9

Book cover design and map illustration by Richard Crookes.

A CIP catalogue record for this book is available from the
British Library

This book is a work of fiction in this earthly dimension.
Some of the locations are real and some are fictitious. All
characters in this publication are a product of the author's
imagination. Any resemblance to real persons or entities,
living or passed over, is purely coincidental.

Dedicated to
The Lone Wolf

A dream you dream alone is
only a dream. A dream you
dream together is reality.
– John Lennon

Reality is merely an illusion,
albeit a very persistent one.
– Albert Einstein

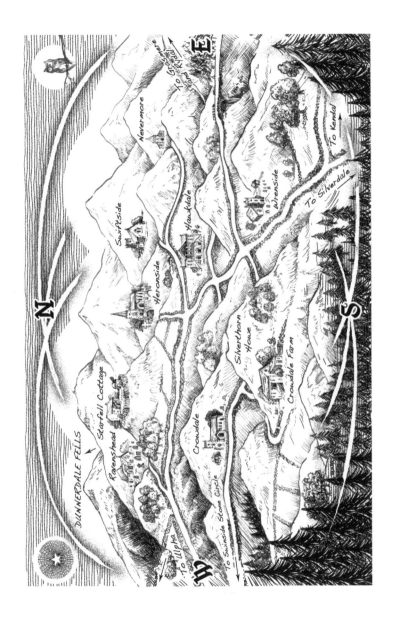

'The conduit is open.'

Prologue

PROFESSOR TRISTIAN NEEBLE'S DIARY

25 January

And so it begins, and I'm not sure whether I'm privy to the most amazing possibility or the most terrible burden. All these years as a theoretical physicist, I lived in hope of some revelation, but nothing could have prepared me for this.

Knowing what I now know has answered the most fundamental questions in physics and yet has raised a thousand more. That's a good thing for a scientist. If I'm honest, though, I'm deeply fearful for the future of humanity, fearful of what some with power and influence might do with this knowledge. And I'm afraid for Tom and Cali.

I could walk away, deny everything, and try to forget what I have seen, but that would go against everything I have ever worked for or believed. My loyalty to scientific discovery means walking away isn't an option. Somehow, I hope they'll understand.

SOME KIND OF BEGINNING

'Question your eyes; there are other worlds within yours that you do not see.'

Seeing a naked woman on the Lakeland fells wasn't a common sight, and certainly not before the last of the daffodils. What's the saying, 'never cast a clout until May is out'? Well, she had cast more than her outer garments, and I was sure my eyes weren't deceiving me.

I lightened my foot off the accelerator and looked beyond the mossy wall to where a copse of hawthorn idled in the sun. There she was, dancing. And she really was naked. She trailed a blue scarf as she skipped and twirled obliviously, charmingly, a slender waif, coal-black hair and all pale honey. I checked the road and slowed the vehicle to a crawl so that I could take a better look. Her wildness, her spirited dance, her audacity left me strangely breathless. I followed her movement, almost hypnotically, as she weaved around each tangled tree. Trance-like, she skipped into a hazy beam of light. The air glimmered for a second like shards of fragmented glass suspended in sunshine – and then something very odd happened. Something very odd indeed! She vanished. She completely disappeared right before my eyes. I stared into the field, blinked, and stared again. What had happened? Where had she gone?

A sudden jolt catapulted me sideways. The mobile library lurched and bumped and juddered as the tyres lost contact with the road. I steered but it was too late. I missed the ditch by a fraction, clipping a hedgerow, and the vehicle shuddered to a halt in an abandoned pasture. I re-started the engine and eased the vehicle into reverse but the wheels spun, sucked into the field's dark muddy ruts. I was stuck. Here I was, newbie to the job, and already in danger of hearing my boss say, 'Tom Philips, you're fired.' I turned off the ignition and fumbled in my coat pocket for my mobile phone. I didn't relish the prospect of having to ask for help, though. I kicked the door panel in frustration as I made my rescue call.

While I waited, I sat in the day's stillness, wondering whom I'd just seen. What kind of a woman danced naked on the fells and disappeared like a magician's assistant, causing me to run off-road in the process? I sank my face into my palms. A crow settled upon a weathered gatepost, feathers oily-black beneath the climbing sun. It glared at me curiously, and then cawed in a mocking tone. 'You can laugh, you scrawny bird!' I shouted. It flapped its wings with a great flourish and took to the sky, circling a couple of times, before disappearing into the woods.

∞∞∞∞∞∞∞∞

*'Life is an illusion. You are the dreamer and
the dream.'*

It's not easy driving a mobile library on the steep inclines
and narrow passages of the Lakeland fells. You need to
know the roads for this job, especially on those frequent foggy
days when the sky's caved in and lost sheep roamed. You'd
think that having lived at least eighteen of my thirty years
perched on the side of one of these unforgiving fells would
give me an advantage but, as I'd demonstrated, there wasn't
much room for error. One moment of poor judgement and you
could end up in a ditch or, worse, careering off the fell-side
into an uncertain predicament or, in my case, stuck in the mud.

A tow-rope snaked from the front of the mobile library to
the back of my brother's tractor. The tractor slowly rolled
forwards, the cable snapped to life, and the library lurched.
My chin banged against the steering wheel and I bit my
tongue. Slowly, the library freed itself from the rutted loam
into which it had sunk half a wheel deep. Pete looked over the
back of his tractor at the cable, at the library, and at me. I did
my best to avoid his eyes. He's shaped to that tractor, born to
it. He had Dad's ox-like back and shoulders and even the same
straggly hairline.

The tractor laboured but slowly released the mobile

library from its muddy confines. We parked up on the road-side. I knew questions would follow.

'How the hell did you manage that, Tom?' Pete released the tow-rope then stared at the straight road in front and behind us, the lines of his forehead creased. 'You weren't reading at the wheel again, were you?'

He gave me a knowing look and I was eleven again, helping Dad plough the bottom field, so engrossed in Orwell's *Nineteen Eighty-Four* that I misjudged the turn, and plunged the tractor into the stinking ditch. That little episode had cost me a whole year's pocket money, and a lifetime's worth of family jibes.

'Well, Pete...' I paused, wondering if I should be economical with the truth. 'I was distracted by something in the field over there.'

Pete eyed me suspiciously, and then laughed, 'Distracted, hey? What was it, a pink giraffe?'

He patted me on the back with his large land-worn hand, and stared at the field. 'You'll be telling me you've seen a bevy of naked dancers next.'

'Well, actually...' I started, slightly flummoxed by how close he was to the truth, but he was already stepping up on the tractor, ready to leave. I decided it was better not to say anything.

'Got to get back to the farm, bro. You owe me a drink later.'

The tractor gurgled and off he went, without a backward glance. I realised I was a good hour late. It wasn't a great way to start the week, nor worth stressing about. As long as the Hawkdale locals received their regular fix of printed or digi-tised entertainment, that's all that mattered. I relaxed, happy to be travelling on, with the lake gleaming silver in the distance, and fells feathering the horizon in such a way that you couldn't be sure if they were real or imagined. The air in the van was filled with the evocative aroma of books, new print mingling with ageing, well-thumbed pages. As for the naked woman doing her disappearing trick, I guessed the circus must have been in town. Maybe she'd show up again later. Yes, maybe she would.

∞∞∞∞∞∞∞∞∞

'The weft of the universe is so finely woven.'

I drove on towards Hawkdale, pre-occupied with the naked woman. Was it possible I'd imagined her? I scoffed at the thought, and also ruled out ghosts and all that paranormal weirdness. As for hallucinations, even with the best attempts at chasing a high in my undergraduate days, I had never experienced anything remotely unusual, whereas my doped-up peers said they encountered giant bananas with legs and other such craziness. Besides, all I had consumed this morning, after the obligatory coffee, was a cup of Yorkshire tea and poached egg on toast – hardly mind-altering stuff. No, it had to be a trick of the light.

The stone marker read 'Hawkdale – 2 miles' and the familiar grey church spire rose out of the green-felted fells. The landscape flattened a little here but the hedgerow-flanked roads twisted, meandering through lowland pastures divided by crumbling stone walls. Generations of my family's sweat and blood had shaped the landscape around here; we were part of the very fabric of this place. I often imagined my father's ancestors chiding me for not continuing the family profession. My father and brother were farmers through and through, their veins threaded into the rich earth. They worked the land as those before us. It was me who didn't fit in. My mind was too busy and my hands too soft for farming. That's what my mother said. I supposedly took after her side of the family: she had a doctorate in plant biology and was the grand-daughter of an Oxford graduate. I had a literature PhD and a fondness for the Romantic poets, but it hadn't materialised into the richly paid job I'd blindly anticipated. And my father wasn't altogether happy about it. 'A PhD... a PhD... and he's driving a mobile library!' At least I was working with books, albeit only as a conduit between bookshelf and reader. And it suited me for now, until something more appealing came along.

I steered the van, whistling a tune, gingerly negotiating the thin roads. As I turned into the next bend, something caught my eye: a pair of legs jutting out of the hedgerow at an awkward angle. 'What on Earth?' I swerved sharply, narrowly avoiding yet another unscheduled off-road excursion. I pulled up, letting the engine idle, and peered through the passenger-side wing mirror. An old lady was reclined in a deckchair on the narrow grass verge. For the second time today, I questioned my eyes. I switched the engine off and glanced round. There was no bus shelter here. No sign of a car. No sign of anyone else with her. She was in the middle of nowhere, basking in the morning glow as if she were sat on Blackpool's Golden Mile. I stepped off the van, filled with curiosity.

'Hello there. Are you okay?'

'Perfectly, young man, thank you,' she replied, squinting over her spectacles. 'Are you?'

'Aye, I am, thanks. I'm on my way into Hawkdale with the mobile library–'

'Thursdays!' she interrupted.

'Sorry?'

'The last chap doing your job used to turn up on Thursdays. They're always changing things. Why can't they stick to routine? It means I have to change my arrangements, which is so inconvenient.'

'Oh, I see. Yeah, I'm afraid it's Mondays now. Sorry.'

She was wearing a long mud-coloured waterproof coat, covering country tweeds. Silver threads of hair, glinting in the sunshine, escaped from beneath her trilby. She had an air of authority about her. In fact, if she were at a country fair, she'd be one of the officials in the show pony classes or even top judge in the jam-making competition. A pair of binoculars rested on her lap.

'Oh, you're bird-watching. I wondered what you were doing out here.'

'No, young man, I'm not bird-watching. Oh no.' She shook her head, slightly bemused. 'I'm looking for *them.*'

I glanced around, over the hedge, into the fields beyond. 'Them?'

'They know I'm watching. They'll be here soon.' Her eyes smiled, mischievously, as she looked me up and down. 'Well, I have to say, you're better-looking than the last chap. A bit too skinny for my tastes, though.'

'Oh, thank you, I think, Mrs...?'

'Verity Lait... Call me Verity. And you must be Tom Philips, the new mobile librarian. See, I keep up to date with all the local news. '

'I dare not doubt it.' I smiled. 'So, are you okay here?'

'Oh yes, don't fuss. They won't harm me. I'm perfectly safe.'

I didn't really want to but I had to ask, 'So, who exactly are *they*?'

'The shining ones, Tom... angels.'

'Angels!'

'Isn't it wonderful?'

She didn't pursue me for a response and I was glad, because what could I say? Poor woman. It must have been her age. She was obviously seeing things.

'Well, I'd best be on my way, Verity. It's nice to meet you.'

'Nice to meet you, too,' she replied in a kind of pre-occupied way.

As I walked back to the van, she began scanning the fields with her binoculars. She seemed to possess all her faculties, but angels? I sighed. Why do people believe in such tosh? I turned the ignition and, as I drove away, Verity was on her feet, smiling and waving towards the adjacent pasture. In that moment, I was sure I saw a blinding light flash briefly in my wing mirror. I shook my head. It had to be the sun bouncing off the glass. That's what it was. There's a logical reason for everything.

∞∞∞∞∞∞∞∞∞

'There is always light in the darkness.'

Hawkdale, one of the newly refurbished towns in these parts, and the main hub for the surrounding villages, was trying to find its personality. Smaller than Windermere or Ambleside, it had already adopted a legion of ubiquitous brand-name high street shops, which did nothing for its appeal. Fortunately, it had an independent bookshop and gallery, which gave it a thumbs-up from me. My father said the town had lost something and wasn't like it used to be, but I think that's just the perspective of someone who dislikes change – any change. In any case, it's people that brought the energy to a place, and there were plenty of characters here to say the least.

'You're bloody late,' one of those characters mumbled, as he placed a stack of books on the counter. 'You weren't abducted by aliens, were you? No sense of missing time or odd symptoms?'

I didn't take him for one of those UFO nuts. He dressed like a gamekeeper, and I thought he must be in his sixties although I was useless at guessing someone's age. He stared at me with penetrating grey eyes: his face was a confusion of angles and shadows and jutting chin. His library card revealed his name: Henry Ligget.

'Sorry, I'm late, Mr Ligget. I had a bit of a delay – a minor technical issue.'

'That'll be those aliens. Did you experience any electro-magnetic interference? Seen any bright lights in the sky?'

'No, the delay was definitely caused by human error – mine, I'm embarrassed to say.'

I swiped his card through the database, and he leant against the reception desk with questioning eyes.

'So you haven't seen any UFOs? No unusual lights? There are strange things going on in these parts, I'll have you know.'

'No, Mr Ligget, I can assure you that I haven't seen any-thing, and I don't believe in aliens or UFOs buzzing around Hawkdale or anywhere else for that matter.' Book lovers queued patiently behind the curious man. 'Now, is there any-thing I can help you with?'

He shook his head and retreated, eyes rebuking me as if I'd said something blasphemous. Two blushing mature ladies giggled as they waited in line. As they approached the desk, I realised they were dressed identically in purple dresses with matching purple hats. One prodded the other, who passed me a piece of paper. The title of the book was *The Ultimate Guide to Tantric Sex*. My eyebrows shot upwards. I typed the title into the on-board database, imagining, or trying not to, what these two old dears wanted from such a book. My operations manager had warned me that I was likely to receive some odd book orders and that I shouldn't react, let alone judge, but it took all my reserve to stifle my laughter.

'Sorry, we don't have this in stock,' I said, clearing my throat. 'Would you like me to order it?'

The ladies looked at each other, blushing furiously, and shyly nodded.

'We're eighty-five, you know,' one of them said. 'Who'd have thought we'd be dancing around like girls again at our age?'

One of them twirled on her pale stocking-covered legs. 'Never had so much energy, thanks to Cali and her healing classes.'

More youthful chuckles followed. I smiled for a very long time because I was lost for words. Henry Ligget continued to lurk around the audio books and DVDs, casting me an occasional sharp-eyed glance. The ladies chirped a giggly goodbye, throwing in a wink as they went.

'Have you any documentaries on UFOs?' asked Henry, spinning the carousel so fast it blurred beyond recognition.

'No, but if you have a title in mind, we can order it for you.'

He mumbled something incomprehensible, sighed, and stopped spinning the carousel. It juddered to a halt. Without another word, he turned his back, and walked away.

Yes, it's characters that made a place.

To make up for the time I'd lost that morning, I skipped lunch and went on to my next stop. The afternoon simmered with the promise of summer. Blue and gold wild-flowers coloured the roadsides, their heads tilted as if in worship of the sun. Meadows were a vibrant green after a recent shower. Butterflies flitted, their new wings bathing in light, and the swooning chorus of birdsong brightened the hedgerows. This was the extra benefit of doing this job, soaking up the lavish unquestionable beauty of Cumbria, and enjoying the sun on my face as the van chugged through villages and valleys. The fells loomed around me in a kind of earthy, protective way and I felt a deep-rooted connection to this remarkable landscape. Everything was in harmony here, just as it should be.

∞∞∞∞∞∞∞∞

'There is always darkness in the light.'

Afternoon turned into evening. I settled in a peaceful corner of the White Crow, reading McCarthy, and waited for Pete to arrive for his good-deed pint of ale. It was strange being here. My last memory of this pub was the night I'd had a row with my father, about moving to Edinburgh for my studies. That was twelve years ago, but there was still an atmosphere. And the way the regulars eyed me, you'd think the argument only took place yesterday. The locals – my father's friends – had long memories, and a resistance to change. There's nothing wrong with that; nothing wrong with the people or the place. Generations of close-knit families shared their lives here in Crowdale. To them, it was the centre of their universe. The fact that I had relinquished the family farming tradition in favour of a life in books, the fact that I'd left for over a decade, now ranked me as an outsider. I was the black sheep returned.

I glanced up from my book. There was Harold in the corner, stone-faced as if he hadn't moved in months. Frank, my father's closest friend, leant against the bar drowning in his pint of best bitter. A few others were dotted around, no doubt positioned at their regular tables, bemoaning the state of the economy, farming yields, and the demise of the village post office. Although I was rarely distracted from reading a good novel, I felt unsettled by the mood and wondered if it had been a mistake coming back.

Life had been good in Edinburgh. Culture oozed from every alleyway. I'd had a rich social life at the university, mingling with thinkers and visionaries, engaging in conversations which had world-changing potential. Granted, I didn't have much money but I had been comfortable, satiated, and reasonably happy. At least, that had been the case until Sylvia came along. Within a year, this crazy woman, who was studying law, had snared me, held me captive, chewed on my emotions, and then spat me out. I never saw it coming; never knew love could taste so bitter. That sorry episode had happened over eighteen months ago and, although I was over her, the experience had changed me, and I wasn't sure whether for the better or worse.

So, here I was searching for something – a new beginning, perhaps. I wasn't convinced I'd made the right choice. I could have remained in Edinburgh and taken a charity bookshop job, despite the low pay. Something else would have come along, such as a role in a publishing house or at a literary trust, and staying there would have meant being amongst good friends. As much as I loved Cumbria, the inspiration of my favourite poets, the city still had me in its grasp.

Unable to concentrate, I closed my book and, as I did so, Pete entered the pub like the good guy in one of those old cowboy films, coolly acknowledging the crescendo of greetings that I didn't receive, and made his way urgently to the pint waiting for him on my chosen table. He picked up the glass, without a word, and drank as if ale hadn't touched his lips in years. He sat opposite, with cheeky eyes.

'Since when did you start wearing the geek glasses?' he asked.

'Since when did you acquire that beer belly?'

He laughed. 'Always the smart arse!'

I grinned, recognising the boy in the man before me.

'I've had the specs for about three years, mostly for reading.'

'If you ask me, those bloody books have ruined your eyes.' He raised his pint glass. 'Cheers!'

'You sound like our father.'

'And there'll be nothing wrong in that, Tom. He's a good man... a bit stubborn, mind.'

'I know. I wasn't implying anything. It's just an observation. You're looking more like him too. Now that's a bit worrying.'

'Cheeky beggar.'

We laughed, and then there was silence for a long moment. This was the first opportunity we'd had to spend time together away from the farm since my return. Pete raised his glass towards the bartender, gesturing for another drink.

'So, Tom, what's brought you back?' he began. 'Is it the scintillating night-life? Or are you missing the stimulating Cumbrian air?'

'To be honest, I don't know.'

Pete guzzled his beer and I stared into mine, as if some answer bubbled within. All I saw was what I'd left behind. Scotland was in my heart, more than England if the truth was known. My mother's Scottish roots anchored me. When I'd started showing academic ability, she'd made sure I spent as much of my holidays in Edinburgh, with my granddad, Professor McBride. My father had been glad to see the back of me. I was, after all, useless on the farm. So, granddad became my mentor and the fatherly figure I aspired to, and Scotland became a more welcoming home.

'Are you glad to be back?' Pete interrupted my reverie.

'In some ways...'

'So, Dad's still making life difficult, hey?'

'He's never accepted the choices I made. But, it's not that... I don't know whether I'll stay for long. I'll see what happens.'

'You need a good woman in your life, bro. That will sort things out.'

'Now you sound like our mother.'

'Mind you, there are days I envy your bachelor-boy life-style, doing whatever you want, with no one nagging in your ear.'

'You have a good thing going with Ellie – and a baby on the way,' I reminded him.

'True enough,' he replied, draining the beer from his glass. 'Time for another drink, don't you think?'

I didn't ever recall Pete being so fond of his ale. He handed me the empty glass and I made my way to the bar. Raucous laughter filled the pub's snug and a strange little old man, with bunion-red cheeks, a sharp pointed nose, and a thin mess of oily hair, jigged around the pub, looking as though he had never known sobriety. Amongst the din of laughter, he was whining out a song of sorts. He spilled out of the snug, heading towards the bar. I tried not to catch his eye but couldn't help but watch him jig, making strange circular movements as he span on his crow-like legs. He moved towards me, his eyes catching mine, and he whirled out a new tune...

'Ta da, ta da, ta da, she comes from afar; the sky will open, and she'll steal your heart, ta da, ta da, ta da...'

He repeated it over and over, until the words were incomprehensible, and his chanting silenced the regulars.

'Shut up, Sam, or you'll be barred again,' the landlord bellowed, shoving a pint of Guinness towards him.

The strange little man quietened, eyes still on me for a few seconds more before darting away. He took the tankard and then cowered in the corner.

'Who's that?' I asked Pete, placing another pint in front of him.

'What, you haven't heard of the singing psychic?'

'The what?'

'Old Sam turned up in the village a couple of years ago and decided to stay. He's become a bit of a celebrity for being able to predict the future through his songs.'

'You're having me on, bro.'

'I jest not. He's foretold lots of things that have come to pass. You ask anyone in the village and they'll all have a story to tell.'

'Argh, stop it. What planet are you on, Pete? I thought you didn't believe in stuff like that. I'm disappointed.'

'So, what did he tell you?'

'I don't know... just some garbage about a woman coming from afar who'll steal my heart.'

'Well, just remember those words, Tom, because there'll be something in them.'

'Yeah, lunacy. It is a full moon, tonight, after all.'

The banter continued, and we spent the waning evening reminiscing, catching up on lost time, and being the brothers that we had always been.

Spirits and tongues lightened with drink, we finally strolled back to the farm. Fragrant wood smoke curled in the night air drifting from huddled cottage chimneys. The quiet lane out of this weary hamlet seemed to reach into oblivion.

'Don't suppose you've seen any naked women dancing on the fells recently?' I found myself asking my ale-filled brother. 'And, I'm talking about a naked woman who sort of disappears into thin air?'

'What have you been drinking, bro?' he replied, swaying slightly, trying to avoid the potholes in the road. 'Because, if you're seeing naked women, I want whatever you're on.'

'So, you haven't seen any strange woman, dancing about... disappearing?'

'You're kidding me, aren't you? You have too much of an imagination – or perhaps you've actually seen the ghost that roams the fells.'

Pete put on a ghoulish voice, which echoed into the star-bathed valley.

'You know I don't believe in ghosts.'

'And I don't believe there are women dancing around naked on the fells. This is Cumbria, Tom, not some Greek isle. You know, it's time you found yourself a real woman, not some imaginary one.'

Pete was right. I must have imagined her.

We reached the gated track that led up to the farm. It was a clear night, and the moon acted as our lantern, casting a sour glow across the undulating landscape as we trundled along. I caught sight of a single meteor, its brilliance short-lived.

'I'll race you,' Pete said, and without warning he pushed me over to grab a head start.

I scrambled to my feet and gave chase. The sobering

night air rushed through my lungs, and everything around me seemed to hang dark purple. I didn't have to run far as Pete tripped and rolled over into a drunken, laughing heap.

The curtains twitched at the lit farmhouse window. Even from here, I recognised my father's bullish frame. Even from here, I knew he was probably moaning, saying how I was leading Pete astray. I grabbed Pete's arm and pulled him to his feet, pointing him in the direction of the farmhouse door.

'Nood gight, bro,' he said, slurring his words.

'Good night, Pete,' I corrected.

He opened the door into the bosom of the farmhouse, where Ellie would probably tease him for being just a tiny bit drunk, where Mother was reading and ending the day with a glass of organic wine, and where Father was probably stewing in his thoughts, while catching up on an issue of *Farmers Weekly*. The door closed on me, and I realised I was sober. I returned to my lodge.

The lodges (aimed at self-catering holiday-makers) and the farm shop tearoom were my mother's venture. The farm would have gone into receivership long ago if it hadn't been for her vision of renovating the old barn and cowsheds. And me coming back to stay on the farm was really her idea. She said there was no point renting somewhere else when I could take advantage of family discount. I was grateful, of course, but being here was a little too close to my father for comfort. If he'd mellowed, made an effort to show me that past was past and that he wasn't bitter about only having one son to farm the land instead of two, then it wouldn't be a problem. But it was clear when he ignored me on arrival that he felt no different to when I'd left. I was just glad I hadn't agreed to move into the farmhouse. I decided that I'd stay here for a month or so and then look for somewhere else to live. If the job continued to go well, then I'd find an apartment in Kendal. I'd be closer to the County Library depot, and there was more going on in town of an evening, a little more culture, and a better chance of making new friends. Who knows? Maybe that special someone was waiting for me there.

The hour was late. I made myself a mug of hot chocolate and attempted to read, but my eyes protested. I had an early start tomorrow so I switched off the light and lay in bed. Through the roof's low skylight, stars sparkled like jewels against the sable cloak of night. In the distance, an owl hooted. I turned on my side. At first I was unsettled, and flitted between dreams and wakefulness. At some point, a deep rumbling sound made me sit stark upright. The bed appeared to be moving, shuddering slightly in the darkness. Odd! The movement stopped and I settled back down, realising that I probably wasn't as sober as I'd thought. Images of the day skipped beneath my closed eyelids. The singing psychic cawed in my ears, his human form turning to a crow. Eventually, I drifted to happily find the naked lady dancing me into the depths of slumber.

∞∞∞∞∞∞∞∞

'Everything is connected to the same source.'

'**I**t's you!'

'Sorry, are you speaking to me?'

I couldn't believe my eyes. It was the naked lady here in my mobile library. I'd been parked in the tranquil village of Ravenshead for all of ten minutes, and she was my first customer. She was clothed, I hasten to add, but I was still speechless for what seemed like a stupidly long time.

'Are you all right?' she said.

'I'm sorry; you must think I'm weird. It's just a relief to know I wasn't seeing things the other day.'

'Seeing things?'

'I saw you dancing on Fellside. I thought I was hallucinating, especially when you...'

'Excuse me? You saw me...?'

'I did...'

'But I was naked! You saw me naked?'

Her cheeks flushed pink, and then she looked at me in a sort of reproving way.

'Don't get me wrong, I wasn't looking on purpose,' I quickly added. 'I happened to be passing with the mobile library on Fellside Road, and with the light shining in that particular way, it wasn't exactly difficult to see you.'

'So, you weren't watching me in a creepy way?'

'No – I mean not deliberately, if that makes any sense. Hell, I'm not doing myself any favours here, am I? Right, okay, you're smiling. I think that's a good sign.'

She laughed, and I was drawn to her lips, soft as rose petals, and her eyes sparkled with a strange familiarity.

'I guess it'll teach me not to go sky-clad so close to the road.'

'Sky-clad?'

'Naked!'

'Right... No, not advisable. You could easily cause an accident.'

She stared at me, her expression quickly moving from questioning to bemused insight. 'Oh my goodness. I remember now. Didn't I see a tractor pulling this vehicle out of the field?'

'You perhaps did.'

'I caused that? I didn't realise. I'm sorry; I shouldn't....' She put her hand to her mouth, failing to shield her amusement, and giggled. 'Sorry, that's really childish of me. You're okay, though?

'Yeah, thanks. Embarrassed, but nothing damaged.'

We stood there for a long moment, eyes meeting then darting away shyly.

'Anyway, forgive me; I haven't introduced myself: Tom Philips.'

'Pleased to meet you, Tom,' she said, placing her delicate hand into mine. 'I'm Cali Silverthorn.'

We shook hands, a bit too formally.

'So, Cali. Do you mind me asking, if it's not too personal, why were you dancing in the woods... in the nude?'

Her eyes, blue like cornflowers, met mine again with that same jolting recognition.

'I was celebrating nature, being alive, that sort of thing. It's something I do whenever the moment takes me.'

'Really?'

'Yes, really.' She chuckled at my incredulity.

Her eyes wandered around the library, picking out book titles from the confines of their shelves, and my eyes wandered too, taking in her every detail. Her knee-length flower-freckled dress shimmied over her petite frame. Well-worn dark blue moccasins hinted of the miles she had trodden. A river of coal-black hair coated her small shoulders. I'd say she was a few years younger than me, mid-twenties perhaps. Her features were delicate and yet incredibly compelling with each turn of expression. She had what I can only define as a raw natural beauty, which probably sounds uncomplimentary, and yet she was truly captivating. I found myself thinking that I'd like to get to know her.

'So, what brings you to the mobile library?' I asked.

'Books,' she replied.

'Ha. Of course; daft question.'

'I'd like to order three books, please.'

'No problem. I'll check whether they're in stock.'

She unravelled a piece of pink paper. She was so close that I caught her fine fragrance, a gentle aroma like wild honeysuckle. I breathed her in.

'I'm looking for *The Shamanic Experiment*, *Psychic Transformation*, and *Astral Travel, The Next Step*. I have the authors' names here.'

'Hmm, well, I can say, without an iota of doubt, that we don't have these in stock.'

'Oh, that's a shame.'

'I'll place an order for you, if you like.'

'Thanks,' she replied. She watched me add her details and name to the database. 'That's Cali spelt with an "i".'

'Cali... as in California?'

'Got it in one,' she said. 'My mother thought it was a good idea naming me after the place where I was supposedly conceived.' She rolled her eyes as if unimpressed. 'My grandmother preferred to call me by my spirit name, Little Songbird, because I'm always singing – but Cali's fine.'

'I like both names,' I simply said, staring at her for a mesmerised moment.

She smiled at me in a way that suggested we shared a far greater intimacy. It felt as if her eyes were reading my every thought. It wasn't disconcerting in any way. Actually, it felt natural – strangely natural.

'These books have been on my list since I moved here in February.'

'So, you're a newbie to the Lakes,' I said, already suspecting so.

'Yes, fresh from England's spiritual heart.'

I looked at her, confused.

'Glastonbury,' she confirmed, 'home to the music festival, Avalon, the goddess energies, Chalice Well, the sacred Tor...'

'Aye, I know of it,' I said, 'but I've never been.'

'Oh you must visit some time,' she said, studying me curiously. 'It has a very positive energy, and there are lots of healing paths there to revive the spirit.'

'I'll bear that in mind, but I find my spirit is amply invigorated by a wee dose of culture and a walk through the landscape. It works a treat.'

She studied me for a moment. 'That's not a local accent... are you new here, too?'

'Actually, I was born and grew up here in the Lakes, but aye, you can probably detect a wee Scottish accent. My mother's Scottish and I studied in Edinburgh for ten years, so I guess I picked up the twang.'

'Well, I like it. And I like the hole in your sweater.' She giggled, eyeing the loose green thread running from the hole.

'Oh, I was hoping you hadn't noticed that.'

Silence stole the next few moments. I found myself wondering about her, wondering who Cali Silverthorn was. She had a kind of bohemian look, something untamed in her flashing eyes... An artist, perhaps, or certainly an artist's model: a dark-haired pre-Raphaelite. Oh but there was something in those eyes, such certainty in her expression, something profoundly knowing in her every turn, her every movement. In a crazy way, it felt like I was with a dear friend I hadn't seen for a while.

'So, are you here with friends, family... partner?' I asked, re-positioning a misplaced book on the shelf.

'No, I'm on my own. Well, actually, that's not quite right. I'm sharing a cottage with others on Ravenshead Pike. It's just a temporary arrangement, really, until I work out what's happening next.'

'Has work brought you here?' I began, and then realised that my questions must sound like I was prying. 'Sorry, it's none of my business.'

'No, that's okay. My work *has* brought me here. I'm a healer. I work with energy to restore health and rebalance auric fields.'

'Oh.' I frowned, unable to contain the trace of scepticism.

'It's not something you believe in?'

'If I'm honest, I don't buy into all that new-age paraphernalia,' I said, possibly a little too bluntly. 'I'm not saying you don't help people. It's just, well, it's just not scientific.'

'Science doesn't yet have all the answers,' she replied, more seriously. 'There's more to life than what we know, far more than we currently comprehend.'

There was an awkward pause. Had I been too forthright with my views? I did, after all, have a habit of speaking my mind. And, in this awkward pause, I wondered if I'd blown my chances of getting to know her. Then she smiled, curling those rose-petal lips and, if I hadn't known better, I could have thought she was using some magic to enchant me.

'Anyway, Tom Philips,' she began, playfully, quite happy to change the subject, 'what do you do for night-life round here?'

'You mean you haven't discovered the buzzing social scene at the village hall?'

She giggled with a lightness of heart that was infectious and uplifting.

'Well,' she said, twirling her dark hair round her fine fingers, 'there must be a live music scene, or some kind of philosophical discussion group, or poetry readings?'

'Poetry readings,' I repeated, my attention instantly caught.

'Yes... you know of any?'

'I do. Poetry is a great passion of mine, and there happens to be a poetry evening at the Lakeside Arms on Wednesday. I'd be happy to take you, if you're not otherwise busy?'

'I'd love to go.'

Her smile dimpled either side of her face. My thoughts

did cartwheels. I noted her address and made arrangements to pick her up on that evening, and although I was in no way making assumptions, it seemed very much like the start of something.

'I'd better run,' she said, curiously checking her wrist for a watch that wasn't even there. 'I'm giving a healing dance session at the village hall for the over-sixties.'

My memory jogged back to the two old ladies who had ordered the tantric sex book. They had actually mentioned attending Cali's healing classes. So, this was the woman responsible for reviving two elderly ladies' sexual appetites. Intriguing!

Two silver-haired men stepped into the mobile library, and we politely exchanged greetings before continuing our conversation.

'So, you're not dancing naked again by any chance?' I said, straightening the CDs in the carousel.

One of the men, overhearing my remark, raised his thick silver eyebrows at the other.

'No, not today,' Cali winked.

'Oh, one last thing,' I said more softly, so as not to be overheard, 'I meant to ask, how did you do that disappearing act?'

'Disappearing act? I'm not sure what you mean.'

'You know, when I saw you on Fellside... dancing...'

'Yes?'

'Well, you sort of disappeared.'

'I did?' She paused, as if thinking back to the event in question. 'Are you sure?'

'Well, no,' I said, scratching my forehead. 'I thought it

must have been a trick of the light. I mean, how could you simply disappear? It's ludicrous.'

For a moment, her eyes glazed as if she was a million miles away.

'Are you all right?'

'Yes,' she said, 'perfectly all right. Anyway, I'll see you Wednesday – around seven.'

She didn't give me chance to reply. Off she ran, with that river of hair cascading over that flower-freckled dress. Within seconds she had turned a corner and was out of sight, but the thought of her lingered with me, like a nostalgic song, an evocative fragrance, a perfect moment remembered, and for the first time since arriving back in the Lakes, I was happy to be here.

∞∞∞∞∞∞∞∞

'Look beyond the equations for the answer.'

The afternoon had passed in a blink, leaving only curious captured fragments: Mr Roberts returning six faded crime novels he'd borrowed some twenty years ago; a ruminating conversation about the beast cat spotted on the fells near Ulpha; and the pale girl with the quirky hat who said I looked like Alex Kapranos from the band Franz Ferdinand and who proceeded to flirt with me, pretending to be a fan of Coleridge's poetry (simply because I mentioned him) when it was clear she didn't know her Ancient Mariner from her Kubla Khan. In the quieter moments, Cali Silverthorn filled my mind, my naked lady, who was no longer the hallucination I thought she was.

The journey home from the County Library was happily uneventful. I parked my old but reliable Land Rover next to the tearoom in the very place where Samson, our shire horse, used to stamp the ground waiting to be fed carrots, apples or Polo mints. He was long gone but the smell of leather and shine of brass teased my memory, reminding me of a different time. Although much had changed here at Crowdale Farm, some things were still the same. The weathered farmhouse, for example, defiant against the backdrop of tumbling fells, was oblivious to its age. According to local knowledge, William and his sister Dorothy Wordsworth had visited the farm in the early 1800s before returning to Grasmere. It was said that Dorothy, upon seeing the stream that runs from the fell-tops past the east field, took off her stockings to bathe her tired feet. I often imagined her sat there, melancholic, with William pacing deep in poetic contemplation. William had loved this area, especially the Faery Chasm at Birks Bridge and all along the River Duddon. The place had inspired a series of sonnets. And thinking that my father's great-great grandfather met the renowned poet sent shivers through me. When I first became obsessed with books and learning, and before I even knew about the Wordsworths' visit, I'd spent idle times by that same stream, engrossed in a novel or a poem, dipping my own feet in the cold water. Funny how the stream still flowed exactly as it had back then: ancient and yet somehow ageless.

My mother was by the farm tearoom, saying goodbye to two touring cyclists, her last customers of the day. She held a basket in her hands: most likely containing her home-grown organic salads and herbs. I had always marvelled at her energy. She never kept still, which probably explained why she was still lithe, dynamic, and much younger-looking than her years. She saw me, and shouted over, 'Would you like dinner with us this evening?'

At that moment, my father appeared from the pasture, slamming the gate shut, and I hesitated. 'Hmm... I'm busy tonight,' I lied, 'but thanks.'

She was probably sick of my excuses. Since returning to the Lakes, I hadn't spent any quality time with her. I think that suited the old man perfectly.

'We'll catch up soon,' I shouted back, loud enough for my father to hear. 'I promise.' And I meant it.

My father didn't acknowledge me but marched past,

bullish faced, eyes narrow as if he was trying to shut out what he didn't want to see. He followed his wife into the house, slamming the door behind him – the same oak door that he had closed on me when I'd chosen academia over farming. I was still the outcast. I couldn't imagine him ever changing.

I sighed and stood by the fence for a while. I was determined not to let anything or anyone spoil my good mood. Swallows swooped into the yard with their stealth wings. They gathered on the phone line that ran from the tearoom to the main house and gossiped noisily.

A door slammed. Pete appeared from the side of the house, carrying two mugs. 'The swallows arrived early this year,' he said, passing me one of the mugs, 'and they're fewer in number.'

'Cheers, bro.' I took a sip of the strong tea, the colour of mud it was, glad he'd remembered not to add sugar. 'Do you think it's to do with climate change? Pollution?'

'I'm not sure. I mean, what do you believe these days? One so-called expert tells you one thing and then another so-called expert tells you the opposite. All I know is that it doesn't take much to knock nature out of balance. Don't need any expert to realise that.'

For more than a few moments we watched the swallows fly in and out of the hayloft, mesmerised by their speed and agility.

Pete emptied the dregs of his tea onto the dusty track, and tapped me on the shoulder, breaking me from the spell of the birds' poetic flying. 'Come with me, Tom. I'll introduce you to our latest addition.'

Curious, I followed him through to the old barn at the rear of the hayloft, which had been converted to stalls for the horses. The place was tidier than I remembered and the internal stone walls were newly whitewashed, creating a lighter atmosphere. It was clear that Pete had been busy with his equestrian project. He beckoned me to the first stall.

'Wow,' I whispered.

There, on a thick bed of straw, was a foal, velvety-wrinkled and as black as coal, stretched out peacefully next to its doting mother.

'He was born this morning,' Pete said, glowing with pride. 'The swallows aren't the only early arrivals. This one came two weeks too soon. Gave me a bit of a shock but, thankfully, he and his mother are doing well.'

'He's a wee stunner.' The foal shifted his head, watching us lazily with his dark eye.

'I reckon last night's earth tremor had something to do with him arriving early.'

I stared at Pete, recalling how my bed had shaken in the night. 'So, that was an earth tremor? I thought I'd imagined it. You felt it?'

'No, I was dead to the world, bro. Think that last pint was one too many. No, I heard about it on the radio this morning. It's the sixth one we've felt in these parts in as many months. If you ask me, there's something going on... something that even the experts don't know about.'

He scratched the side of his head just like he always did when something was baffling him.

'So, there's a bit more seismic activity than normal. I don't think it's anything untoward, Pete.'

'Hmm,' he simply replied.

There was a pre-occupied pause for a minute or so. Pete seemed somewhat more contemplative than I remembered him to be, and certainly more tense. The way he guzzled his beer last night was also unexpected, as if he was trying to blot out something that was worrying him. And yet there didn't appear to be any problems – certainly nothing obvious.

'So, is everything going well with the equestrian venture?' I asked, wondering if business was on his mind.

'Yeah, better than anticipated. Two other mares are in foal. We recently backed and sold three youngsters, and there's a stallion arriving soon.'

'Things have really changed round here. I take it the old man approves?'

'He wasn't keen at first, but said if it brought in extra income for the farm, then he'd leave me to it.'

'That was generous of him,' I said, unable to contain my sarcasm.

'Yeah, well, you know what he's like, Tom. He's practical and the survival of the farm comes first. I have to say, he's been easier to live with since Mum began profiting from her lodges and tearoom. These days, he only has to worry about the sheep and there aren't many of them now: just a few Herdwick, and they mostly look after themselves. It's taken the pressure off but he's still as grumpy as ever.'

'I guess some things don't change.'

The foal scrambled up, shaking gawkily on his spindle legs. I patted Pete on his shoulder, happy for my older brother, happy that he was carving out his own niche and doing what he loved.

'So, did you find your naked woman?'

Pete's change of subject took me by surprise. I laughed. 'I thought you'd had one too many pints to remember that conversation. Hmm, well as it happens, aye, I found her.'

'You did! And...?'

'I'm seeing her tomorrow night.'

He grinned, 'Well, it hasn't taken you long to pick up a date, that's for sure. Why do girls fall for daydreaming green-eyed poets? It's always been a mystery to me.'

'Who said it was a date? I just offered to take her to a poetry reading, that's all. Not sure if anything will come of it.'

He kept on grinning, as if he didn't quite believe me.

'Remember Charlene Barrow?' He nudged me with his elbow and winked. 'She worshipped the ground you walked on. She still has a crush on you. So, if things don't work out with this "date", then I can let her know you're back in town.'

'Thanks, bro, but I'm not interested. Charlene's lovely, but if I'd wanted to date her I'd have done something about it years ago.'

We walked back outside into the evening light. A torrent of silver-lined cloud billowed, pocketing the fell-tops, and an image of Cali blossomed in my mind's eye. Instantly, I lost touch with the moment as I imagined her dancing in and out of those billowing clouds like the May Queen, dressed in a garland of sweet wild flowers.

'Look, what's that?' Pete pointed at the sky. 'Is that love in the air?'

He thumped my back, laughing so loud that a flock of sparrows squawked and darted from the hawthorn hedgerow. I rolled my eyes. Who said anything about love?

∞∞∞∞∞∞∞∞

'Do not be confused by conflicting voices.'

I showered and chose clothes to wear for my evening with Cali Silverthorn: slate-grey drainpipe trousers, grey shirt, a dark purple v-neck tank top (one without a hole), and my slate grey jacket. My wardrobe was sparse, and what I had had seen me through the best part of university. Surviving on a student budget had instilled in me a respect for economical living. I reckoned, though, it was time to buy something new to shake off the faded and worn look.

I posed in front of the mirror, combed my fingers through my hair, shifting back a far-too-long fringe, and saw this slightly pale, thin, serious-looking guy staring back. Did I look like a poet? I laughed at myself: probably more like a world-weary academic who was a little unsure where to go next on life's journey. I grabbed my watch, wallet, mobile, and keys. I checked my side-pocket for my notebook and pen. I was all set to go. A Monet print (my mother's choice, not mine) hung askew on the wall so I straightened it. I considered how much better the sparse room would be with floor-to-ceiling book shelves across the back wall, filled, of course, with a selection of my favourite authors and poets: Kerouac, McCarthy, Orwell, Coleridge, Keats, Dylan Thomas, and so on. I stared at the bare wall and was left with the feeling of how temporary it all seemed. With a sigh, I closed the door behind me.

An unusual rush of excitement or nerves skipped in my stomach as I drove to Ravenshead. I was looking forward to seeing her, of course, but the feeling gathering inside me was much stronger than I could comprehend – as though I was rushing to meet a lover I hadn't seen in a while. Again, I tried to squash the feeling. Although a poet at heart, a lover of swooning words and rare thoughts, I wasn't really prone to flying away on a fantasy cloud of high romance. I was far too grounded and sensible and logical. Yet she'd been on my mind... *constantly*... and I couldn't hide the anticipation growing within, hoping something would actually develop between us.

The evening sky was an unusual palette of pale turquoise and apricot with a burning red streak over the western fringe. Even though the nights were lifting by approaching summer, there remained a shy coolness in the air. I turned into Damselfly Lane and realised I was unfamiliar with the road. It rose sharply, and then twisted a little. I drove slowly, searching for signs of Cali's place. The road climbed higher still and I shifted into a lower gear. The weakening sun cast a syrup glow, and midges hung thick, dancing in the dusty light. Higher still, and tree cover dispersed, and a house perched on the ledge of the fell came into view; a house with an observatory in its grounds, sat on a promontory, commanding the best possible views of the sky.

A weathered plaque, with 'Starfell Cottage' hastily painted on it, was awry on the gatepost. I resisted the urge to stop and straighten it, and drove through the opened gateway and parked on the gravel drive. The views from here reached out to the west, with the sea just visible in the distance like a silver chain. I stepped out of the Land Rover and took a deep breath.

Yes, I was more nervous than I should be. I was about to knock on the imposing arch-shaped door when Cali appeared, opening the decorative wrought-iron gate at the side of the house. She was wearing a pretty blue tea-dress, the colour of summer skies, which sat just above her knees, revealing slender, tanned legs. It was the kind of tea-dress that would have sent Dylan Thomas' pulse soaring. She wore a necklace clasping a crystal. I recognised the gem as a piece of labradorite, flashing blue-green and silver. It was difficult not to look at this dazzling crystal without noticing the dazzling female landscape beneath. My eyes lingered, perhaps too long, until the soft melody of her voice broke the silence.

'It's a fine night for a poetry reading, don't you think?'

'Inspiring,' I replied, momentarily dragging my eyes away from her to view the sky.

I wanted to say how beautiful she looked, but how, without it sounding predictable or disingenuous? Why was I finding this so bloody difficult?

Her hair settled easily on her shoulders like a dark cape. She moved a strand away from her face, revealing the fine pink rounds of her delicate cheekbones, and her cornflower-blue eyes flashed keenly. My palms felt unusually clammy.

It took eleven minutes to reach the Lakeside Arms. The pub nestled in a wooded area with the shores of Coniston Water just a stroll away. To quell nerves, I rambled on about poetry, and about how a poem can move us to distraction. I talked about Wordsworth and Coleridge and how much of their poetry had been inspired by their time in the Lakes. I told her about William's doting, wild-eyed sister, Dorothy, and how they had all travelled together, walking through the landscape seeking inspiration. She listened and smiled. As I pulled into the pub car park, I realised I'd done a lot of telling and had hardly given her chance to speak.

'Sorry,' I said. 'I've been rambling.'

'You've not been rambling at all.'

'Yes I have. I tend to do that when... well, when I'm a bit nervous. And, I'm sorry for not saying earlier how beautiful you look.'

There, I'd said it.

'Well, thank you, kind sir.' She beamed, and my nerves fell away.

The pub was surprisingly busy, but we found a cosy table for two in the corner. It had a reasonable view of the hastily prepared stage, which was simply a cleared space on a slightly raised area occupied by a microphone stand. I ordered drinks: cider-blackberry for Cali and a lemonade shandy for me. An eclectic mix of people filled the space, buttering the atmosphere with a sense of anticipation. I carried the drinks back to our table, nodding hello to a couple of familiar faces I'd met in the mobile library, conscious of not bumping my head on the low dark ceiling beams.

The proceedings began as soon as we settled down. For the next hour, we listened to an array of poems from amateur and seasoned poets alike, and grew steadily intoxicated by their words. Then there was a lull. Cali stood up, and I thought she was about to visit the ladies' room, but she winked at me and made her way to the stage. My mouth dropped open. She adjusted the microphone, composed herself, and the room quietened with anticipation. She seemed ever so slight and vulnerable, and yet there was a fearless spark in her eyes, something assured in her manner, and she had an irresistible light about her. My heart drummed. She began to recite a poem from memory. Her voice, soft and melodic, reminded me of a blackbird's morning song, and I was mesmerised. I listened intently right through to the last stanza...

'... Young swallows test their wings,
Gliding on summer's song.
And lovers linger beneath the crystal moon,
Lamenting the turning of days.
No need for more than this.
Wood smoke memories; Leaf-blown kisses.
All that is, is now.'

A hushed moment followed and then the room vibrated with applause. Cali took a modest bow, and skipped back to our table, beaming, surprised by the hearty reception.

'You're a poet,' I said, still applauding her.

'Not really,' she replied, blushing a little, 'certainly not of any standard, but I do like to write when the mood takes me.'

She took a sip of her drink. I simply stared at her, captivated by this spirited woman, this rare rose blooming before me. And as we settled into each other, I wondered what other surprises Cali Silverthorn had in store for me.

∞∞∞∞∞∞∞∞

'Listen to the ancient ones. Wait for their signs.'

The poetry readings concluded, and the air seemed to sigh as poets, poetry lovers, and pub regulars melted into the evening's relaxed ambience. I relaxed, too. The wall lights in this aged building dimmed and brightened occasionally, casting an orangey-yellow glow that swelled the mellowing mood. In the quiet setting, our eyes would linger as they met, holding each other a little longer as the night crooned. I was filled with curiosity. I felt the most profound recognition, which left me wondering if we'd met before somewhere. I wondered if she felt this too.

'You have familiar eyes... the eyes of an ancient soul,' she said, as if reading my thoughts.

'What, blood-shot from too many caffeine-filled nights reading into the small hours?'

'No,' she giggled, 'I mean you have the eyes of someone who's been reincarnated over many lifetimes.'

'I do? Hmm, well you might think that but I'm of the belief that we only come this way once.'

'Oh, and then what?'

'We are gone... forever.'

She smiled into her glass, and I knew she didn't share the same belief. Her eyes glinted with a kind of quiet knowing.

'So, tell me more about Cali Silverthorn.'

'What do you want to know?'

'How about you start at the beginning?'

I was but a breath away from her in this cosy corner. Her right hand curved round her glass, long fingers with short manicured nails gently tapping out a rhythm, and I thought how neatly her hand would fit in mine.

'The beginning... Well, I'll keep it simple and start with this lifetime,' she said, grinning. 'I was born somewhere on the side of Glastonbury Tor. Apparently, I was two weeks overdue and my mother was desperate to bring on labour, so she thought a walk up the Tor would help speed things along. Well, it did. On the way down, her waters broke and I made a rapid appearance. I was delivered by a Japanese tourist and a druid priest beneath the midday sun of summer solstice.'

'That's quite an entry into the world.'

'A little unconventional, some would say. Anyway, Mother stuck around until I was three and then decided to take off to America in search of my father, leaving me with my grandmother. I don't know if she ever found him as I've never seen her since.'

'Hell! I'm sorry – that must have been tough.'

'Not really. I was too young to know different, and my grandmother brought me up as her own child. She said it had been meant to be – that it was written in the stars.'

I regarded her with growing intrigue as she told her story and the noise from the rest of the pub seemed to fade away.

'My grandmother was called Mea Drodan, but everyone in our healing kinship knew her as Star-maker. She was an ancient soul with clear memory of all her past and future incarnations. She even remembered her origin planet.'

She paused to take a sip of her drink, but I had the distinct impression that she was giving me time to digest what she was saying, to see how I was taking the odd information. It all sounded far too otherworldly for me to consider seriously, and so I simply regarded her story as some folk-tale passed on from whatever belief system she had belonged to. After all, this talk of origin planets seemed to be something plucked from the library's sci-fi section. Still, there was no falseness in her tone of voice nor concern that what she was telling me would make me think she was crazy or deluded.

She continued. 'In this lifetime, grandmother Star-maker had been given two tasks. One was as an earth healer to help maintain this planet's equilibrium, and the other task was to prepare me for my destiny.'

I peered over the rim of my glass, aware of shandy froth bubbling along my upper lip. 'To prepare you...? For what?'

She shrugged her shoulders. 'To be a healer, like her, I guess. I'd been told something else too but I don't remember what, and when I was old enough to question, it was too late. My grandmother passed over when I was eleven. She knew she was going – even told me the date – and she reassured me that her work was done and that everything would be fine.'

I simply nodded, playing with the button on my shirt-sleeve.

'My grandmother's wish was for me to be fostered by one of the elders in her healing commune, but it wasn't to be. My grandmother's younger sister, a deeply influential woman, took the matter to court, and I was taken into her care. As my great aunt had never approved of her sister's activities, she certainly didn't want me to be involved with the commune. She tried to mould me into a very different way of life: one that didn't suit me, and I was quite the rebel teen.' She giggled at this point, as if recalling moments of anarchy. 'What she didn't realise though was that I continued to learn the old ways in secret. The healers kept a close eye on me and were always there for me. My grandmother watched, too, from the other side, of course.'

She paused, again, to sip her drink and to let me digest her story. I had to admit, it all sounded very strange and certainly far beyond anything I'd experienced. Her eyes sparkled with a kind of vitreous glow.

'When I turned eighteen, I went travelling all over the world... on a spiritual quest to understand my journey as a healer. When I returned to England a few years later, I discovered that my great-aunt had passed on. Some of the healing kindred were in Glastonbury, and so I went to live there to continue my work.'

'And now you're here in Cumbria.'

'Yes, I'm meant to be here right now, in time for my twenty-sixth birthday. It's my destiny.' She held me in her eyes, as if searching for something.

'Destiny,' I repeated, churning my thoughts. 'I'm not sure I like that word. It's too self-assured and always makes me think of endings. To be honest, I don't believe in destiny, as in a pre-written life. There's only one certainty in my mind, and that is we all die. The rest is made up as we go along.'

She eyed me inquisitively, smiling easily, clearly not swayed by my outlook on life and death.

We didn't talk for a minute or two. I stroked my chin in contemplation. I considered what an unconventional childhood she'd had, and I understood how isolating it must have been. And then there was her grandmother, who had obviously been a major influence. All that talk of past lives, origin planets, and fate would have left their mark. After all, children are impressionable. Often, we grow up believing what we've been taught whether it's proven fact or fiction. Cali was simply telling me the crazy truth as she believed it to be.

'So, you now know the quick version of my life story,' she said, smiling.

'Life story so far,' I corrected.

She nodded, thoughtfully. 'Anyway, enough about me; I want to know about Tom Philips.'

'Ah, there's not much to tell.'

'No way; let's hear from the beginning.'

She leant forwards, waiting for me to start, hands rested on the table and held tantalisingly close to mine. The crystal at her neck flickered.

'Okay, well, I was born at the family farm at milking time, which wasn't the most convenient moment to make an appearance. Unlike my older brother, Pete, I didn't take to farming. I seemed more of a hindrance than helpful, and my father was always on at me because of it. Anyway, to cut a dull story short, I spent time with my granddad, and his love of academic life inspired me. That's when I fell in love with books and poetry.' I paused. 'Am I boring you yet?'

'No, not at all. So, you decided to follow the academic route.'

'Aye, I applied to the University of Edinburgh, was accepted, and lived the student life. Way back, I had this romantic idea of being a poet. I do write and I had some poems published, but I soon found that it was notoriously difficult to make a living purely from writing poetry. For a time, I shifted from writing poetry to writing song lyrics and I formed a band. We played a couple of gigs in Edinburgh bars, but we were notoriously lacking in musical prowess so we gave that up, and probably saved our audience's eardrums. Not long after, I enrolled on postgraduate study, hoping I'd find a job I loved at some point in the future. I remained in Edinburgh until recently.'

'So, why have you returned to your roots?'

'I don't know; things changed. I turned thirty back in February. It was time for a new direction, I guess. I applied for the position of mobile librarian on a whim. There was no one more surprised than me when I found out I'd been offered the job. I accepted, and here I am.'

'And are you happy being back?'

'Too early to say,' I replied, draining my glass. 'But I'm happy right now, right this moment.'

'Well, that's all that matters. After all, the world is not to be lived in the past or the future; it's to be lived in the now.'

This time, I held her in my eyes. There was a shy moment between us, and then we both tried to speak at the same time, which made us laugh. This was followed by a rally of 'before you' and 'no, you first', and then I asked if she'd like another drink, and we spent the rest of the evening together, closed off from the world. And I was happy. I think she was too. We talked about a diverse range of topics, from the mundane to what I considered the crazy weird. I wasn't sure about some of the esoteric subjects she brought into conversation, and I tended to respond with a questioning frown, a few choice words of scepticism, or a confused silence. Still, the overall mood was uplifting and we were so engrossed in conversation that we were surprised when last orders were called.

'The landlord's throwing us out,' I said, standing up, narrowly missing hitting my head on the low ceiling beam. 'C'mon, I guess we'd better go.'

I held out my hand and she took it. The moment seemed to stand completely still. A surge of energy shot through my fingers, up through my arm, and seemed to explode in my head like a sudden burst of sunlight emerging from a cloud. I savoured the moment I'd been waiting for all evening: that first touch. Everything seemed brighter, and I was filled with a sense of what could be.

∞∞∞∞∞∞∞∞

'They walk upon the Earth with you.'

Nevermore was a tiny hamlet of thirty residents. Apart from a dotting of weathered cottages and a farm, it had a general store, which functioned as a post office, meeting place, and tearoom for passing walkers, mountain bikers, and explorers. It was also the stopping point for the locals to receive their library and community services. There was only one road in and out, leading from a lane to the boundary of Hawkdale, and that road just happened to be two miles long and frustratingly narrow: a nightmare when driving a large, lumbering vehicle such as the mobile library. It was a feat just to visit or leave this time-forgotten place. There was only a handful of passing places, and if you met another vehicle at the wrong time in the wrong spot, you had to reverse back to the last passing place. It's a bit like a game of Snakes and Ladders.

On this occasion, I was attempting to leave. At this time of year, with day-trippers and holidaymakers using the road, it was a frustrating journey. Normally, I would find it tedious. But today, I was smiling. Today, my head was full of Cali Silverthorn. I didn't mind if it took all morning to drive the two miles because I was happy, day-dreaming, thinking of where to take her next – maybe into Kendal to watch a film. Or a weekend trip to Edinburgh. Now there was an idea. Then my imagination flew into the future – a tour into Europe, perhaps. In my mind's eye, I imagined us setting up home, even having children together.

'Get a grip, Tom,' I reminded myself, 'we've only just met.'

Yes, only just met and yet it was as though I'd known her all my life. What was that about?

My thoughts drifted back to last night, how good it had been to be in her presence, growing drunk on her. She was a little strange at times. I mean, I didn't really understand this ability she proclaimed to have in seeing people's auras. Hell, I wasn't sure I even believed in auras. And, although she had attempted to explain how she used the light to heal, it didn't really make much scientific sense. And, if truth be known, she had a hippy presence about her which sat right at home with the most ardent Glastonbury Festival followers. I could imagine her singing and chanting around a camp-fire, probably naked. Despite the giddy goddess-worshipping spiritual stuff, she was captivating. She giggled a lot in a sweet way. Even in the darkness, outside her door at midnight beneath a canopy of budding Wisteria, she sparkled. Oh, but why hadn't I kissed her properly instead of on her cheek? What was wrong with me? It seemed ridiculous now.

I reversed the van into a passing place for the third time as a stream of cars edged their way forwards along this forsaken lane. Two buzzards circled high over the adjacent rock-strewn pasture. A raven perched on the passing place sign, regarding me intently. I allowed the slow procession of cars through. While waiting, my eyes idled over the adjacent wall into the rolling field. A group of men – seven in total – were sat around a small fishing pond. There was nothing particularly strange in that, only they didn't have any fishing rods or nets.

They simply stared into the still water, heads bowed like meditating monks. Now that *was* a bit weird. I couldn't make out their features because they were too far away, but they were all dressed in dark clothing – that I could see. I watched for a few seconds more, trying to work out what they were doing. The road ahead was clear so I drove on, my questioning frown in danger of becoming a permanent feature. A burst of light brightened the valley. Ever curious, I was tempted to stop, go ask the men what they were doing, but I wasn't sure I wanted to know. In any case, I was on the home straight now, where the road widened as it met the junction, so I kept on going. Finally, I emerged from Nevermore and from my wishful reverie and the weird guys round the pond, and drove onwards along the tranquil back-road through Hawkdale.

∞∞∞∞∞∞∞∞

'The ancient ones are kindred. Listen to their song.'

Fine tendrils of cirrus cloud streaked the sky. Cali continued to invade my thoughts. The image of her was firmly imprinted in my mind, and those eyes of cornflower blue possessed me. She was beguiling. She had a determination about her, a quiet wisdom, something instilled perhaps from her upbringing. There was a whole lot to like about her. So, maybe, just maybe, I could overlook her strange outlook, her new-age beliefs, and the fanciful stuff I was at odds with.

I eased the van round the next bend, glancing into the landscape's belly and up over the fells. An unsettling sensation rose in me like a barometer's mercury, something primitive and instinctive. A herd of ponies grouped on the fell-side, ears twitching, heads alert, and they cantered away, shying at the invisible. Further on, sheep were flocking, running this way and that, clearly agitated. I wondered if a dog was on the loose, or perhaps that wild beast cat that people had been talking about. There had been regular sightings of a large black panther-like creature over the years. Whatever it was, the animals were seriously spooked. I scanned the fields but saw nothing untoward.

Just past the milestone, I found Verity Lait wandering in a field. Now, that was not so unusual, as I had come to realise. Upon seeing me, she waved frantically so I pulled up at the

51

roadside. She made her way to the mobile library, awkwardly running on her arthritic legs with a kind of excited urgency. I wound the window down.

'Morning, Verity. Are you all right?'

'Ecstatic, Tom, thank you,' she wheezed, catching her breath. 'Can you see it?'

'See what?'

'The angels... they've left a sign.'

'A sign.'

'Yes, and you can take that bemused look off your face, Tom Philips. I'm not a crackpot or crack-head or whatever you young ones call it. See, look over there.'

Verity pointed to the far corner of the field. I wasn't sure what I was supposed to be looking for, so I scanned the line of trees, the wall, and the woods beyond.

'Look at the ground, Tom. It's in the grass. Can you see?'

I made out the edge of what looked like a depression in the crop. 'I can't quite see from here.'

'Well, get up on the roof then,' Verity ordered.

'What?'

'C'mon, a young agile man like you. Get up on the roof and you'll see it.'

I couldn't believe I was doing this. I rolled up my sleeves, opened the van door, and scrambled up the side of the mobile library, using the open window as a foothold. For some reason, I was reminded of my ten-year-old self, trying to climb over the seven-foot-tall vicarage wall in the neighbouring village, lured by the promise of ripe apples on the other side. Pete had bounded over like a cat but I, all gangly-limbed, just wasn't built for climbing, and it took me ages. I wasn't faring much better now, but I did manage to heave myself onto the roof. As soon as I was steady, I turned round, impressed with the views my vantage point gave me, and then I looked to the corner of the field. What I saw almost knocked me backwards. Wide-eyed and loose-jawed, I stared down at Verity in disbelief.

'Well?' she said, with an 'I told you so' look on her face. 'Impressed, hey?'

I couldn't quite take in the immensity of it, and my stomach tightened with excitement or apprehension or something. There, swirled into the long green grass, was a pattern, a complexity of circles, and it was so precise and so big and so unusual that my logical mind was threatening to go absent without leave.

'It's one of those crop circles,' I said, composing myself. 'They are common down south but they're man-made...'

Verity was shaking her head from side to side, and grinning defiantly.

I ignored her for a moment, trying to estimate how long something like this would take to create, how it could be done so precisely and without leaving a trail of evidence. I remembered there being a study group at the university that investigated this kind of phenomenon. Although the group were funded year-on-year, they were certainly on the fringe and never taken seriously by the scientists amongst us. I recalled sitting in on a debate entitled *The Physics Behind the Unexplained* with my good friend, Professor Tristian Neeble, who went on to graduate in theoretical physics. One of the speakers put across some nonsense that crop circles were the physical result of space-time dimensional disturbance. Even now, I could hear the laughter that filled the halls of academia.

Verity was still grinning, confidently, and then I realised, and asked, 'Am I right in thinking you saw this being created?'

She nodded, and I swallowed so hard that it hurt my throat, as if the stuff of reason had lodged itself there. I swallowed again and found my voice.

'And, you're sure it wasn't students on a drunken binge?'

She nodded, still grinning, and I kind of knew what she was going to say next. I looked at her, eyebrows raised in question.

'I told you, Tom. It was done by angels.'

I sighed and my shoulders slumped. Angels. There had to be a logical explanation.

Awkwardly, I slid down from the mobile library's roof.

'And do these angels have wings?'

'Well,' Verity began, 'they're really nothing like our tradi-tional view of an angel.'

'Okay, so Michelangelo got it wrong.' I tried not to be facetious, but I couldn't help myself. It all seemed too absurd. 'So, if they don't look like angels, what do they look like?'

'Bright balls of light.'

I tried to stifle my laughter but failed. 'How on Earth do bright balls of light translate into angels?'

Verity eyed me fiercely. 'Stop your smirking. I just know that's what they are.'

Her indignation quietened me, and I knew this was an argument I could not win. I leaned against the side of the mobile library, contemplative. 'So, how long did it take for these bright balls of light to create this?'

Verity rubbed a crooked finger over her bold chin as if the very action was computing her answer. 'Oh, I'd say about thirty seconds.'

'Thirty seconds?'

'Yes, that's what I said, Tom.'

I suddenly needed a strong coffee.

A cool wind slithered over my bare forearms, and I was consumed by a strange sensation of being watched. My stomach contracted and I had an overwhelming but completely illogical desire to leave this place, and now.

'C'mon, Verity, I'll take you back to town.'

I opened the passenger door for her.

'What for? They may come back.'

'That's what I'm worried about. They – whatever they are – might not be friendly.'

'They haven't harmed me,' she replied.

'No, but it's best the experts take a look. I mean, if you've seen some kind of energy source–'

'Angels, Tom.'

'Well, whatever those lights are, I'm sure there'll be a logical explanation. It could be a military project for all we know, or simply some natural phenomenon. After all, there's been plenty of seismic activity in the region of late.'

Verity's face fell. 'Well, I don't think it is and I'm not sure about calling experts in. It'll only cause trouble, you mark my words.'

'C'mon, I think we both need a coffee.'

Reluctantly, she stepped up into the library's passenger seat, grumbling away to herself. As we travelled into Hawkdale, I wondered what Cali would make of it all.

∞∞∞∞∞∞∞∞

'They speak in symbols and whispers.'

I'm not sure who had needed the coffee more: Verity or me. It had been a strange kind of morning and my head felt woolly. Verity said it was likely to be the effect of coming into contact with angel energy. I exhaled deeply, shaking my head at the mere suggestion, and the lines round her mouth tightened to vent her disapproval at my dismissal. I shrugged my shoulders in a kind of resigned retaliation. She wouldn't be budged on her views, so there was no point discussing it.

I guessed it was time to return to my day's schedule, and it was probably as well. I couldn't sit here and listen to another rendition of Verity's version of events. The café was busy now and she had a keen audience of locals with eager ears, including the town's newspaper journalist who had just come in for his lunch, ready to take in the grossly flamboyant detail about her experience with the angels in the field. Verity certainly had a penchant for dramatics but I'd seen and heard enough weirdness for one day, and welcomed the fresh air as I stepped out into the high street.

Despite the morning's kerfuffle I was ahead of schedule, so I decided to take another gander at the work of Verity's angels. I parked the mobile library close to the hedgerow, leaving enough room for passing vehicles. I locked the van's door and entered the field. There was now a stiff wind blowing from the west, which rustled through the standing remains of the meadow grass, creating a silvery-green weft. When I reached the edge of one of the three large circles, the wind dropped.

Tentatively, I stepped inside the circle. All was still. I hesitated as it felt like I shouldn't really have been there. The first thing I noticed was the extreme cold. The downed stalks were springy underfoot and had a frozen blue-tinted hue. Goose pimples raced up my arms and I realised that it really was markedly colder. And again, I had that feeling of being watched. I turned full circle and caught a glimpse of something sparkling within the adjacent woodland. I thought of Verity's angels and shook my head. There really had to be a scientific explanation. What with the recent earth tremors, perhaps the light was plasma escaping from a fault line in the underlying rock. I was sure my granddad would have known, him having been a geologist.

I walked towards the small woodland to take a closer look. The earlier irrational fear I'd had was gone, replaced now by a healthy stoicism and a need to know the truth. A line of oak trees, all twisted and knolled, lurked like a row of old crones, dividing the wood from the field. The woodland itself was a mixture of silver birch, beech, hazel, and hawthorn: a small coppice that had been left to nature's wisdom. With only a fine canopy of spring leaves, there was enough light shining through to illuminate the early spread of bluebells. There was no clear path through the wood so I loitered at the edge, enchanted by the perfect poetry of those shimmering blue flowers, like the blue of Cali's eyes.

Movement in the woods slapped me out of my daydream. Branches were breaking underfoot. And there, fleeting shadows – something dark and quick moving... and something else

– flashes of light caught my peripheral vision. And then, out of nowhere, a voice.

'Are you looking for something, Mr Philips?'

I near jumped out of my body. I turned round to find a vaguely familiar face. It was the old guy who had visited the library earlier in the week, the one obsessed with UFOs. I placed my hands on my knees and bent forwards, recovering from the shock of him creeping up on me.

'Where on Earth did you come from?' I asked, slightly exasperated.

'I was passing and saw you up here so I thought I'd see what's going on.'

'It's Henry, isn't it? Henry Ligget?'

'That's right. You remembered me, then.'

How could I forget? I thought. I straightened myself up and took a slow breath.

'Not surprised you're jumpy, lad,' he continued, looking back over the field. 'I see you've discovered one of those alien-made patterns. Don't suppose you've seen the little grey ETs about – in the woods, perhaps? Those little blighters are everywhere.'

I gave him the 'are you serious?' look, and then sighed. Verity thought angels were visiting us. Henry thought it was aliens. What next, ghosts, zombies, or little green elves?

'If you want my opinion, Mr Ligget, I think this has something to do with the earth tremors – something geological, something very natural, something that can be logically explained by science.'

'So, you haven't seen any ETs roaming around in these woods?'

I hesitated. After all, I thought I'd seen something – shadows, flashes of light – but I couldn't be certain. 'To be honest,' I began, 'I haven't seen anything definitive.' Henry had a confused expression on his face, so I clarified. 'I haven't seen any aliens, ETs, or whatever you want to call them.'

'Oh well,' he said, looking around, 'I expect they'll be long gone by now.'

'And I think it's time I should be gone, too,' I said, jangling the van's keys. 'If you'll excuse me, Mr Ligget, I have to be on my way.'

He tipped his cap at me and stepped aside to let me pass. I walked round the edge of the field rather than cut through the crop pattern again. Henry followed me, quietly keeping pace like one of those snappy heelers. When we reached the road, he promptly perched on his bicycle, which he had leant against the side of the van, and lurched forwards into the road in an ungainly and quite comical fashion.

'Don't forget to stock some UFO books and films, Mr Philips,' he called out as he pedalled away. 'And stay vigilant. Those ETs will be watching.'

He didn't give me chance to reply, which was probably a good thing. I'm not sure he'd have liked what I was about to say. UFOS: what a load of tosh!

∞∞∞∞∞∞∞∞∞

'The time has come to awaken.'

I relaxed by the window in Ravenshead's one and only café, and glanced at the menu. A lady appeared from the kitchen, wispy greying hair clipped back from her flushed round face. She beamed a generous smile that was directed at me.

'Ah, you must be Tom,' she said brightly, pulling up her sleeves to reveal her thick vinegar-tanned arms.

I nodded with a surprised expression.

'Cali said to look out for a tall, handsome man, and there aren't many of those about these parts, so I knew it was you.'

Now I was the one feeling a bit flushed and I smiled, bashfully, not sure what to say.

'She told me to tell you to place an order for lunch, and that she'll be along shortly.'

I glanced at the menu again, wondering what to order for Cali. I hadn't known her long enough to be aware of what she liked or didn't like.

The lady studied me with warm grey eyes and pointed to number eight on the lunch menu. 'She doesn't eat much, that I can tell you, but I know she's one of those vegetarians, so I'd suggest the summer salad.'

'Right, I'll order two of those and...'

'Elderflower cordial – it's one of her favourite drinks.'

'Okay, so two cordials it is, please.' I smiled, and she tootled off to the kitchen, humming a song that was vaguely familiar.

I checked my watch. It was just gone midday: 12.11 p.m. to be exact. Cali had said she would meet me here as soon as she'd finished her healing dance class at the village hall.

The café snuggled into a high bank overlooking the weir. The slow water, a tributary of the River Duddon, met the weir's inescapable rushing force: it was like two distinct worlds colliding. The river's hiss provided a constant background noise which was pleasantly invigorating. I hadn't been here before. It seemed quiet for a Saturday, but I guessed that many locals would have travelled into Hawkdale or Kendal for their main shopping. A few tables away, a middle-aged couple were chatting over lunch. Their accents were American so I imagined they must have been tourists passing through. In the corner, at the table ahead of me, an old chap was reading the local newspaper. The front headline caught my attention: 'Mystery lights over Coniston spark UFO hunt', and part way down the page, 'Local lady sees angels', with a picture of Verity with super-imposed wings on her shoulders. I laughed out loud.

'Unbelievable!' I couldn't help saying. What rubbish they were using to sell newspapers these days.

The old chap dipped his newspaper and peered over the top. He grinned at me for a few seconds, the lines of time and experience etched on his face, and then he disappeared between the pages, more than likely engrossed in a made-up story. After all, what was news but a tiny window of events retold through a narrow version of subjective reality? To my mind, there seemed to be a fine line between fact and fiction.

Sunlight streamed through the window and reflected off the table's glass vase, creating a prism of colour, which danced on the opposite wall and ceiling.

Outside on the veranda, overlooking the weir, two jackdaws watched the day's turning. They perched beneath the slated overhang of the café's roof, bobbing their grey heads. A single white feather dropped from the sky and appeared to be suspended in mid-air. I watched it quiver on the faint breeze and wondered where it had come from.

'That's a message from the angelic realm.'

I turned to find Cali standing just behind me. She continued to watch the feather, eyes wide and sparkling, whereas my attention was now most definitely on her. She was radiant in a light purple summer dress. Her river of dark hair tumbled over her bare sun-kissed shoulders, and my senses were sweetly intoxicated with the heady aroma of honeysuckle.

'The feather is for you,' she continued, dreamily, as if she was seeing something else that wasn't there. 'It means that you'll have to make a decision – sometime soon.'

I studied her, curiously. Before I'd even had chance to say anything, the lady reappeared from the kitchen, carrying our meals.

'Lovely to see you, Cali, my dear,' she chirped, as she put our plates on the table. 'And you're right – he is tall and handsome.'

This time, Cali blushed, and the lady chuckled as she scurried back to the kitchen. A moment later, she returned with our drinks.

'Now, you will look after our Cali, young man,' the lady said, raising her finger like an exclamation mark, 'because she's a true gift – heaven-sent, I'd say, and I'm not even religious.' She chuckled again, and then added, more seriously, 'You know, I wouldn't be here if it wasn't for this young lady. Brought me back from the brink with her healing, she did. She's like a daughter to me, and I only wish the best for her.'

A moment passed between the two of them: something unspoken, something significant.

'Oh, you mustn't make a fuss, Grace, but thank you,' Cali said, quietly humbled.

'Well, enjoy your lunch,' she chirped, and off she went back to the kitchen, humming that familiar song again, which I knew but just couldn't remember.

After lunch, Cali and I strolled, side-by-side, along the riverbank. The afternoon had that simmering quality about it that was more late summer than spring. Despite its unquestionable beauty, it was undisturbed here, a forgotten domain off the tourist trail, and we walked in comfortable silence for a while, lost in nature's offerings. Frequently, our arms brushed together as if magnetised. Frequently, she gazed up at me with that knowing look in her eyes, which left me feeling naked and separated from my senses. And she was more alive here in nature's sanctuary. Every few steps, she stopped to marvel at a butterfly. She delighted in the song of birds, such a bright melody lifting above the constant babble of water. Her nose crinkled appreciatively as she breathed in the sun-kissed meadow's drowsing aroma. Now and then, she would stare into space and I'd follow her gaze, trying to decipher what remained hidden to me.

Soon, we reached a bend in the river. The water seemed to inhale and exhale, exposing sandbanks and drawing in the light that fed it. Part of the bank had eroded, creating a generous sandy shelf and an irresistible little rest spot. Cali grabbed my hand and playfully pulled me along, until we were on the sand bed. She kicked off her sandals and paddled ankle-deep in the clinging clear water.

'Isn't it cold?' I asked.

'Just a little, but it is so refreshing and energising.' She waded through. 'I love being in water. When I was in Arizona, I bathed in the sacred springs by Oak Creek Canyon and received a powerful purification healing.'

'I bet it was a little warmer there than it is here.'

'Yes, I was sky-clad for most of the time. There's nothing like being at one with nature.'

Images of her bathing naked stoked my imagination. I grabbed a handful of sand as a distraction and let the grains drain from my clenched fist. She tiptoed out of the water and rested cross-legged beside me, dress gathered up to reveal the smooth honey curves of her knees. Sand stuck to her toes, glistening in the sun like tiny jewels.

'So, what do you think of Cumbria?' I asked, rolling up my shirtsleeves to take advantage of the spring sun.

'I love it here, Tom. It's magical,' she said, and then with a slight frown, she added, 'although the vibe is a little weird at times.'

'How do you mean?'

'Well, I'm usually very good at interpreting and working with energy, but that's all been a little strange and inconsistent since I've been here. Sometimes, the vibration is strong. My astral journeys, for example, have been very... well, very tangible, of late, and also incredibly exhausting.'

I didn't know how to respond to that. I'd always thought astral travel was the result of vivid dreaming or an over-active imagination.

'What about the cottage... your house-mates?' I asked, preferring to focus on the ordinary stuff I understood. 'Is that working out for you?'

'Considering the very different personalities in the house, it works out well,' she said. 'There's Jake Quake, who's a singer in a band. I was invited to have a glimpse into his future and he's going to be famous. Then there's Rachel. She travels a lot with her job as an art buyer. I've only met her once. She's very nice but constantly pre-occupied with making money. Then there's the owner, Matt Darker. He's an astronomer, I think...'

'That'll explain the observatory in the garden,' I said. 'Sounds like an interesting bunch you're sharing with.'

'Yes, but I don't see much of them. Really, the house is just a base for them as it is for me. I'm always busy with my healing.'

I rubbed my chin. 'Your work is important to you.'

'It is, Tom,' she said, turning to look me straight in the eyes. 'There is much healing to do... so very much.'

I frowned. 'I didn't realise there's so many ill people out there.'

'It's not just people,' she said, and then paused as if unsure whether to continue. 'I mean, healing is needed on many different levels. For example, the Earth needs healing just as much as anyone who is sick. Our earth mother used to be self-healing, but now, because of the impact of human activity, she needs help. Some of my healing involves taking care of mother earth and continuing my grandmother's work.'

'Hmm, well, I agree about the state of our planet but I'm not certain what any one person can do to change anything.'

'You'd be surprised, Tom. If we each play a part, we can make a difference on the whole. Individually, we all have more power than we think. You see, I'm not so unusual where my healing gift is concerned. Anyone can learn to do what I do. It's just a matter of focus and belief. It's a matter of living from the heart and not from the head. Love is the way, Tom. It's the answer to everything.'

I laughed. Perhaps I shouldn't have done but I couldn't help myself. 'If only life was that simple... I'd like to see love stop famine or prevent all the devastation caused by environmental catastrophes. I'd like to see love launch a rocket into space.'

'Love is where it all begins,' she continued, untroubled by my dismissal. 'When we live with love, we find positive solutions to these and other problems. We resonate from a very different space. Love has the power to change our world.'

'I'm not convinced but I respect your viewpoint, despite its sentimentality. In my opinion, more brain-power needs to be applied. More brain-power and more logic. For example, consider all the strange stuff going on locally, at the moment.'

'Strange stuff?' Her forehead wrinkled, and I considered that what I found strange might not be at all strange to her.

'You know, the crop circle that appeared in the field near Hawkdale, and the strange lights and shadows, all the earth tremors, and so on... many locals are saying it's all to do with aliens or angels or some other ridiculous suggestion. But where's the proof? Where's the logic behind such assumptions? It's totally absurd. If you ask me, people would sooner believe in a fantastical explanation because it's more exciting than the mundane truth. Either that or they're just too lazy to find a rational explanation.'

Two ducks flapped their wings, splashing and quacking noisily through the water as they took flight. I realised I was ranting with a bit too much gusto. Cali maintained a serene but faraway look in her eyes. She didn't respond. But what was there to say? Deep down, she must have understood.

My mind quietened, as if the river had taken my thoughts and carried them away downstream. I closed my eyes and tilted my head back, enjoying the sunshine on my face.

Cali nudged me. 'Look, Tom. Open your eyes and look.'

There, over the river, blowing in from the fields, were thousands of dandelion-seeds floating in procession on the breeze. The air was thick with them as they passed over our heads.

'Wow,' I said, surprised by the sheer volume. 'I've never seen so many.'

The tiny cotton-like parachutes spun and tumbled, their destination in the hands of the air that carried them. Cali stood up, giggling with excitement, and she reached out to catch the white seed bundles. I saw the girl in the woman. And, in that moment, despite our very different outlooks, I felt a profound connection, something inexplicable emanating from deep within. I knew so little about her, and yet I wanted to be there for her. I wanted to protect her. I didn't understand why.

The dandelion snow dispersed and Cali sat down again with a bundle of hairy seeds in her palms. One by one, she blew them away, surrendering them to the breeze.

'We can spend a lifetime finding truth,' she said, holding up the last dandelion seed and then letting it go, 'and if and when we find it, we realise it's never whole, it's never constant. Truth is as fleeting as a dandelion seed.'

Sunlight glazed the water like a sheer of varnish. Her eyes glazed, too, taking on that vitreous film, as if hiding something beneath. In this moment, there was uncertainty: something unspoken. I was sure I had a thousand questions for her, but I couldn't find the words. It's as if all my thoughts had drifted away with those dandelion-seeds. A sudden sullen wind rustled the laden willow branches hanging over the river. The water rippled silver raising momentary flashes, as if a thousand tiny sticklebacks had turned their bellies to the sun.

'Can you hear the river song?' she asked.

'I hear the water trickling by, if that's what you mean.'

'Listen very closely,' she whispered into my ear. 'You can hear its ancient song... the one it's been singing since the beginning of time.'

I strained my ears but I heard nothing other than the familiar flow of water and the steady climb of my pulse as she leant her head against me. Tentatively, I put my arm around her. It felt right. It felt like the way it had always been between us.

∞∞∞∞∞∞∞∞

'Thought is energy.'

When I accepted the position of mobile librarian, I was told that one of the great educations of working in the community was meeting such a diverse range of people. I now understood why the word 'education' was chosen. As I listened to the strange banter between the bookshelves, I was clearly learning that some of the people in Wrenside were particularly weird or, to be fair, had a weird outlook. They were nice weird, polite weird, on the surface quite normal weird but weird all the same.

Take Mrs Mannering, for example: a lovely, recently retired civil servant, courteous, intellectual, and sharp-witted, but she talked to her dead husband, Victor, as if he was still standing next to her. She'd returned her books this afternoon and while I was scanning them through, she'd turned to the space at her side and asked the invisible Victor if there were any books he wanted this week. I didn't hear his reply – because he wasn't there. He's dead – but she continued to have this conversation with him. To me, that was weird.

Then Merlin appeared. Yes, Merlin: long silver-haired, silver-bearded former window cleaner now pagan psychic who believed he was the reincarnated magician of Arthurian legend.

Dressed in his magician's outfit, complete with black cloak, his presence was difficult to ignore. Most people talked about the weather while they were waiting. Not Merlin. He simply said, 'The veils between worlds are thin at the moment. There's something moving in the ether, some kind of special magic.' And then he launched into that song by Queen: 'It's a kind of magic... it's a kind of magic.' And then he gave a curious wide-eyed grin, long white eyebrows flying upwards like owl wings, which would probably scare small children. 'Have you noticed the magic?' he asked.

I shook my head. The worst thing I could do was engage in conversation in case I provoked a tirade of cursing. I'd already witnessed him cast an evil-eye gesture on a tourist who had jokingly asked him where he could find Camelot. Although I didn't believe this particular Merlin had any powers, I didn't want to be fired from my job for duelling with customers. With a great flourish of his cloak, he took out a piece of paper from his velvet waistcoat pocket and ordered a book on alchemy and one on car maintenance. I was tempted to say that if the magic didn't work, good old tried-and-tested mechanics would fix his car, and that was the real magic. I thought better of it, though, and wished him a good day.

Then there were twin brothers, Leo and Nick: two bright boys, with a healthy interest in current affairs, hopeful of gaining employment in the city after completing a college course in business studies. Now these two weren't really weird at all: over-active in the imagination department, yes. They were discussing the earth tremors, and I couldn't help capture some of the conversation.

'I reckon they're tunnelling underground,' Leo said, sweeping his long fringe to one side.

'Nah, why would they do that? They can hide in the lake,' Nick replied, scratching his aquiline nose, while flicking through a book about city trading.

'They're mining, taking the minerals they need from deep underground. We obviously have something on Earth that they haven't got on their planet.'

'I don't know, bro. I think there's a more logical reason for the tremors.'

'And what's that?'

'They're being caused by the force of their propulsion systems or whatever it is their crafts use to fold space when they travel here. Makes sense, eh?'

My face must have seemed like it had hit the floor. Disappointed? Yes. I was expecting a sensible discussion from these two.

They leant against the desk with their chosen business books on how to make a million on the stock exchange, and I scanned them through.

I don't know why I bothered but I just had to open my mouth. 'I couldn't help overhear you guys talking about the earth tremors. Are you saying that they're caused by something not of this world?'

'Yeah,' they both said.

'Do you mind me asking how you've come to that conclusion?'

'We've seen them,' Leo said. Nick added, 'We've seen their crafts going in and out of Coniston Water.'

'You've seen? Are you sure it's not just a trick of the light?'

They looked at each other as if I was the crazy one, and laughed.

'Nah, man, definitely of ET origin, because we definitely don't have the tech they have.'

They picked up their books.

'We might have,' I challenged. 'It could be top secret stuff.'

'What, along with the little silvery-grey guys that fly those things at speeds that defy all known forces? Nah, man, you really have to see to believe.'

They smiled, said cheerio, and left, giving me that sorry expression as if I was the deluded one. I tapped my fingers on the desktop. They obviously believed that they'd seen something not of this world, but seeing wasn't necessarily proof. And this was what I'd tried to explain to Cali at the weekend: that such unexplained happenings required logical analysis, measurement, and scientific testing to determine their truth. How could anything be deemed something without the application of rationality?

I drove away from Wrenside, convinced that local people were simply overreacting to all the gossip and rumour. When someone reports seeing a UFO, it's obvious more people would look to the skies and, inevitably, convince themselves they'd also seen alien spaceships, when in actual fact it was a Chinese lantern, cloud, star, passing satellite, helicopter, or simply the sun rising. There was always a rational explanation.

At lunchtime, I escaped the weirdness and parked the mobile library in a lay-by on Moon Howe Road. I was a few miles from civilisation and, today, that suited me just fine. I ate my cheese and pickle sandwich, poured a cup of strong tea from my flask, and lost myself in the real explainable magic of the landscape. Here, the earth seemed to dither and slouch, bracken-coated, stretching wide until the fabric rose to form an undulating ridge on either side. Bristled knolls pocked the fell and sheep grazed on rough terraces. The odd tree clung to life, roots clawing brittle earth and rock. In front of me, road and land gently sloped away to softer contours of green, then rushed headlong into pockets of grey villages and, further still, grey towns like bruises on nature's skin. Beyond was the glint of estuary and sea. Here was a place of ever-moving shades of light and dark, a place shaped by fierce westerly winds, a place still being sculptured year on year.

I turned the radio on. My look-a-like was singing 'Katherine Kiss Me' and I mouthed the words 'Cali kiss me' and imagined how that would be. Then I wondered, realistically, whether things could possibly work out between us. After all, she was a bit weird and I was probably not weird enough. We had very different outlooks and ways of thinking: a collision in the making. I turned the radio up. I closed my eyes and dozed in the sun for ten minutes before setting off to my next destination.

That evening, I held tight to the ordinary. After leaving County Library, I stayed in Kendal for a few hours. I had dinner at the arts centre, watched a documentary film shot in black and white about a woman who gave up love for art, and then ended the evening drinking non-alcoholic wine in the Café Bleu bar. I eavesdropped on conversations about the lack of arts funding in a time where art was needed more than ever to save people from tedium. I quietly enjoyed the overt flirting of ideas and emotions. I was alone. Oh but it was good to have a few hours of normality.

∞∞∞∞∞∞∞∞

'Be settled in your heart. You will know.'

Cali Silverthorn! Why was this woman overwhelming my thoughts, day and night? The alarm clock glowed 4.31 a.m. I turned over, punched my pillow, and tried to sleep. She was still there though, teasing my dreams with her naked fell-side frolicking. Her eyes filled the darkness and I wondered what power she had over me. I knew she was in my waking and sleeping thoughts because I liked her. If I was honest, 'like' wasn't the right word; it didn't even begin to sum up how she affected me, and yet I couldn't possibly use the other 'L' word. After all, I'd known her all of five minutes and I wasn't one to express love so lightly. Besides, as captivated as I was, in my most rational moments I knew there were issues. She believed in stuff that my logical mind couldn't assimilate or accept.

Earlier this evening, we'd met at the Fox and Jackdaw in Ravenshead, a pub run by an ageing former rock guitarist. The place was effectively a shrine to all things musical. Cobweb-coated vintage guitars, mandolins, saxophones, and drum-skins hung from grim wood panelled walls. Framed platinum records, music posters, and black and white photos of past musicians, many long gone, littered the remaining wall space. It was as if we were in a musical graveyard, and yet there was a number of young people at the bar or gathered round the jukebox, particularly skinny-jeaned boys wearing black eye-liner. It reminded me of a Berlin bar scene. Anyway, Cali and I had talked about poetry again but the subject drifted towards the issues concerning my father:

'You still hold a lot of fear in your heart where your father is concerned,' she'd said.

I'd straightened up, sort of defensively. 'You're wrong. I'm not frightened of him.'

'No but you're carrying some fear because of him... fear of loss or rejection.'

'I left all that behind when I moved to Edinburgh. All that was years ago. It doesn't bother me now.'

'Time matters not if healing hasn't taken place... if you haven't forgiven him.'

I'd fidgeted, pulling on the cuff of my shirt, and I'd felt... well, I'd felt irritated. What did she mean about forgiveness? Surely my father should be apologising to me for making my teen years difficult. 'He's the one with the problem,' I'd sniffed. 'If he wasn't so bitter... so challenging to get on with... then maybe...'

'It's okay,' she'd said, resting her hand on mine, soothing the agitation, which had built far too easily within me.

For a moment, I thought she'd offer to heal whatever she thought needed healing, but she didn't. She'd simply waited until the tension dissipated and I was centred enough to see sense.

'Sorry,' I'd said. 'He obviously still gets to me. You probably have a point, but I'll deal with it my own way.'

It had been a strange and unsettling conversation, which left me awkward, embarrassed for over-reacting, and annoyed that I'd allowed my father to make me feel this way. After that, the rest of the evening had settled into a more relaxed mood, although the weirdness loomed.

I mean, how was I supposed to react to her telling me that her deceased grandmother, the one who had died when she was eleven, was now visiting her in the form of an owl? Of course, I had laughed. I think I told her that she had a vivid imagination. I even gave her one of my looks, the look that clearly said 'nonsense!' She had been resolute though, and seemed sad that I didn't believe her, and there had been a longer silence between us. Fortunately, we talked about normal everyday things too. Yet the strange stuff kept finding its way into conversation. Visions, healing energies, spirits, nature elementals, and the like didn't fit into my vocabulary or my ordinary experience, and as much as I understood the positive placebo benefits of her work as a healer, I struggled to accept the obscure explanations behind what she did. Without evidence, without scientific basis, it was simply wild conjecture. This was what was causing the conflict... more for me than for her. Oh but there's a lot about her that did make sense: her passion for helping people, her love of nature, her philosophy for living lightly on the Earth, her zest for life, and the way everything lit up when she was present.

My bedroom shrank in the darkness. There were no stars this night. Suffocating cloud filled the skylight and I felt lost in the rectangle of grey-black. I knew I shouldn't allow myself to be swept away on this tide of feelings. She was beautiful, without question. I was attracted to her, without question. I couldn't explain it but I felt like I'd known her all my life. But, the airy-fairy stuff, the unsubstantiated assumptions accepted as fact, challenged the academic in me and would most likely drive me to despair.

I sighed. I punched my pillow, and turned over again. Sometimes, I wished I didn't think so much. Why couldn't I just go with the flow? Eventually, sleep started to dissolve me but not before realising that it was too late to rein in my feelings. It really was too late. You see I knew, without doubt, I'd already fallen for her.

∞∞∞∞∞∞∞∞

'Thought moves through dimensions without limits.'

A pewter sky clothed the fells in dullness. All was quiet in the mobile library. The relentless drizzle, a rarity in the Lakes this year after a particularly dry winter, had driven the Heronside locals to their fire-sides or, more probably, to the Bee Inn on the brow for a pint of best bitter. I checked my watch: it was time to call it a day. I stared at the rain-blistered windscreen, reflecting on the semi-abstract world beyond. There was something comforting about sitting in a vehicle listening to the rain. I lost myself in the memories rain summoned, happily recalling my student years in Edinburgh. It momentarily transported me back to a café on Princes Street: in the late afternoon. The air was suffocating. A smell of coffee and wet clothes lingered. Rain was lashing at the window, and life on those city streets seemed distant. But I didn't mind. I was too busy watching the pretty waitress, who I'd had my eye on for a couple of weeks. It took three lattes before I plucked up courage to ask her on a date, only to find that she was already spoken for. I remembered the disappointment as if it had only happened yesterday.

I snapped out of my reverie. Rain trickled, creating short-lived rivulets and tributaries on the glass. Through the windscreen, a blurry figure, almost intangible, appeared on a push-bike pedalling towards the van. A customer! I opened the door in anticipation, watching the thin rain drift eastwards. The drenched figure stepped inside.

'Hey, there,' said the familiar voice. It was Cali. Her face glistened with tiny rain pearls.

'Hello,' I replied, surprised. I clumsily dropped the Coleridge anthology, painfully aware that I was doing a poor job of remaining unflappable in her presence. 'I didn't expect to see you today. I take it you don't mind the rain?'

'Of course not,' she laughed, hair dripping, 'I love all nature's gifts.'

She wiped her brow with the back of her hand. I noticed the hem of her flower-speckled dress was rain-soaked and clinging to her naked legs.

'I've just finished a healing session. I knew you would be here and couldn't pass without saying hello.'

'Well, it's good to see you.'

Eyes met eyes. The moment seemed to stretch and all our unspoken thoughts held us silent. My neurons fired great big banners past my mind's eye, neon-lit banners that said, 'I want to spend the rest of my life with this woman', and I tried shaking this mad thought, because it really was too mad to deal with.

Water dripped off her coat. 'Here, let me.' I stepped forwards to help her remove the wet garment, which I placed over the guardrail by the door.

I had an overwhelming urge to kiss that sweet petal mouth of hers. I was still annoyed at myself for not doing so when I'd had the first opportunity.

'So, you've been working?' I realised I still wasn't comfortable using the term healing.

'Yes, and I've had a lovely chat with Verity Lait.'

'So, you know Verity?' I said, not really all that surprised. 'Then you'll know about these wee angels she keeps harping on about. The old girl certainly has a vivid imagination.'

'Perhaps that's just what Verity sees,' Cali replied, brushing off my raised eyebrow with a gentle unwavering expression. 'One person's reality can be quite different to another's. It's all relative, don't you think?'

'Yes, but angels?'

Cali dismissed my incredulity with that beguiling smile of hers. She traced her hand along the middle row of books, stopping twice to read the finger-brushed titles. This wild and intriguing woman mesmerised me. Oh but I was more than mesmerised.

She turned to me and, in a forever moment, she held my gaze and I knew that she knew. No words were needed. We were falling into each other, so sweetly, so effortlessly.

There was a heated stillness. My pulse rushed. I really had to kiss her. Could I be so bold? What if I was reading all this wrong? I couldn't be absolutely certain. Maybe if I asked her out again. I could take her for a romantic meal. There was a restaurant by the shores of Coniston, which would be the perfect setting.

'I'm wondering,' I began, spinning the book carousel. I stared out at the dark smudges of rain-misted fells beyond the village car park, pausing to find the words, wondering why I found it so difficult to simply ask her out. 'I'm...'

I turned back towards her and froze. A strange cloud of smoke billowed through the rear of the mobile library, and an odd humming noise penetrated the air. For a second, I thought the van was on fire but realised this wasn't smoke and there was no fire.

'Cali...? What's happening?'

I edged forwards, slightly, but the uncertainty manacled me, pulling me back. This cloud, or whatever it was, had completely engulfed her. I watched as the plume spread out in front of me, hanging like a sheet of sun-kissed ice. It totally obscured the rear of the library.

'Cali?' I shouted. 'Can you see me? Follow my voice. Walk towards me.'

There was no reply. The humming noise suddenly stopped. Then, as quickly as it appeared, the mist spiralled away towards the back of the van. I stepped back, instinctively guarded. As I did so, the mist dissipated and *whoosh*, a slim meteor of light rapidly shot out of sight. There was silence. Cali was no longer here.

My heart thumped against my chest. I steadied myself against the counter, searching the space where Cali was only seconds ago. I stared at the floor, the bookshelves, and the roof lights. There was no other way out. She couldn't have passed without my seeing. What was this? Some elaborate trick?

'Cali? Where are you? How did you do that?'

All was silent.

I trembled backwards, stumbling into the doorway, falling against the guardrails. Cali's coat was still dripping Cumbria rain onto the floor. Panic set in. I opened the door, and ran out into the rain. I ran round the mobile library, round the empty car park, looked up and down the street, and ran back to the van, like a man whose sense of reality had abandoned him. The rain drove in, stippling my skin, and I wiped my eyes and face with my shirtsleeves.

'Cali,' I shouted, again.

There was no reply.

I leant against the van, and took a deep breath. Her silver-framed bicycle was propped against the side, just where she had left it. Anxiety turned my insides, and for a moment I was afraid to go back into the van. Was I losing my mind? I stood in the rain, wondering what to do. 'Okay, I need to calm down', I assured myself. I counted to seven, a totally irrational habit stemming from when I was a boy, trying to soothe my equally irrational fear of the demon closet in my bedroom. Seven was my favourite number. Counting to seven made everything right. On seven, I stepped back into the van, re-proaching myself for being so fearful, hoping Cali would jump out at me, laughing, having fooled me with her magic trick, but she wasn't there – and what kind of magic trick makes you disappear so completely?

I slumped sideways in my driver's seat, eyes searching, mind racing as fast as my pulse. I only half-registered the passing time, the fact it was no longer raining and the sky had shaken off its grey cloak because I was stuck with a situation that made no sense. I couldn't leave without knowing what had happened to her, whether she was all right. All kinds of thoughts tormented me. Had I imagined her? Of course not! Her coat and bicycle were here – physical proof. I went over and over what had happened. I played back what I had seen in slow motion. I searched for a logical explanation but conclud-ed there wasn't one. So, I sat and waited.

∞∞∞∞∞∞∞∞

'Time is immaterial.'

E ach passing second raged as anxiety stabbed the empty slab of my stomach. I glanced at my watch again. Two hours had passed since Cali disappeared into, well, into thin air. Ridiculously, I was still wondering what to do. I couldn't go to the police. What on Earth would I say? 'Excuse me, constable, but my would-be girlfriend has gone missing in the back of my mobile library.' They would probably breathalyse me. I was damn sure they wouldn't believe me. I could just go home, but what if I did and Cali couldn't return as a result? Why was I even thinking like this? Oh, but what if she didn't return? I churned the thoughts over and my stomach churned too in sympathy, as nervous energy ate away at my already wiry frame. I decided to wait for one more hour. I couldn't think beyond this.

All I could do was go over the events leading up to her vanishing, trying to find a sign or something to explain what happened. I remembered the day when I first saw her, dancing naked amongst the hawthorn trees, and how she had disappeared in much the same way. At the time, because I had been some distance away, I thought it was the light or my eyes playing tricks. Now I'd seen it happen right in front of me, I was at a loss. What could cause such a thing? Was it an illusion? If it wasn't for her coat and her bicycle, I could have questioned whether she had actually been here at all.

My reflection in the side window startled me. The face staring back was drawn, fearful. It was the face of a man on the brink of loss or madness, and I didn't recognise myself at all. Maybe I was the one who had disappeared? What if I was dead and didn't realise it? I pinched my arm. Ouch! Pain was a good sign. A red mark flared my skin and I was sure I hadn't died. From where I was parked, I could see signs of life playing out on the main street. One or two people darted about, not seeming to question why the mobile library was still in the village car park. I was surprised no one had been to investigate, surprised but glad because I wasn't sure I could deal with anyone right now.

I drummed my fingers on the steering wheel, growing more impatient and frustrated at not being able to do anything constructive. Then, out of nowhere, a low electrical hum assaulted my ears, the kind of sound that generates from electricity lines on a damp day, and I stopped drumming my fingers. My skin prickled and adrenalin began to flow again. The van was shaking. The humming grew louder, and a sparkle of light appeared at the rear of the van, followed by a silvery-grey mist, billowing like smoke, creating what seemed to be an oval doorway. The light brightened. I stood up, not really sure whether to run or hold my ground. My heart thundered against my chest and I found I couldn't move. Then I saw a figure appear from the shimmering mist. It was Cali. Relief flooded through me. She stepped forwards. Her face was as pale as a winter's moon. Her eyes stared wildly. She stood there in her summery dress, the hem of which was now bone-dry, and her lips moved but her voice was lost to her. The mist spiralled to a dot, and then promptly disappeared with another *whoosh*.

'What the... Cali, are you okay?'

She was motionless; her eyes momentarily met mine, and then lost focus as her body crumpled. I moved towards her, catching her as she fell, and I lay her down onto the van's crimson-carpeted floor. She was barely conscious, just a feather in my arms.

'I'll take you to the doctor's,' I said.

'No, Tom,' she whispered. 'Please take me back to the house. I'll be fine... Just tired.'

'What happened? Cali?'

She closed her eyes and her body went limp as she fell into a deep sleep. I placed her on her side, remembering my first-aid training. I crouched there for a minute or two, shocked and confused. I watched her body gently rise and fall with each slow breath while my own pulse thundered perilously. As she slept, the colour slowly returned to her face. There didn't appear to be any injury. In fact, apart from her sleeping on the library floor, no one would be any the wiser of the strange event I'd witnessed. It was as if it had never happened.

I checked her pulse on the inner side of her wrist. It beat strong and normal. I covered her with my coat and then secured her bicycle inside the doorway, and set off for Ravenshead. Thoughts were racing, and I drove quickly and erratically. I constantly checked my interior mirror to make sure she was still with me. The mobile library laboured on the ascent of Damselfly Lane, dispersing the midge clusters hanging like filigree in the evening light. On reaching the house, I realised there wasn't room to drive the library through the gates so I parked on the narrow roadside. I opened the door, threw the bicycle on the grass verge, and then went back for Cali.

She was a sleeping beauty. Her river of hair settled round her face and shoulders. I gathered her to me, breathing in her sweet honeysuckle aroma. She was so light in my arms as I carried her with ease to the front door of Starfell Cottage. I used my elbow to press the doorbell, and waited. Her head was against my chest, dark hair spilling over my arms. I pressed the doorbell again. 'C'mon,' I muttered, impatiently. Perhaps there was no one at home. I wondered whether to take her back to the library and call at the village surgery for the out-of-hours emergency number, but then I saw a figure dart from the raised platform of the observatory. It had to be the owner, Matt Darker, if my memory served me right. Gorse bushes, thick with yellow flowers, blocked my view, but then I heard foot-steps crunching the gravel. A dark-eyed man appeared, with swept black hair flecked grey. He was younger than I'd envis-aged – early forties perhaps – broad-shouldered and unex-pectedly athletic. For some reason, I'd imagined him as a younger version of Patrick Moore, perhaps minus the mono-cle, and certainly less attractive than he was.

'Hello. Are you...?'

'What's happened to her?' he said, cutting me off mid-sentence.

I wasn't sure what I could tell him. I wasn't sure he'd believe me. 'She fainted,' I lied.

He opened the front door, eyeing me suspiciously. I moved forwards with the intention of carrying Cali inside the house, but he stopped me at the door.

'It's fine. I'll take her from here.'

He stole Cali out of my arms and into his. Some other feeling rose inside me, momentarily overriding all the confu-sion and strangeness of what had happened in the mobile library. I didn't want to let her go. She was still in a deep sleep, and vulnerable. And I didn't know this guy. Was it safe to leave her here with him?

'I'll wait... to see she's all right.'

'No, that won't be necessary. I'll call the doctor to be sure, but there's no need to worry. She'll be absolutely fine with me,' he said, and then added, 'We're together, you see.'

For a second, I stood there dumbfounded.

'Together?' I questioned, as if I didn't quite understand what he was saying, and then it began to sink in and my heart sank, too. 'Oh, right,' was all I could say.

He just stared at me with his dark eyes, deep-set and framed by equally dark brows, and then he kissed the top of her head. 'Let's get you in, my dear,' he said to her. Her eyes were still shut. He turned to me, briefly. 'Thanks for bringing her home.'

I nodded, and then he shut the door on me.

For several seconds, I stared blindly at the door, my mind blank except for the words that spun through my ears like an angry wasp: 'We're together, you see.' Cali and him: together, as in boyfriend–girlfriend, as in a couple.

The realisation slammed in my face. How come I hadn't known? Why hadn't she told me? I couldn't make any sense of it. I walked away, confusion and bitter disappointment rattling around my shattered head. Her disappearing trick was one thing, but finding out she was already in a relationship sliced through me. I drove away, ivory-knuckled hands gripping the steering wheel. I kept telling myself that, at any moment, I'd wake up, relieved that it was all a crazy nightmare, but I knew my reality well enough to know: that wasn't going to happen.

∞∞∞∞∞∞∞∞

'What you see in the physical realm is temporary.'

Somehow, I managed to return the mobile library to the county depot and drive away in my Land Rover without incident. But I wasn't ready to go back to the farm and I didn't want to speak to anyone. My thoughts were in such a jumbled mess, I couldn't even remember if I'd had plans for this evening. Of course, that didn't matter; not now. Everything had changed.

I just drove, letting the road take me, and the miles and the evening vanished in a blur. Eventually, I found myself on the lofty sway of Kirkstone Pass, disappearing into fog. I slammed on the brakes and shifted to a lower gear, crawling along the climb more cautiously. The fog instantly reminded me of the strange mist Cali had disappeared into. I shook out the thought, reasoning that this was simply atmospheric, a low bank of cloud: quite normal and expected for this high fell pass. Still, this white wall surrounding me was suffocating, detaching me from everything except a sense of loss and confusion growing cavernous inside me. I concentrated on what I could see of the tarmac and tried to keep to my side of the road. I wondered how many people had been caught out here by the fog. How many had hurtled off this high fell to their deaths? I wasn't ready to go over the edge, despite how I felt right now. Soon, the road dropped, and I came out of the grey cloud, and into the lap of Ullswater. I released my grip on the steering wheel and drove into Glenridding.

Tired and blurry-brained, I parked by the lake and turned off the engine but my thoughts were still in motion, hurtling around my mind, ricocheting off the edges of reason. I wound the window down and welcomed the cool air. I leant forwards over the steering wheel, resting my head on my forearms, and listened to life on the water. Daylight was fading fast, leaving just a silvery glow upon the dark lake. Two lovers held hands, silhouetted in the dusk. They stopped to steal a kiss under the sliver of moonlight. The village slipped into its nightgown and I watched the ordinariness of day's end, embracing the normality, the stuff of reality. I sat here for some time, chasing the thoughts round my head until numbness set in and I couldn't think any more. I couldn't think and yet Cali's sweet face was all I saw, and I tried to shake her away because it was clear she already had someone in her life – that, and the fact that she did extraordinary things like disappearing into thin air. It should have been enough to extinguish the dreams I'd had of our future together, enough to evaporate any thoughts of love. I closed my eyes and her face was even more vivid.

A rag of grey streaked the pink-plumed sky that draped the fell-tops and darkness crept in from the east, bringing with it the uncertainty of night. Cold spread like a rash around my face, neck, and hands. I should never have allowed myself to fall for her, not so soon, never have allowed myself to dream of what could be. Like Icarus, I'd flown too high, too wrapped up in my soaring imagination, too lost in romantic possibilities, without really knowing who or what she was. I swallowed hard. My throat felt like sandpaper. And my stomach growled, now from hunger rather than anxiety, but most of all I was exhausted and ready for my bed. My brain hurt a lot. My heart hurt even more. It was time to head back, but I didn't expect to sleep much this night. After what I'd seen and how I felt, I wasn't sure I'd ever sleep properly again.

∞∞∞∞∞∞∞

'Your world has many doorways into other dimensions.'

Here I was, thirty-year-old Tom Philips, the mobile librarian for South Lakeland. What made my world tick in its welcoming, predictable way? Well, I liked a strong black coffee in the mornings while I read the latest issue of *Poetry Now, The Bookseller* or *Literature Latest*. I enjoyed the simple things in life, such as poetry, a good meal with friends, visiting art galleries, walking through Edinburgh's yellow glow on a misty night, cycling so fast my legs burned, and watching nature's changing seasons. Sometimes, I'd daydream about how, someday, I'd be married and have children and be set up in my own publishing company – someday soon, perhaps. Aye, I welcomed the ordinary, everyday life, and its predictable rhythms. So, what was with all the weird stuff? Why had Cali come into my life and turned my world into chaos?

Days had passed in a haze and I'd made no attempt to contact her. I thought it would be for the best. What's the saying, out of sight, out of mind? Only, it wasn't really working. It was a typical White Bear Syndrome. I tried not to think about her but the more I tried, the more she loomed in my thoughts. I decided that the best way of dealing with it all was to keep myself busy. So, after completing my mobile library schedule, I took on a couple of evening shifts and Saturday duties at the County Library to help with organising two 'meet the author' events and the monthly book club. When I wasn't working, I watched old black and white thrillers at the local arts cinema and immersed myself in reading non-fiction: mostly travel journals about road trips through Europe. I avoided poetry, for now. My feelings were still too raw for that. Despite the avoidance tactics, Cali remained like a siren in my thoughts. It became so bad that I spent a night in a bar, taking one shot of vodka after another in the hope of obliterating her from my mind. It almost worked. Somehow, I must have staggered through town to the depot, and settled down in the mobile library for the night. I had no memory of how I got there. For those few short hours I managed to sleep in alcoholic oblivion, but Cali was back in my thoughts as soon as I woke up. I realised then that she wasn't going to disappear from my life that quickly. And that's the weirdest thing. It's not like I'd known her that long. We hadn't made love. We hadn't even kissed. So why was this hitting me so hard? Why couldn't I move on?

Today was Sunday and I was trying another tactic to forget her. This tactic involved replacing one difficult situation with another – in this case, having dinner with my family for the first time in years. I sat at the kitchen table across from Pete and Ellie. My dear mother was at one end and my miserable father at the other. I occupied one side as if I was on trial. The awkwardness of the situation was palpable in the silence. But I didn't mind. Even my father's seething face offered welcome familiarity. Yes, this was what I needed right now, the ordinary that was life, the stuff I could deal with.

The kitchen hadn't changed much over the years. It had the same enduring oak cupboards and cheery yellow and blue accessories. In fact, the only difference was the presence of a new green range. A painting of Samson, ploughing the lower field, still graced the wall by the dresser, a reminder of the old days, and the antique wall clock, which had been in the family's possession for several generations, still kept time. The kitchen was smaller than I remembered but the aroma of freshly cooked food filled the air as it had always done. Pots and pans; willow-patterned china; ladybird fridge magnets; recipe books: I immersed myself in the familiar and yet couldn't really settle. Questions kept surfacing. Strange questions such as 'is this all real?' We finished eating dessert: my favourite, rhubarb pie and custard.

'So, Tom,' my mother began, breaking the post-meal silence, 'are you settling into your new job?'

'I am, thanks.'

'Any more off-road episodes?' asked Pete, smirking.

'Oh, yes, Pete mentioned you'd had a bit of an incident,' my mother said, frowning with concern. 'How did you manage that?'

'It was a one-off,' I replied, not wanting to be reminded. 'It just took me a day or two to get used to driving the van.'

Ellie cleared the table, her pregnancy clearly evident through her mushrooming t-shirt, a reminder that there would be a new addition to the Philips family before autumn was out. 'Pete can laugh,' she said, 'he nearly ditched the tractor last week on seeing that crop circle in the field by Hawkdale. Have you seen it, Tom? It's almost as big as a football pitch. You can see it clearly from the top road.'

My father sat stone-faced and silent. Being together, in such close proximity, even after all these years, was clearly uncomfortable for him as it was for me.

'All kind of rumours are flying around,' Ellie continued, eyes wide and glinting with curiosity. She swept back her short fair hair and began speaking in a whispered tone, which added to the drama. 'Some say there's some kind of military experiment going on, but Dee Pemsitt from the bakery says it's the work of aliens.'

Mother poured steaming tea into our mugs, shaking her head and smiling in a dismissive way. She didn't have to say anything. It was clear she didn't believe in the paranormal stories being bandied about. How alike we were. I took a sip from my cup, not realising just how hot the tea was. The liquid burnt my top lip.

'She's been watching too many episodes of *X-Files*,' Pete laughed, tucking into a second helping of rhubarb pie.

'No, Pete, she's actually seen things – strange moving lights in the woods below the fells.'

'It'll be poachers with torches. I mean, has she actually seen an alien or a spacecraft?' Pete paused, wiping custard from his chin. 'Anyway, it's well known that those crop circles are made by people – people who have far too much time on their hands.'

'I don't know,' Ellie persisted, 'but there's apparently a woman in Hawkdale who saw the crop circle appear. She says angels made it.'

I listened to the conversation unfolding, finding it hard to believe that, even here, the extraordinary was finding its way into everyday life. I didn't mention that I had been there with Verity Lait just after the crop circle formed. I didn't mention that my would-be girlfriend – could I even call her that now? – had a tendency to disappear into the ether. I didn't tell them because it would only fuel the furnace and steal the ordinary that I craved.

I cleared my throat. 'So, how are things here?' I asked, eager to change the conversation.

My father shifted uncomfortably in his chair, and slurped his tea, avoiding eye contact.

'Fine, son,' my mother replied. 'It's certainly busier with the tearoom and the lodges. Never have a moment to myself, these days. I can't complain, though, as it brings in good money, and I enjoy meeting people who visit.'

'We've been lucky,' Pete chipped in. 'Harold's place went to auction last week. We've had to change to survive.'

'Well, it looks like you made the right move,' I replied, attempting to remain upbeat, 'considering the fate of the other farms.'

Father stood up, scraping his chair against the tiled floor. 'I'm off for a pint,' he mumbled, clearly agitated. 'Are you coming, Pete?'

Pete looked at me, then at Ellie. 'I'll be along in a while, Dad.'

'Please yourself.' He grabbed his tweed cap, and left without another word.

'Was it something I said?' I asked, already knowing the answer.

My mother's shoulders slumped as she sighed. She shook her head, running her fingers through the wisps of silver around her forehead. I realised, in that moment, how much the frazzled relationship between the old man and me must have taken its toll. For years she had been in the middle, like some referee unable to contain two unruly fighters.

'It's fine, Mum,' I reassured. 'It's just the way he is; it doesn't bother me.'

'He's a stubborn, grumpy old man,' she said, irritated, 'old enough to know better. Life's too short for harbouring grudges – and ridiculous ones at that. It's about time he got this out of his system and moved on. It doesn't do anyone any good.'

I listened to her words, as wise as always, but it wasn't my father I was thinking about now. It was Cali. I realised I had to face her to resolve what I was feeling and to gain some answers. Ignoring her wasn't going to help. I didn't want to be seething like my father for the rest of my days. I needed to understand. I needed to know what was happening with her disappearing trick and her relationship with Matt Darker. Only then would I be able to move on.

Nothing more was said about my father. We chatted into the early evening about Pete's equestrian plans, possible names for Philips junior and, to my mother's delight, news about the latest books on the literary best-sellers list. I even laughed at some of Pete's terrible jokes. For a time I wallowed in the normality, but Cali and the weird stuff never really left me. The thoughts just hovered in the background like gathering storm clouds.

The light was already dimming when I said goodnight. I walked the short distance across the yard to my lodge. Pete caught me up, zipping his coat to deter the evening chill.

'Fancy a pint?'

I imagined Father at the bar, ranting. 'I think I'll give it a miss, bro,' I said, wondering how he managed to put up with the misery that was Philips senior. 'I have an early start tomorrow and I haven't had much sleep lately so thought I'd catch an early night.'

'Not much sleep, hey?' He winked. 'Don't suppose that has something to do with the new lady in your life?'

I frowned and sighed. I couldn't manage any other response. I couldn't find the words. In the emotional vacuum, there was just a lonely wind and tumble-weed.

'Oh, a sore point,' he simply said, realising it best not to say anything.

We stopped outside my door. Rustic benches stretched along the porch, one for each of the six lodges, and potted shrubs added colour to the veranda. All that was missing was a rocking chair and perhaps a guy in a Stetson strumming a guitar. I leant against the slatted railing. Pete stood with his hands in his pockets, not really sure what to say. Wood smoke scented the air, drifting on the breeze from the neighbouring cottage half a mile away. I breathed in the hint of seasoned pine but felt nothing. Beyond the fledgling apple orchard and fields criss-crossed with stone boundaries, the creeping darkness began consuming the familiar. The derelict stone barn in the furthest field was barely visible and the clashing fell-sides were now cloaked and featureless. The darkness advanced but still I felt nothing.

'Does all this seem real to you?' I asked, throwing my hands up as if to dramatise the question's weight.

I didn't have to turn to see the confused expression on Pete's face.

'What are you on about?'

I wasn't sure I could answer. I mean, where would I begin? How would I explain what I'd seen happening to Cali? People just didn't disappear like that. They just didn't. And yet here I was wondering... wondering about the meaning of reality... wondering why I'd gone numb and bereft of feeling.

'Will you do something for me, bro?'

'Yeah, sure,' Pete replied.

'Will you hit me?'

'What?'

'Hit me. Just a quick punch in the stomach or something.'

He laughed. 'What do you want me to do that for? Are you crazy?'

'No, but if you don't hit me, I'm in serious danger of losing it. So please,' I shoved him hard against the shoulder, 'bloody well hit me. Go on! Have you gone soft in your age?'

'If I hit you, it's going to hurt,' he said, stating the obvious.

'Aye, I know and that's what I need.'

I pushed him again and he pushed me back. Although we were both just under six feet tall, he was broader than me, good farming stock as my father often said, born to work the land. If we were in a serious fight, I'd definitely be in trouble. I moved forwards again, jabbing him in the chest and, this time, he retaliated by throwing a hesitant punch, which glanced meekly across my jaw.

'Is that the best you can do?'

I shoved him again... and again... and – thump!

The punch to my stomach sent me reeling backwards. A strange wheezing sound escaped from my mouth and I dropped to my knees, clutching my ribs.

'Bloody hell, Tom,' Pete hovered over me, 'I didn't mean to hit you that hard. Are you okay?'

I found my breath, and winced at the pain over my left ribs. It hurt. It hurt like hell. And I was relieved that it hurt. After a few seconds, I pulled myself to my feet, slowly straightening my torso. I hissed at the stinging sensation.

'Thanks, bro,' I said, grinning through my grimace, 'I needed that.'

I patted him on the shoulder, impressed with his boxing skills.

'Any time, you mad fecker.' He sort of smiled and frowned at the same time, and shook his head. 'Now, can I go for my pint?'

He didn't hang around for an explanation but I guessed that he'd already assumed my weird mood had something to do with Cali. Some things didn't need to be explained. I opened the lodge door and leant against the door frame for a minute, watching Pete march his way to the pub along the winding farm track. His figure melded with this moonless evening as if he was the very fabric of this darkened landscape. Soon, he was out of sight. I gently prodded my lower ribs. Ouch! No doubt there'd be a meaty bruise there by morning but, yes, it was exactly what I'd needed. I was losing my mind, losing all sensation, losing my grip on reality. I was like a boat without an anchor, drifting further and further out to sea. But now I could feel again. The pain around my ribs was real enough and, in some strange way, that grounded me, reconnected me to my reality. And grounding was exactly what was needed if I was going to confront Cali and find out what was going on.

∞∞∞∞∞∞∞∞

'Open your mind and you will see.'

Another couple of days had passed before I plucked up courage to phone her. She seemed happy to hear from me, and her voice had the usual effect of scattering my thoughts and making my pulse rush. She asked why I hadn't been in touch before now. It was as if nothing had happened that day she'd disappeared, which I found odd and unnerving. I stumbled over my words. I made excuses, saying I'd been busy; it wasn't really what I wanted to say, but nor did I want to blurt out how I'd been going out of my mind. In the end, I asked if we could meet up on Saturday and then, to give it the necessary gravitas, I said we needed to talk.

Saturday arrived soon enough. I'd turned up at Heronside earlier than I needed to so I had breakfast in Swan's Café, a cheese and tomato toastie, thinking that food would settle my anxiety. It didn't. Nerves somersaulted and jolted my insides. As arranged, I waited for Cali by the stone fountain in the market square. The church clock tolled. She'd said she would be here just after eleven. A tide of people passed by: young and old, browsers and buyers, going about their weekend shopping, pre-occupied with bargain hunting and the price of butter. The pretty market-stall awnings fluttered in the breeze, and the chatter of traders and potential customers scattered the air like indistinct voices on an ill-tuned radio. A busker set up his pitch and belted out a random medley of both popular and obscure songs on his amplified acoustic guitar. Some songs I recognised, and provided a pleasant distraction, like Belle and Sebastian's *Le Pastie de la Bourgeoisie*, which I used to listen to in my bed-sit in Edinburgh, dreaming of eucalyptus fields and what it would be like to nearly go too far in the church bazaar. I had a talent for remembering song lyrics as well as poems. The busker was far too good to be playing on a street corner although, ironically, he probably earned more money there than on the live music circuit.

A sharp gust of wind stole in from nowhere. It whipped up the brightly coloured sales leaflets from one of the market stalls selling villas in the sun, and whisked them into the air like paper aeroplanes. The trader and his assistant, both sporting fake tans and smiles to match, began chasing round the square to retrieve them. One leaflet landed at my feet. I picked it up and read the headline: 'Make Your Dream Come True!' The words bounced back and forwards in my brain. Cali would probably have said this was a message for me, whereas I was inclined to think we read into whatever we want to see. But it made me wonder: if only I could make my dream come true. Seven crows gathered on the bakery rooftop, keen-eyed, waiting for discarded food offerings. I turned the leaflet over. 'Travel to paradise,' it said, in bright red letters. Is that where Cali went when she disappeared?

My watch beamed 11.11 a.m. I heard her unmistakable sweet laughter before I saw her. Further along the street, outside the Seven Stars Inn, a white-haired man danced on age-bowed legs to the busker's music and Cali was dancing too, smiling, and weaving round him as if casting a spell. I tried to remain hidden by standing behind the small crowd that had gathered to watch the impromptu duet. She danced without inhibition, and each movement expressed her joy for life. Her long blue skirt swished like it was trying to keep up with her. Everyone was clapping along, tapping feet to the hypnotic rhythm. Everyone had a smile. She seemed to have that effect on people. Once the song had finished, the old man took a bow and graciously kissed the back of Cali's hand to much applause and cheering. The crowd dispersed and then it was just the two of us, eyes meeting eyes, holding each other in a forever moment. If she were able to see all the questions and uncertainty flooding through my veins, she wasn't show-ing it. Instead, she gave me her brightest smile: the kind of secret smile reserved for a lover.

'Can you believe Bill is ninety-one?' she began, glancing back at the white-haired man, who was now sat at a table outside the inn, drinking his beer. 'He's really taken to my healing dance sessions. Apparently, he's been caught dancing on the table, serenading one of his lady admirers.'

She chuckled, and then grabbed my arm and walked me through the busy market square and into the peaceful em-brace of the churchyard. It took all my resolve to stop my mind falling south into my heart.

The churchyard slipped quietly away from the busy mar-ket streets. Behind the austere grey building, an avenue of toxic yew trees, their lance-shaped leaves shivering, led to the cemetery. Beyond the cemetery wall, rich pastures rolled and sidled, rising steadily to the crown of Ravenshead beyond. You could just about see the observatory dome perched on the peak at Starfell Cottage. I imagined the man in her life spying on us with his telescope. The thought reminded me of why I was there.

'Strange places, graveyards,' Cali said, touching one of the lichen-mottled headstones. 'People come to talk to their loved ones, not realising they can communicate with them at any time and most usually in places where they have shared happy memories... not here under these cold stones.'

Two tar-black crows skipped from one grave to another, scolding the bones beneath while remaining indifferent to our presence.

'I guess whatever gives people comfort,' I said, finding my voice again.

'True, but if only everyone could see what I see...'

'Then the world would be full of Cali Silverthorns... Hmm.' I thought. 'Not sure if I could cope with that.'

I grinned. She feigned a disgruntled expression and poked me in the chest. In pretence, I jumped back, and the action jolted my still-sore and badly bruised ribs. I bent over, hissing at the sharp pain.

'You okay?' she asked, touching my arm.

'Aye, it's nothing. Just bruised ribs.'

'Let me see.'

Before I could stop her, she grabbed and lifted my shirt, revealing the pale slab of my stomach.

'Honestly, it's nothing,' I protested, embarrassed, but she had already seen the bruise on my lower ribs, which stretched like a blue-purple nebula on my milk-white skin.

'There's a hairline fracture,' she said, studying the bruise.

'How do you know?'

'I just do. I can see... intuitively.'

She placed her hand over my ribs. I closed my eyes. Her touch was warm, and grew warmer, until it became unbearably hot, like an iron held against my skin. I began to feel uncomfortable and aroused and also self-conscious. Here we were amongst an audience of gravestones: me holding up my shirt and Cali with her hand on my naked middle like she was performing some kinky ritual. I hoped the vicar wasn't looking, or Cali's boyfriend for that matter. Call me old-fashioned but I felt guilty for just being with her, feeling the way I did. My mind hurtled to its senses. I opened my eyes, cleared my voice and pulled away, now pre-occupied with what needed to be said.

She followed me to a bench in the corner of the cemetery, normally reserved for those mourning or remembering lost loved ones. I rolled up my shirtsleeves, biding my time, trying to glean where to begin. The mood was weight-weary with unknowns. I clutched to the pure simplicity of being here, the pure simple reality, because I knew deep inside that my life was going to change today.

'I need to know,' I began, fidgeting with the button on my shirt cuff.

She seemed to hold her breath in anticipation. We perched like bookends with a gulf of unspoken emotions swirling between us. I stared at the gravestones, all of them marking the end of days for someone, and a miserable cloud hung over me.

'I need to know... How long have you been seeing Matt Darker?'

The question seemed to hover in the air and take her completely by surprise. She stared at me, confusion wrinkling her forehead.

'What do you mean, Tom?'

'That day... that day I took you back to the house when... you know, when you kind of disappeared. Well, he met me at the door and told me that you and he are together.'

'What?' Her raised voice startled the chaffinches feeding on the path, and the button fell off my shirtsleeve.

Her mouth was agape; she was clearly having difficulty believing what she was hearing.

'You think me and Matt Darker are together, as in a couple?' She shook her head from side to side, dumbfounded. 'I'm not sure whether to laugh or cry. Did he really say that? Are you sure?'

'That's what the man said. It's one of the reasons why I've stayed away this past couple of weeks.'

'Well, it's a complete lie.' Her voice was uncharacteristically angry and her lovely eyebrows pinched together in torment. 'Why would he say such a thing? I just don't understand.'

So, it wasn't true after all. They weren't together. My sigh of relief was audible.

'Maybe he fancies you and it's his way of telling me to get lost? I have to say, it almost worked, and I feel a fool.'

Hawthorn blossom shimmied in the breeze. Every now and again, a flurry of pinkish-white petals fell and scattered, a reminder of how quickly the season was gathering pace.

'Well, you now know the truth,' she said, touching the back of my hand. 'And let me make it clear: I'm not even remotely interested in him.'

I took her hand in mine and turned it over, tracing my thumb across her palm to sketch invisible spirals.

'I'm happy to hear it. I mean, if you were with him... you know, as a couple... then, I'd be happy for you as long as you were happy... but I'm happier that you're not with him... for reasons which I think must be pretty obvious now.' I cringed at my clumsy admission.

'I know, Tom,' she said, her expression softening, 'and I'm hoping it's pretty obvious that the person I *really* like is sitting real close to me right now... a mobile librarian who has a fondness for holey jumpers and shirts that seem to lose their buttons.'

She smiled and squeezed my hand. I sat there, kind of wide-eyed. How could I have blindly believed Matt Darker and put myself through emotional hell these past two weeks? It seemed ridiculous. So, maybe there was hope for something developing between us after all. One major hurdle surmounted, but there was still the other question, the one that in many ways would elicit answers far more challenging... far more unpredictable.

'I have something else to ask.' I said, frowning again, 'but you already know that because it's the question you've been anticipating.'

She nodded and stared at the ground. We prolonged the silence, clinging on to the ordinariness of the day, and then I locked our fingers together. The warmth of her touch was reassuring – reassuringly real. Our fingers remained woven, drawing strength from each other.

'You really did disappear that day in the library, and also when I first saw you dancing naked around the hawthorn trees.'

'Yes,' she admitted, without any hesitation.

'What happened to you?'

'At first, I didn't know. I thought I was having visions or that I was in some kind of dream trance. More so, it seemed like I was astral travelling, but then I discovered the truth.'

'And, what is the truth?'

She faltered. Her mouth opened and then closed. Then she straightened her back, taking a deep breath, as if she was about to dive into an unfathomable abyss.

'I'm disappearing into other worlds, Tom. I know it must sound totally crazy, but that's exactly what's happening. I'm being taken out of Earth time and space and transported elsewhere into other dimensions... to other planets... in other star systems.'

Even as she explained, I was shaking my head, my logical mind refusing to accept.

'No, no way, that's impossible. How? I mean, I saw you disappear. I saw it happen and yet, all the time, I've been thinking – hoping – it was just some clever illusion.'

I was still shaking my head. I exhaled a dismissive but uncertain laugh. I had lived with logic, in a world that could be explained by science. This... this was just too crazy.

'I grew up experiencing the extraordinary,' she said, 'and yet, over time, I forgot most of what I'd seen with my grandmother. I forgot, or thought they were dreams. What's happening to me, however, isn't a dream. It is very real. For many reasons, I wish it wasn't.'

Anxiety spread through me like wild fire. I wasn't sure I could deal with this. I wasn't sure I wanted to. Her warm hand tightened in mine, giving and seeking reassurance. Inside, I counted to seven, trying to find the mind space for this, trying to make sense. I considered how my granddad would have dealt with it. He always used to remind me not to judge anything, not to react, until there was enough information to make an informed response, until every possibility had been considered. I had always found it sound advice.

'How long has this been happening to you?' I asked.

'A few weeks, I think.'

'You're not sure?'

'I used to be aware of travelling at night, using astral projection. It is something we are all capable of doing so I didn't think it so unusual. But this... this is different.'

'What do you mean?'

'Well, with astral projection, you travel out of body. With this, I'm travelling with my physical body – fully conscious – into other dimensions. I'm being taken out of this reality.'

I wasn't even sure what to think about astral projection, let alone anything stranger. I scratched my head. I stared at the gravestones, imagining the dead staring back at me. My button-less shirt cuff flapped in the breeze. Questions continued to surface.

'When you say taken, do you mean without your consent?'

'Well, not exactly,' she said, frowning, as if unsure. 'I mean, it just happens, as you saw when I disappeared in the mobile library. I am called, often unexpectedly, and I have to go.'

'So who or what is taking you? Is it these angels that Verity keeps harping on about?'

'Verity calls them angels, but I know them as guides and star-beings. We have a long association with entities from other star systems and realms. I have vague memories of being told stories and being part of the ceremonies that invoked these beings when I was with my grandmother at the healing community. I have memories of that time, of unearthly lights spiralling over us, of energy vortexes, stars dancing in those big dark skies, and I never questioned. I was brought up to accept what others would believe extraordinary or paranormal. I know now that, even when grandmother passed, the connections I made during my childhood remained with me, and now I am to fulfil my life's purpose, it seems.'

Adrenalin darted through my stomach like a thousand agitated starlings. Fulfilling her life's purpose, fulfilling her destiny. There was finality about it, a sense of being on a runaway train and being powerless to stop it.

'You have no control over this?'

'No,' she said.

'So, when you say you are to fulfil your purpose...?'

'It means that soon I will go and won't be able to return.'

∞∞∞∞∞∞∞∞∞

'We are one of many walking beside you.'

There were books to help you deal with the end of the world. There were even books to advise on what to do if you encounter extra-terrestrial intelligence. But, as far as I knew, there wasn't an instruction manual for how to cope with your girlfriend disappearing into another dimension. My brain began to spin. Despite the relief of discovering that she wasn't shacked up with Matt Darker, it seemed I was going to lose her anyway.

'Strong tea is good for shock,' Cali said, leading me out of the churchyard and to Swan's Café, where I'd had breakfast earlier. 'That's what we both need right now.'

The tea was indeed strong, almost strong enough to stand the teaspoon in. It took two cups before I felt present again. We sat at a table outside, allowing the street bustle to provide a reality buffer to stop me sliding helplessly into The Twilight Zone. Cali held my hand across the table like the perfect nurse. Down the street, the busker was crooning Louis Armstrong's 'We Have All the Time in the World', and I thought, if only. The café sign spun on its axis in the wind, so fast I thought it might flicker and disappear. For that reason, I started thinking of H. G. Wells' time machine.

'It's a lot to take in,' Cali said. 'Even I'm struggling with it all.'

'What can we do?' My voice sounded hollow in my head.

'I'm not sure, Tom.' She picked up the spoon and stirred her tea, as if hoping for something miraculous to spring forth. 'I know you must have lots of questions, but I can't answer them all right now... not sure I can cope.' Her voice faltered and she stopped stirring her tea. She looked away for a few moments, and then asked, 'Do you mind if we just do something normal for the afternoon, just for an hour or two?'

'Normal is good,' I said, welcoming the suggestion.

'I reckon it's what we both need right now. You see, you're the only person who knows about what's happening to me and just by sharing it with you... well, it's made me realise what a big deal it really is. I guess I've been in denial. So, yes, a bit of normality would really help.'

I spun my cup around then sat upright. 'Okay, normal it is. How about something poetic for the girl who loves poetry? Have you ever visited what William Wordsworth described as the most delightful spot on Earth?'

She shook her head. 'I don't think I have.'

'Well, drink up and I'll take you there.'

Despite the strangeness of Cali's revelation, which sent my thoughts to a place I hadn't dared to venture, the prospect of spending a couple of hours pretending all was well was preferable to the swollen emotions festering like a fog in my mind's dark recesses. In any case, Cali needed this space just as much, so it seemed. And it was a treat to return to Grasmere and Rydal and to introduce her to the place that had been home and inspiration to the great romantic poet. And being here connected me to what was familiar and real, allowed me to lose myself in the landscape, giving me some distance from the weird.

We did the normal stuff. We started with a tour of Dove Cottage and its busy gardens. I imagined Wordsworth pacing the upper terraces, searching for words, while Dorothy worked her own poetry amongst the flowers. I imagined other literati of that bygone age arriving at this tiny idyll to visit the poet and his sister: the comings and goings in a world now so remote that it seemed oddly questionable. After Dove Cottage, we went on to Rydal Mount. This was Wordsworth's final home, something more becoming of his Poet Laureate status, before he died in 1850. Even though my head was still throbbing from Cali's revelation and even though so many questions were gathering, I honoured her wish to have a few hours of normality.

And so we talked about normal things, such as art (she was into the Pre-Raphaelites, naming her favourite painting as the Lady of Shalott, whereas realism was my preference: the likes of Edward Hopper and Jules Breton), music (we both discovered we shared a diverse taste in tunes, tending to favour specific songs rather than follow groups or singers), and travel (I'd visited France, Germany, Malta, and some of America's mid-west on various literary pilgrimages, while Cali's focus had been on spiritual travel – Sedona, Arizona; Egypt; Peru; Hawaii; and, of course, going where few had ever dreamed possible – into other worlds). Little reminders of the mind-blowing weird kept creeping through the conversation and were quickly averted, but we both knew that we couldn't hold back the tide for long.

After our tour of Rydal Mount, we walked a little way on one of my favourite paths along the belly of the fell, which overlooked Rydal Water and Grasmere. To our right, woods and pasture continued their lofty climb against the rugged face of Nab Scar and, to our left, a mixed assembly of trees, mostly ashes and birches, punctuated the crags on a downwards slope towards the glassy lake basin. Being in the landscape held me in awe. If I were to believe in a god, then I was certain I'd find one here.

We stopped to rest and admire the views in a lovely spot full of fond memories for me. It had been a number of years since I was last here so I was happy to find that my favourite oak, with its exposed, rooted veins, was still standing sentinel on its precarious shelf of dry earth. This was quite a feat when so many neighbouring trees had uprooted during winter storms in a cruel and somewhat crude way, with their roots violently untethered from the ground.

'How's your ribs?' she asked.

In all the mind chaos, I'd completely forgotten about it. I placed my hand on my side and took a deep breath. The pain had completely gone. I lifted my shirt and couldn't believe my eyes. The bruise had disappeared too.

'How...?'

'I'm a healer, Tom.' She giggled at my dumbfounded expression. 'I took care of your injury.'

'But the bruise has vanished... and there's no pain at all... Nothing can heal that quickly.'

'I know, Tom, and I can't explain how it works. All that matters is that it does.'

She knelt down between the tangled tree roots and ran her hand over the cracked earth. Sunbeams dappled the side of her face, and she was all a glimmer.

'The trees are waiting for rain.' She traced her fingers along the thirsty bark.

'According to my brother, the last year has been the driest ever known in these parts.'

The sun hid behind a sobering grey cloud and the landscape plunged into sudden dullness.

'Mother earth and father sky are struggling to maintain equilibrium,' she said, tapping the ground to prompt me to sit by her side. 'Some of the changes are natural as our earth mother grows and responds to universal energies, but most of the serious problems have a human cause. We are the only species unable to live in collective harmony with nature. We are the only species destroying this planet.'

'Aye, and it's a sad testimony to humankind seeing that we're supposed to be the intelligent ones.' I sat beside her, and sighed. 'I caught the news yesterday that large pods of pilot whales have been gathering by the shores in various parts of the coastline. Quite a number have beached and died. There seems to be a lot of this going on.'

'The whales are mourning, bringing their dying family ashore to tell the human species that "this is what you're doing to us with your poison and pollution", and I know this because I've seen and heard what is taking place...'

Her voice trailed off as her eyes brimmed. I wondered what she had seen and heard. I wondered if this had something to do with her disappearing into other worlds. So many questions, but it just didn't feel like the right time to ask. I gathered a handful of dusty earth and let it fall through my fingers.

'Wordsworth lambasted man's alienation from nature in one of his sonnets,' I said, bringing to mind the poem. I recited a few poignant lines: 'Getting and spending, we lay waste our powers; little we see in nature that is ours; we have given our hearts away...'

The poet's words resonated as sharply now as they had done during the industrial revolution. I turned my eyes to hers and caught her quietly studying me. The sun reappeared. Insects hummed hypnotically in the ripening light of late afternoon. It was easy to forget everything in nature's sweet embrace.

'You have a strong connection with our earth mother,' she said. 'I can see the reverence in your eyes when you speak of her, when you're in her embrace.'

'Aye, I guess I do.'

'And you know this path well,' she said.

'I used to walk here with my granddad. We spent many hours exploring these fells. They were special times... quite ordinary, really, but special.'

'Your granddad passed over into the spirit world, right?'

'Yes, he died about twelve years ago.'

She gazed into space as she often did, and a soft smile lit up her face. 'Don't be alarmed,' she whispered, 'but your granddad is here right now.'

I bowed my head and sighed. I was about to say how ridiculous... how the dead are just that: dead. I was feeling a rant coming on about how we only come this way once, how there's no scientific proof of an afterlife, but then she giggled in that captivating way that softened my rational thoughts and made me lose track of them.

'He's asking me to tell you to forget what he told you about there not being an afterlife because he says it's not the absolute truth. He's asking if you remember when you and he were last here. He knew then that he didn't have long in this reality and that's why he gave you his silver pocket watch... almost right here where we're sitting now...'

My mouth gaped like the mouth of Rydal's cave. How could she possibly know that?

'... but he stumbled over his words, just like you do sometimes,' she continued, looking ahead of her as if she really could see him, 'and he couldn't tell you what he really wanted to say because, well, as you know, he was a man of science, of reason and rationality. He was a bit old-fashioned... He's laughing now, Tom. He's stood here, wearing his favourite waistcoat and striped scarf...'

Yes, I thought. He used to don a particular waistcoat and often wore his striped scarf. Where was she getting this information?

'He's quite a handsome fellow. He's here as his younger self. You so look alike; it's uncanny. Anyway, what he wanted to say was that he loved you, Tom; he still loves you. And he was very proud of you then just as he's proud of you now.'

I swallowed hard. I knew he loved me and I loved him. I knew, and there wasn't any need for words to express that. He was the best granddad I could have had and I was so grateful for everything he did for me.

Cali placed her hand on mine. I realised I was holding myself rigid. I looked in her eyes, into cornflower blue, wishing I could see what she could see. 'How could you possibly know about the pocket watch?'

She smiled, in a tender and understanding way. 'I didn't know until your granddad just told me.'

'And you can see him... like a ghost?'

'Your granddad... those who have passed... often appear in their spirit light form but, if they wish to be recognised, they assume a holographic image of themselves as they used to be in the physical realm. We share our breath with all that is visible and with all that is invisible.'

I couldn't say anything for a time. I tried to find a logical explanation for her knowing all this but couldn't, so I put the thoughts aside. In any case, there were really more important things on my mind.

∞∞∞∞∞∞∞∞

'We are one of many just a breath away.'

C louds tumbled overhead and sunlight cut through at random moments, illuminating the landscape, slowly changing everything. We both knew we couldn't stay on this fell forever, pretending everything was normal when it wasn't.

'I've known you many lifetimes,' she told me, staring right into my eyes and holding my hand like she'd never let go.

'I know... I don't understand it but I feel that too. That's why I can't walk away. I don't want to walk away.'

She leant her head against my chest. A robin landed on the tangled boughs above and sang a bewildering song. The afternoon's heat soared and we melted together, like one heartbeat, basking under the sun's healing balm.

'Where do you go?' I asked, unable to stop the gathering questions. 'What's it like? How do you get there?'

She did not move her head from my chest but replied, sleepily, as if hypnotised. 'I travel in a vessel of white light. I'm still not sure what it is or how it works, but it takes me to different worlds, some not too dissimilar to our own.'

'How do you know they're different and not some place here... on Earth?'

'There's much I still need to understand so I can only go by what I see, what I experience. And there are plenty of signs... some places I've visited have more than one moon, and star formations I don't recognise. And there are other beings, some similar to ourselves and others very different.'

I nodded, silently, searching for clues, searching for some link to everyday reality.

'I'm still acclimatising to what's happening, Tom; I'm still working things out. As wonderful as it seems to be able to travel to other dimensions, and the fact that it's some ancestral duty, I'm really not ready to go. That's the difficult part for me. I have a life here, things I want to do.'

She leant forwards and clasped the labradorite necklace round her neck as if drawing strength from it.

'If I hadn't seen you disappear I just wouldn't have accepted it. Even now, after what I've seen and what you've told me, it's a struggle to believe, and yet it's really happening, isn't it, and I feel so bloody useless.'

'I'm sorry, Tom. Truly sorry that I've burdened you with all this.'

'Do you know how long–'

She cut me off before I could finish the sentence. 'Before I'm gone for good? It could happen at any time but I'm still being prepared for the transition. The physical as well as mental impact of travelling between dimensions is immense and requires time to acclimatise.'

'Okay. So, where do we go from here?'

'I don't know. One moment at a time, I guess.'

Silent thoughts interrupted the conversation. Charged thoughts; impossible thoughts.

'I keep thinking I'll wake up later, you know, the nightmare scenario, only that's not going to happen, is it?'

She shook her head. 'Just go with the flow, Tom. That's all we can do.'

'Go with the flow... Okay.' I frowned.

The trees swayed, creaking and shifting. Cali stood up, stretching the raw feelings out of her muscles, and then started to hum a tune, and the mood seemed to lighten, instantly. It never ceased to amaze me how she could do that. She skipped and danced and then she grabbed hold of my hands and pulled me to my feet. We spun round and round until we grew dizzy and I started laughing, giddy as though drunk.

'That's better. I like it when you smile,' she said, as we clung on to each other to stop us from falling.

'So, we should be in the moment,' I said, thinking it really was the best philosophy for life.

'Yes, Tom. We're truly alive in the moment... everything is so much more real.'

For the first time, I held her to me. Her tiny bird heart raced, and for this everlasting moment, I wanted to believe. I wanted to believe she'd always be safe in my arms, and as long as she was in my arms we'd always be together. She stood on her tiptoes and we kissed, and it seemed that all time had surrendered. When we finally stopped kissing, we were lost in each other knowing only what was unspoken.

Roe deer watched us from thick fell terraces and sunlight filtered gold through woodland clearings, illuminating fairy-like insects flying in clusters. I was touched by nature's majesty, suddenly more aware of worlds within worlds, even within our own dimension. More so, I was touched by love, the very essence holding the universe together, it seemed. Dared I believe this might prolong the time we had left?

'Do you hear the trees whispering?'

'I hear the leaves rustling in the wind, if that's what you

mean,' I replied, scratching my neck, 'but you hear more than that?'

She nodded. 'Sometimes they tell me their stories. Sometimes they ask me questions. There is much a tree knows but also much they can't comprehend. Human nature, for example; they have a hard time understanding the things some of our kind do.'

'I can empathise,' I replied, with a half-laugh. 'Talking trees, you disappearing into other dimensions... Have I fallen down a rabbit hole?'

'If you have then I'm there with you.'

But for how much longer? I wondered. And to what depth am I likely to fall? I swallowed back the sadness. I was right in thinking that this day would change everything, but I'd never anticipated just how much. In normal circumstances, I'd be filled with joy at the prospect of sharing what we had. Instead, uncertainty cast a long shadow.

The only definite was the realisation that all we could ever have was now, but wasn't that the same for everyone?

∞∞∞∞∞∞∞∞

> '*We are all energy, resonating at different rates.*'

And so it began, like a scribble on blank canvas or a first word in a poem. It only took a spark, something momentary and minuscule to ignite the emotions. One kiss and *whoosh*, it was too late. Every thought and feeling burned with such intensity. Today, that moment of no return had come and I knew that my life was with her, however extraordinary, no matter what the outcome, and regardless of how short our time together. I didn't mind admitting I was frightened. Yes, I was scared out of my mind. I thought I knew of love before she slipped into my life, but nothing – absolutely nothing – could have prepared me for this.

Time moved on. Reluctantly, we left Rydal and Grasmere. There were questions that couldn't be answered. There were feelings I couldn't deal with. There were practicalities that needed to be considered. It had been a long day, though, and I was too exhausted, both mentally and emotionally, to think with any clarity.

I parked outside the pillared gates of Starfell Cottage. I didn't want to take her back and leave her there. The house seemed sulky in the sullen light.

'What about Mr Darker?' I asked. I didn't know the guy. He probably had good reason for telling me he was with Cali.

Maybe it was an innocent wish, or perhaps he was doing what he thought was best. After all, he didn't really know me either. Still, I wasn't sure I could trust him. 'If he gives you any trouble...'

'Don't worry, he won't.' She touched my hand, reassuringly. 'Will you be okay?'

I wasn't sure I could answer with confidence or if I'd ever be okay again, but I smiled – my most convincing smile. 'I'll be fine.'

'Good. Remember, let's go with the flow.'

She smiled, and I knew she was right. I needed to ground myself in everyday normalities. Keep busy. It'd settle my mind, stop me going insane.

'Call me in a few days,' she added. 'Give yourself some time to think. I know you said this afternoon that you wouldn't walk away, but–'

'I won't. That's a promise.'

She lowered her head. 'I know, but I'd understand if you didn't want to be involved – if you preferred that it didn't go any further between us – because it's going to be difficult...'

'Too late,' I said. 'I'm committed... as long as you want me to be. Besides, who else is there to help you through this and apply some much-needed logic?'

She shook her head.

'Anyway, something might change. Maybe you've got it wrong. Maybe you'll be able to stay here. Surely, nothing is set?'

Both of us hung our hopes on the huge question mark hovering between us.

I kissed her. She kissed me. It was the kiss of lovers who weren't sure how much time they had together, and that made it all the more heightened. We let each other go, and I drove away resisting the urge to look back, afraid that if I did she might not be there.

∞∞∞∞∞∞∞∞∞

'Do you hear the rhythm in your veins?'

Coniston Water glistened beneath the sun, revealing nothing of its cold inky depths and choking secrets. I picked at my sandwich, focusing on satin waters licking the shore. I welcomed the soporific rhythm – anything that would numb me for a while. Behind the mobile library, a shawl of sentinel pines and unfurling ferns provided some respite from the blistering light, from the uncertain truth. On the surface, Coniston appeared much as it had done in Ruskin's day with its unruly fells, boats bobbing at their moorings, and those hallowed paths trodden by many a bright soul. It sang of permanence. A world captured in a snow globe. Yet, even here things were changing. The earth was trembling beneath our feet. Scientists had recorded unprecedented seismic activity in the area and far too many strange weather days. The locals were blaming climate change, but the problems, as I was coming to realise, went much deeper. And other changes were taking place: strange, inexplicable changes.

Normally, I'd throw my troubles into the lake and leave them there. Not today. Cali was on my mind. When was she never on my mind? I'd done what she'd suggested by spending a couple of days away from her in an effort to gain perspective, but I had no doubts. I wanted to be with her. Yet I felt ridiculously impotent. Blood thumped through my veins. The hole in my jumper was growing in tune to the gaping hole in my understanding. I moved from wishing I'd never met her to feeling euphoric she was in my life – at least for now. I scratched my bristled jaw. I didn't have a clue about what I was dealing with here. Who else had a girlfriend travelling between worlds and communicating with alien beings? It seemed ridiculous. I needed to talk to someone about it, but who? I'd never really bought into the whole counselling scene. As for my family, they would think I'd lost the plot. My father would blame it on my heathen outlook and have me carted off to some forgotten place.

I shifted my thoughts to *Swallows and Amazons*, and the *Gondola* cruising to Brantwood. I grasped logic, facts and figures, to that which could be measured and quantified... Coniston Water, five and a half miles long, half a mile wide, 180 feet deep, stretching beneath The Old Man's 2,635 feet. Facts and figures anchored me, usually, but now they fell away and my thoughts slid. At some point, Cali would disappear and there was nothing – absolutely nothing – I could do.

Sunlight danced on the water, pretty much as it had always done since the lake's beginnings. It had been on these shores that my granddad explained the electro-magnetic spectrum to me, and we'd spent a good hour or so sitting on the jetty with our feet dangling in the water, discussing light, and how rainbows appear. 'You'll always find answers in science,' he'd once said. My logical world had always had a scientific basis, had always been rooted in proven facts and figures. Yet could science provide answers to what was happening to Cali? I guessed there was one way of finding out.

I grabbed my mobile phone and found the number for Tristian Neeble. I needed to share this with someone I could trust, someone who would be honest, and tell me whether all this was real or not, because I was damned if I knew. I pressed the call button.

'Trist, it's Tom. I'm wondering... any chance we can meet up as soon as possible? There's something happening here, something that will blow your mind.'

∞∞∞∞∞∞∞∞∞

'Listen! We are all one song.'

I made my way to Ravenshead. Before I knew it, I was parked outside Starfell Cottage and knocking at the door. After living in my head for the past day or so, I just had to see Cali again. I had to make sure she was still here.

Chattering swallows swooped around the eaves, going about their chores, feeding their young. They had no thoughts of what had passed or what was to come. The door opened and Cali beamed at me. She had that knowing look in her eyes, the one that made me lose focus, the look that turned me from confident communicator to jabbering idiot.

'Hi... you're here! I was passing and thought I'd say hello – is that okay? I should have phoned, and, well...'

'I had a feeling you'd call and of course it's okay. In fact, you're in time for supper.'

She grabbed my hand and I followed her into the house. She was barefoot and wearing a long peacock-coloured summer dress. Her dark hair was loosely tied back, revealing her slender neck and the gentle curve of her shoulders. I imagined my kisses journeying over her skin. We passed through the shadowed hallway into a surprisingly light and spacious dining kitchen. The slow strum of guitar playing resonated from a man who was sitting at the kitchen table. He was wearing sunglasses and a camouflage-patterned beret over long straggly brown hair.

He stopped strumming. 'Hey there, man. Pull up a chair, help yourself to cornflakes.'

'You must be Jake,' I said. So, this was Cali's soon-to-be famous songwriter house-mate. 'I'm Tom... Tom Philips.'

He formed a peace sign with his fingers, and saluted me.

'I'll make you guys one of my special herb salads.' Cali opened and closed cupboard doors, gathering utensils and ingredients.

'Cool. Breakfast straight to supper... way to rock,' said Jake, lifting his shades to let in the light. It was obvious he hadn't been awake for long. He reminded me of a twenty-something version of John Lennon meets Julian Cope.

He tuned his guitar and then played a melody, filling the room with the sweetest sound. Cali chopped chives and parsley. Every now and again, she glanced over at me. I expected she was wondering if I was okay about what I knew. Right now, everything seemed normal. Right now, it was as if I'd imagined Cali's disappearances into other worlds, imagined everything she'd told me about meeting other entities and this role she'd been chosen for. Perhaps it was all a dream. How much easier it would be if it was.

'I've been hearing super-cool vibes about your healing sessions,' Jake said, tuning his strings again with his serpent-tattooed left hand. 'A friend of mine says they're wild. We could do with you on tour, help me and the band deal with excesses, you know?'

'What? Turn you into a mellow rocker before your time?' Cali smiled. 'I don't want to be responsible for that.'

He laughed, amber eyes staring into space for a moment, and propped his guitar back in its case. Cali dished out the herb salad platter, a vibrant tangle of greens, punctuated with cherry tomatoes and sprinkled with seeds and seasoning. She sat next to me, her elbow touching mine.

'So,' he said, regarding us both, 'you two are together.'

It was more a statement than a question. Cali and I silently quizzed each other, as if seeking permission. After everything we had talked about at Rydal, after kissing her, after realising we shared some profound connection, then yes, indeed, we were. Neither of us answered, though, but I guessed we didn't need to.

'Kindred souls,' he said, taking out a bottle of elderflower wine from the fridge. 'I can see that.'

He poured the wine into fluted glasses. A bee flew in through the open window, hovering around the lavender pot on the sill.

'The humble bumble,' he crooned, studying the bee and gulping down the wine, 'does he know how important he is, going from flower to flower, doing his thing? Without the humble bumble, life would be very different on this little planet.'

'Aye, true,' I replied, nodding thanks as Jake passed me a glass.

'Life... reality as we know it... is just a fine balance of so many factors coming together,' he continued, chasing a tomato round his plate with his fork. 'Wasn't it Einstein who said that if all the bees disappeared, the human race would be extinct within four years?'

'I believe the quote was mis-attributed. It appeared in a bee-keeping magazine in the sixties,' I said, remembering a heated conversation on the topic between a group of literature and physics students in an Edinburgh bar some years ago. 'Anyway, quote aside, yes, I reckon we'd have a hard time surviving.'

The bee danced from one flower to the next.

'I always send love to the bees,' Cali said.

'Too right, sister. Peace and love to the humble bumble.'

Jake stared through the window, squinting into sunlight, his amber eyes flashing gold. The bee buzzed and flew away.

'So, where's the dark dude tonight?' he asked, tracing his finger clockwise round the rim of his glass.

'Matt? I expect where he usually is,' Cali said, unconcerned.

We all gazed through the opened conservatory doors at the pale domed observatory at the top of the garden. Just the mere mention of Mr Darker agitated me. Although I had tried to rationalise why he had lied to me, uncertainty still dripped like a leaky tap. What probably made it worse was that I knew so little about him.

'I take it he's a keen astronomer,' I said, pushing the uncertainties aside.

'Yeah, man, but I believe he's really searching for extra-terrestrials, although it's all hush-hush.' Jake tapped the side of his nose twice, and winked. 'You see, I overheard a conversation he was having with an American guy. Don't think they knew I was in the house,' he sniggered, biting into a celery stick. 'Anyhow, the dark dude said he'd found a signal in the constellation of Sagittarius – that has to mean ET is calling, right?'

'Don't pulsars give out signals?' I said, offering a realistic explanation.

'Then, why would he say they'd sent back a response? They're in communication, if you ask me.'

I shook my head. There was a long pause of staring into vacant spaces. Lately, I'd been doing a lot of that, hoping for some nugget of understanding.

'Anyway, I don't know why they're looking out there,' Jake continued, pointing skywards. 'Aliens are already walking amongst us, have been for years. Some of us have extra-terrestrial DNA, you know, alien hybrids. David Bowie's one of them.'

I flashed my eyes briefly at Cali, raised my eyebrows at Jake, and laughed.

'Well, he's gotta be... the ultimate star-man's too much of a creative genius for a mere human.' He grinned, plucked a string on his blue guitar and closed the battered case. He drummed his fingers against his chin, contemplatively. 'You know, I think we're all children of the stars, and the dark dude sat in his observation tower out there already knows more than most. We're not the only sentient beings in the universe, and that is a fact.'

I imagined Cali saying, yes, it's true, there were other life forms, aliens, ETs, inter-dimensional beings, whatever you wanted to call them, but she said nothing. Jake nibbled on a plectrum, and the house creaked in the evening's soporific mood.

'Anyways,' he said, standing up, stretching his gangly limbs. 'I'm meeting the guys at the Fox and Jackdaw. Fancy joining us?'

'Thanks, Jake, but it's an early night for me. I'm running a healing session at the village hall in the morning.'

'I have to get back soon,' I said, 'but maybe another time?'

'Okay. If you change your minds, I'll be in the pub... at least for the next few hours. After that, who knows? What with all the weirdo happenings going on locally, maybe ET will beam me up.'

After having seen Cali disappear, the thought of ET beaming any of us up didn't seem that absurd.

'One thing, Cali, before I go,' Jake said, scratching his chin. 'Earlier, while in the land of nod, I dreamt I had to pass a message on to you. It was so vivid I thought I should mention it.'

Cali's eyes met Jake's as if already anticipating what he was about to say.

'I have to tell you not to worry. Everything will be okay. You just have to remember what it is you've forgotten... Crazy, hey?'

Cali nodded her head, and smiled. 'Thank you, Jake. I think that makes sense.'

She didn't say any more. I wanted to ask what she thought the message meant, but the moment passed. Jake winked, drank up the wine, wiped his mouth on his shirt-sleeve, and thanked Cali for supper, and then he and his guitar were gone.

'So that's the soon-to-be legendary, Jake Quake.'

'He'll have the world at his feet within the year.' She winked, knowingly. Her absolute certainty made me shiver and I was reminded, once more, that the woman in my life appeared to know more than logic would explain.

I helped clear the plates. Cali introduced me to dandelion coffee (more delicious than I anticipated), and then we wandered into the garden. The evening clung to the day's warmth. Grasshoppers fidgeted. The lilac and honeysuckle grove was a contradiction of wild and cultivated flowers, and the cottage itself was just as incongruous, with its modern appendages, a satellite dish and solar panels, contrasting with its aged stone walls. And then there was Cali and me, another incongruity. She was all ethereal, and questionable, like a rare glint of sunlight on a dull day, and I was... well, I was pretty much rooted in rationality, or I had been. Now, it was as though my feet were being pulled away from their once-firm earthly footholds into an airy-fairy world where nothing made sense.

'Meditate with me,' Cali said, as she sat cross-legged on the lawn.

'How do I do that?'

'Just sit next to me and close your eyes. I'll guide you.'

I'd never meditated in my life but, being ever curious, I did as she asked. Sitting cross-legged was the easy bit. I tended to sit like that on the floor, on the sofa, or under a tree, reading my books.

'Just relax,' she whispered, 'slowly breathe in... and breathe out... Let your mind settle.'

At first, a torrent of everyday thoughts flitted past my mind's eye, and my ever-active neurons fired off in all directions. Letting my mind settle wasn't easy at all. Unless I was in a deep sleep, I was always thinking. Her voice soothed, though and, after a few minutes, my thoughts did quieten, and I began to drift. The world around me seemed to fall away or become less than what it was. I was in that space just before sleep, and images flashed before me, like unfolding dreams. First, I re-lived the moment I'd kissed Cali at Rydal. The picture melted into a vision, and we were no longer in the English Lakes but somewhere else... somewhere dry, dusty and hot... and we were on horseback, beneath red-hued cliffs, riding through a valley in the long shadows. I was bare-chested. My usually pale skin was surprisingly bronzed. Cali was wearing a necklace of silver and turquoise, my gift to her. We were happy in this timeless place. What a wonderful dream, and yet it felt so real, so now. A voice whispered in the breeze. 'Consciousness is a singularity,' it said. 'We are all one.'

Startled, I opened my eyes to a burning sunset. The cottage walls were brazen orange, such a vibrant colour like saffron robes worn by Buddhist monks. I tilted back my head and refocused.

'You had a vision,' she said, eyes searching mine, 'of us both together, riding horses through a valley. I'm wearing a necklace of silver and turquoise. You are bare-chested and all angles and shadows beneath a blazing sky. Your walnut-coloured hair is sun-streaked...'

'Yes... yes, that's exactly what I saw. How do you know?'

She took hold of my hand and pressed her palm against mine. 'I know because I had the same vision.'

I didn't know what to say. Was she reading my mind? Was it just coincidence that we had seen the same dream? I stretched my arms out in front of me, and shook out those unanswerable questions.

Cali stood up and hummed a tune. She twirled elegantly in her peacock dress, barefoot dancing on the rich green, and then she stopped still, like a statue, all wide-eyed. I must have had a quizzical expression on my face because she laughed. 'You can't see them?'

'See what?'

'Hundreds of sparkling orbs drifting past us.'

'Orbs?'

'Spirits... conscious energy,' she replied, holding her arms out, as if to greet whatever was plainly invisible to me.

'You'll be telling me you've seen a Tizzie-Wizzie next.'

'A Tizzie-Wizzie?'

'It's a creature of legend, seen on Bowness by a boatman in 1900. Apparently, it has a body of a hedgehog, the tail of a squirrel, and bee-like wings.'

Her expression was one of fascination. 'Well, I haven't seen one yet but I'll sure tell you when I do.'

She winked at me, and twirled back round, eyes following what I couldn't see.

'The spirits are whispering,' she said. 'They are saying that consciousness is a singularity... We are all one.'

'Now you're freaking me out. That's what I heard when I was meditating.'

She didn't seem at all surprised. She took hold of my hands, eyes all reassuring. 'There's nothing to fear. There are worlds within worlds. We are all travelling together in a way.'

My brain jammed. I wasn't afraid. I was just... well, confused, at odds with what she could see, frustrated, too, that I wasn't seeing and understanding the same things. How could this possibly work between us?

I glanced at my watch: it was later than I thought. 'I have to go,' I said.

She walked with me to the front of the house. The evening was wild-flower scented. As night drew its shutters, tiny orange lights glowed from the houses and streets in the villages carpeted below. The glow offered a comforting familiarity.

'Just go with the flow,' she reassured, sensing my insecurities. 'I know everything must seem strange and incredible, but there is a reason we have met and connected in this way. We'll learn as we go along. I'm trusting in my Great I Am, and you must also trust in your Great I Am. For now, just think from your heart.'

Unless my brain decided to migrate into my chest, I wasn't sure how I went about doing that. Oh, but Cali was full of strange sayings and notions, so I nodded and smiled.

'If you're in the area tomorrow, around noon, meet me at the village hall. I'm doing a crystal healing ceremony, just a short walk from there. I'd love you to be with me.'

'Okay,' I said, quickly calculating tomorrow's schedule and route.

'It won't take long,' she added. 'I want to share a sacred place with you.'

The light faded and stars pierced the encroaching darkness. Two pipistrelle bats flew around the roof arch, almost blind to the world yet knowing exactly where they were going. We kissed, a little awkwardly, bumping each other's noses. It made us laugh. We said our good-nights and, as I set off back to the farm, I dared to be hopeful of having all the time in the world with her.

∞∞∞∞∞∞∞∞∞

'Why seek what you already have?'

Tuesday's schedule took me to the small township of Swift-side. A constant stream of people visited the mobile li-brary. This was good because being busy kept me grounded. I thought I could take my mind off the weird stuff, only it wasn't to be. Just about everyone was talking about the strange dis-turbances in the local crops, UFOs skimming over the fells, lights and shadows in the woodlands, and I'd overheard every-thing from intelligent theories on the physics of light anoma-lies to scaremongering banter that there was going to be an alien invasion of body-snatchers.

Oh lordy! Another small group was gathered in the back of the van: a middle-aged man, dressed in hiking gear; a slim, smartly dressed retired gent; and two full-figured elderly la-dies. They were having a heated discussion about crop circles.

'Hell's bells,' the smart, retired gent said to the other man, 'you don't seriously believe in aliens? How completely absurd. Trust me, this design in the crops is a man-made affair... probably created by some drunken yobs or that graffiti artist whatshisname.'

'There was a witness,' one of the ladies timidly replied, 'and she says it's the work of angels.'

'Yes,' the other pink-cheeked lady confirmed, 'it must be the work of Angel Gabriel.'

'Poppycock!' the smart retired gent blurted out. 'If you believe that, you're clearly deluded.'

Not long ago, I would have said exactly the same as the retired gent. I'd have laughed at such talk because I, too, didn't believe in such things as aliens, angels, or spirits. The extraordinary belonged to the world of fiction, to the realms of celluloid and movie screens, served up with large bowls of popcorn. It didn't spill out into the seams of everyday life and if it did, it attracted eccentrics and people with overdeveloped imaginations. I was neither, and yet my whole world had turned around; reality was not what it seemed, and ET was probably out there still trying to phone home.

I leant on my elbow at the reception desk and listened to the group sounding off their beliefs, their expressions more animated by the second. They were standing in the very place where Cali had recently disappeared through some incredible porthole of light. If only they knew.

The group's conversation fizzled out, all agreeing to disagree. One by one, they borrowed or ordered books, and by the end of the morning the small stock of esoteric mind body and spirit titles had gone from their shelves, with orders placed for many more books on angels, extra-terrestrials, ghosts, and all aspects of the paranormal.

My last customer before lunch was a boy, no more than eleven. He quickly darted round the library, flitting urgently like a dragonfly from shelf to shelf.

'Can I help you?'

He unfolded a scribbled note with his small fingers. 'I'd like to borrow *Why Does E=MC²?* by Professors Brian Cox and Jeff Forshaw.'

He was freckled-faced, with short-cropped hair sprouting awkwardly with the effect of having a double crown.

I found the book on the third shelf up. 'Is this for school homework?'

'No,' he replied, disgruntled. 'We haven't started sciences yet. My dad says it's because of those bloody budget cuts. But I'm going to be a professor in any case and make an important discovery one day.'

He had the eyes of an ancient soul, as Cali would say.

'Well, young genius, introduce yourself, as I'd like to know the name of the man who will one day make such a discovery.'

'It's Jonathan Ellise, sir.'

'Well, pleased to meet you, Jonathan.' I passed him the book and considered the revelations to come, and wondered what Albert Einstein would have made of Cali's otherworldly travels. 'Make sure you study hard,' I offered, 'and keep an open mind because things aren't always as they appear.'

He considered this with a frown, smiled widely, and held the book to his thin chest. He said goodbye and walked away up the street, already reading the first page. I wondered how the world would have changed by the time he became a man.

Seven magpies landed on the speckled wall opposite the van. Time was pressing on, and I was due to meet Cali at noon. I turned the ignition and the mobile library shuddered to life. The magpies took flight, scratching the sky and squawking furiously. I made my way over to Ravenshead, driving past the latest strange pattern in the crop just on the edge of Heronside. There were people there, in the field, with instruments and cameras and tripods. I suspected they were paranormal researchers, documenting the event. I wondered what Tristian would think of it all. I wondered what he would make of Cali.

∞∞∞∞∞∞∞∞

'Work with the elements and symbols.'

I arrived at the village hall ten minutes early. Music played: a slow earthy drum beat resonated from inside the hall and soft flute tones rose through the air like the skylark, drifting above slated rooftops to the fells beyond. Cali was still running her class. I didn't want to disturb the flow but I was curious, so I went round the side of the building and peered through the dusty window. The room was a blur of people of mixed ages. They were dancing, well, sort of swaying, with their eyes closed, moving to the beat. Cali was dancing, too, weaving between everyone, and there seemed to be a strange glow emanating from her. I wasn't certain if it was the light in the hall or something otherworldly, but it illuminated those around her. Moments later, the music stopped as the session came to a close.

People left the building, all smiling and glowing. I listened in to their excited chatter. 'I've never felt so well,' one woman was saying. 'I've had ME for years. My husband had to bring me here this morning because I didn't have enough energy, but look at me now! It's like I have a new body.' 'I'm ninety-five and feel like I'm twenty-one again,' someone else said. 'She's a miracle worker,' another remarked.

Cali was making such a difference to these people, but it worried me. What if her gifts attracted the wrong kind of people?

Last to appear, Cali had that special sparkle about her, which I couldn't clearly explain. It's like she had the sun shining on her, even when it was cloudy. Her eyes met mine, and something inside me danced. The sun broke free of cloud, and she was even more radiant.

'Come with me, Tom,' she said, skipping child-like through a gap in the hedgerow, swinging a rainbow-coloured bag over her shoulder.

We ascended a common covered by ankle-length grass flicking silver in the breeze, and this slow ascent led up to a bank of sycamore trees. Soon, we were above the village, above its grey-slated buildings, looking out to the shapely peak of Stickle Pike and more distant fells fringing the sky. Cali nimbly negotiated the rising landscape as easily as a mountain goat. She wasn't even out of breath.

'You've obviously done some walking in your time,' I said, as we tackled a steep slope.

'Grandmother said I had good travelling legs, much better than hers, but I always found it difficult to keep pace with her on our pilgrimages. At times, she moved like the wind and was as sure-footed as a cat.'

'Well, I don't know about your grandmother but you make it look easy,' I replied, tripping over loose stone. 'Better than me, that's for sure.'

The path flattened, and we came to a meadow splashed yellow with buttercups. We climbed over crags, where roe deer grazed on tree-lined terraces watching us with inquisitive eyes. We stopped by a fragrant tree-clustered hollow. Gate-keeper butterflies flitted and danced, seeking out clover blossom, and rabbits basked beneath a mellow sun. The place had a wild beauty that called out to me, and yet there was order here, nature in balance. Would William and Dorothy Wordsworth have stumbled upon this place, perhaps on one of their walks with Coleridge? I imagined their rapture on being here, poetry spilling from their hearts, Dorothy so affected that she would have had to lie down for a while to settle her tender heart.

'This is my favourite contemplation spot, and that is the mother tree,' Cali said, pointing to the oak. 'Here is where I will perform the crystal ceremony.'

The oak tree stood proud in a bodice of green ivy; branches spindled out either side of her like a mother's outstretched arms. From her ivy-coated head, a twist of fine branches created an elaborate headdress. Around her were smaller hawthorns, rowan, holly, and crab apple trees, gathering like children. In a clearing, there was a stone labyrinth and, on the wider periphery, a sentry of tall trees – the tallest I'd ever seen in these parts. I could see why she had chosen this place. It was special. I even went as far to think it had a special energy.

'What's the purpose of the ceremony?' I asked.

Cali opened her bag. She unwrapped the crystal from its cotton covering and I recognised it as being a piece of clear quartz, and a large piece at that.

'For some time, my guides have instructed me to plant sacred crystals back into mother earth to help rebalance her energies and strengthen the ley lines. Others, like me, are also reconnecting the crystals. Right now, it is important work for the health of the planet and for all her living entities.'

I couldn't quite bend my head round how crystals would make a difference, and I didn't even begin to contemplate ley lines.

'Why is it important now?' I asked.

'Our mother is weak. The crystal ceremony honours her, and helps enhance her energy.'

I scratched my forehead. 'But it's only a crystal... I don't understand how it could make a difference.'

Her eyes grinned at me. 'It's not just the crystal, it's the intention energy sent through the crystal. Thought is powerful. Our thoughts and beliefs carry weight. Our song resonates, implanting the crystal and making it more powerful.'

My logical brain questioned. It was written all over my face.

She added, 'Whether you think you can or think you can't, in either case, you'll be right. That's the power of thought. When my thoughts are of pure love, the frequencies in this crystal will increase and do the work that is needed.'

She held the crystal up and sunlight sent shards of light streaming in all directions. I moved back, arms folded, not sure what to do or what to expect. She closed her eyes as if in prayer. A few moments passed. She then burst into song. It was a song without words and her voice resonated, each tone vibrating the air around us. The crystal seemed to brighten and sparkle with a greater luminescence, sending out brilliant rays like the beam from a lighthouse. The breeze lifted and changed direction, gushing suddenly, and then there were other voices, subtle at first and rising to a crescendo like an invisible choir. They were singing along with Cali. I looked around. Where were they coming from?

The wind stirred bracken and ferns, whistling through the trees, swirling pollen and seeds. From nowhere an eagle owl swooped across the craggy hollow, screeching as it flew. I ducked, surprised by its presence, and almost lost my balance. It circled us, wings silently treading air, before landing in the oak tree.

Cali turned to me. The light around her, emanating from the crystal, was blinding. She had tears in her eyes, tears of joy. 'They are here... with my grandmother, too.'

I smiled, nervously, but I didn't know what to say so I said nothing. A sudden rumbling noise, like a train rushing through, knocked me sideways. I knelt, thinking it was another earth tremor, but realised it was a gust of air, breaking over the fell like a ravenous beast. Complete stillness followed, so still it was as if time had stopped. From nowhere, a silvery mist billowed around us, removing us from the familiar. Even the blue sky above was shrouded as if a cloud had descended. My stomach tightened. This was like the sparkling mist I'd seen in the mobile library when Cali was taken yet this time there was more of it. The mist encircled us and the mother tree. Lights flickered in the mist and, slowly, tall willowy figures emerged, half-hidden within the vapour and behind the surrounding trees. My knuckles were white knots. Were these Cali's ET friends?

Cali stopped singing and approached the oak tree. She knelt by a small mound of soil and lifted up a moss-covered stone slab to reveal a hole in the ground. Carefully, she placed the glowing crystal into the hollow. 'In honour of our earth mother,' she said, and then started shovelling the rich soil into the hole with her hands. Once done, she patted the earth and replaced the mossy slab. She gazed at the owl just above her. Something unspoken was shared and then the owl extended its grand wings, took to the sky, and was gone. Seconds later, the tall willowy figures seemed to fade away and the silvery mist retreated as quickly as it came, with a final *whoosh*. The distant fells were visible again together with the blue sky.

'All done,' Cali smiled, rubbing the soil from her hands, as if what had just happened was a routine event.

My face must have been a picture. My mouth gaped. My eyes stared wildly. This was the most bizarre lunch break I'd ever experienced. How could anything ever seem normal again when everything in my life had changed, when reality, or my version of reality, was no longer true?

'You okay?' Cali asked, sunlight dancing on her hair.

'Wow!' was the first word I could muster. 'That was... unexpected. Where on Earth did the owl come from? And those beings... what were they? I mean, I didn't see them clearly but they were watching in the mist.'

'The owl was my grandmother,' she smiled, unfolding my clenched hands. 'She's never far away when I'm doing a ceremony.'

'Okay.' I resisted the urge to add sarcasm or incredulity to my tone of voice. She had previously mentioned that her grandmother had returned as an owl, but I had laughed at the ridiculousness of it all.

'And the others were star-beings – in fact, higher-dimensional star-beings, collectively known as cosmic light-workers. I'm happy you've seen them, Tom. Not everyone does. I think that must be a good sign.'

'What do you mean?'

'Well, if they were in any way unsure of you, they just wouldn't have shown themselves as they did. So maybe, just maybe, things will be different when I next commune with them. Like you said, nothing is set in stone.'

We sat below the mother tree in her rooted lap, and I attempted to restore much-needed normality. I poured coffee, and unwrapped my sandwiches. Cali crunched into an apple. All the while, I was shaking away the thoughts in my head as if the very action might erase what I'd just witnessed, or at least discard it as some kind of waking dream. I listened to breeze-blown wishes and the minute creaks of the tree's weary branches. Nothing else should have mattered but this moment – a daisy chain of moments – but my thoughts were tumbling out of control. My rational brain was on a protest march, attempting to maintain hold of the normal, everyday reality I'd once known.

'You know, I thought you were a mad woman at first,' I admitted.

She laughed, stretching out her slender legs. 'And what do you think now?'

'I think I'm the one going mad.'

I guzzled what was left of my coffee and tilted my head to the sky. Fine wisps of cirrus cloud drifted high above, changing shape with each passing second. I followed the clouds' movement, taking comfort in the familiar.

'I understand it must seem that way when you've grown up with different beliefs,' she said, now nibbling on sunflower seeds. 'It takes a while to adjust.'

With Cali at my side, and some kind of normality resumed, I settled into approaching summer, of greens, blues, yellows, and drowsing aromatics. Seed-heavy grasses swayed in tune with life's rhythm. I listened to Earth's gentle breathing, surging bird song, the afternoon's turning, and I was comforted by the mother tree's embrace. It would be so easy to linger here, to forget my day's schedule, to forget what was happening, to let go of everything.

I glanced at my watch. 'Blast!' I shot upright, realising that my lunch hour had been and gone 'Why does time pass so quickly?'

Cali laughed. 'Clock-watching is such a curious thing. I was raised knowing only the cycles of nature, of day and night, of the changing seasons, of the drift of moon and stars. Even now, I still rely on my instincts, still turn to nature's cycles. I eat when I'm hungry. I sleep when I'm tired. Who needs a clock to know that?'

'It's an idyllic way to live,' I said, quickly packing away the cups and flask, 'but sadly not that practical when you have schedules to keep. I need to be in Ulpha... like ten minutes ago. I don't suppose you can wind back time?'

She shook her head, and I sighed. I was glad that she couldn't distort time, that there were things beyond the scope of her gifts, because it reminded me that she was really just an ordinary woman, a woman I had inexplicable feelings for. We walked back to the village, hand-in-hand. My bare forearms prickled with the sun's rising heat.

'How about I take you out for dinner this evening?' I suggested. 'We can talk more and just chill out for a while...?'

'I'd like that very much,' she replied, with a broad smile that dimpled her cheeks.

We reached the village hall where the mobile library was parked. Apart from a graceful flame-haired lady, like a Pre-Raphaelite vision, walking past with her green-eyed cat at her heels, no one else was around. The village was draped in a sleepy afternoon ambience. Cali collected her bicycle from the village hall's foyer and we made arrangements to meet later.

Just as we were about to go our separate ways, a bus pulled up at the stop across the road. There was some commotion inside. The door hissed open and the burly bus driver grabbed an old man by his coat collar and deposited him in the lay-by.

'I've told you, Sam, about messing about on my bus. I won't tolerate it. You can wait here for the next one,' the driver shouted, to the amusement of the other passengers. 'Let that be a lesson to you.'

The driver returned to the bus, closed the door, and drove away. It was only when the bus had gone that I recognised the old man, dressed in dusty black. He had been at the pub, that night I was with Pete. What did he call him... the singing psychic? The man focused on us like a beady-eyed hawk, and began bellowing out a tune, dancing up and down the pavement on his spindly crow-like legs. He crossed the road, all toothless grin and red cheeks, and sang to Cali.

'Deedle, deedle, dee, a star traveller you may be, the way will set you free, only then will you see. Deedle, deedle, dee.'

He chanted louder, hopping around like a possessed crow. Cali simply smiled at him, and he was still grinning, still singing, still dancing, as he disappeared into the public house at the top of the street. I stood spellbound for a long moment, silently mouthing the singing psychic's words. I didn't realise that Cali was already cycling away.

'See you later,' she called to me, hair softly lifting on the breeze.

All I could do was wave, until she turned the corner and was gone.

∞∞∞∞∞∞∞∞

'In nature, everything is as it's supposed to be.'

I'd always been a pragmatic type of guy. Even as a wee boy, I didn't believe in the tooth fairy or Father Christmas or God. Neither did my granddad. It had caused a lot of trouble at home. My father was a godly man, you see, and had always made time for the church. For many years, I had been made to go to Sunday services; that was until my thirteen-year-old self began challenging the concepts that couldn't be proven by science. One day, I had asked the vicar some testing questions about God after one of his sermons, and my father never lived down the embarrassment. After that, I wasn't allowed to go again, and that actually worked in my favour.

Thinking back, that was probably the point where the relationship between my father and I faltered. Being a heathen, as he liked to call me, had never boded well. He still thought I'd been sullied by the Devil. Just as I'd been on my way to meet Cali this evening, he had stared at me like I was the product of evil. I'd half-anticipated him holding up a crucifix against me. It was laughable but sad to think how expectations and beliefs can ruin relationships. I didn't want to be like him. I didn't want to be limited, and yet my own beliefs were being tested by Cali and this strange reality.

The restaurant was new and housed in an imposing Gothic mansion on a promontory of glacial rock jutting from the fell's midriff. Crows crooned around its turrets. Gargoyles grimaced although in a comical way, their terrible expressions softened by the elements. Cali and I had a table for two by the window, which offered generous views of Coniston Water. Around us were silver suits of armour, a stuffed brown bear, coats of arms, a chalice, and a sword plunged into a fake rock. There was certainly an Arthurian theme going on, although I wasn't sure why. Perhaps someone had spotted the Lady of the Lake in Coniston's waters with Excalibur in her ethereal hands. An entire industry could (and often did) arise from our fair isle's myths and legends. We ordered our meals: two decidedly un-Gothic Italian vegetarian dishes from the specials menu. I half-expected Merlin, the former window cleaner, to appear to provide magical entertainment.

'So, how are you feeling?' she asked.

'Fine, thanks,' I said, twiddling another loose button on my shirt. 'Actually... I'm still overwhelmed. I expect that's because I'm seeing the world with different eyes, and it's no longer a world I understand.'

'How do you feel about that?'

'I don't know. Weird, I suppose.'

'Weird is okay.'

She studied me for a moment and then shyly averted her eyes, her heart-shaped face flushing pink, as if she was privy to my innermost feelings. The wall light close to us started flickering and a frown creased my brow.

'Sorry,' she said, squinting at the light. 'This is a kind of side effect of what's happening to me. It's the energy, some kind of fluctuation, I guess. It's been happening with increasing regularity over the past week or so.'

'Is it just happening with the lights?'

'No, I seem to have an impact on other things. For example...'

She took my hand and placed her index finger on my wristwatch. The digital display flashed and the numbers accelerated. My eyes gaped as wide as my mouth as the hours on my watch sped by.

'How did you do that?'

'I don't know,' she said, shaking her head. 'I just focus my thoughts and it happens. Oh, and in case you're wondering, it is still Tuesday evening, 8 p.m. I'm not bending time or anything.'

I stared at her, fascinated. All she did was giggle, seemingly just as amazed as me.

'Some things are random, like the flickering lights, and I don't have any control over it, which is a little annoying. However, my healing and psychic abilities are stronger. As you've already discovered, I'm able to direct the energy in a way that brings about instantaneous healing. Even for me, that is quite remarkable.'

We ate our meals, washed down by a glass of non-alcoholic Chardonnay. The waiter returned to our table, concerned about the flickering light. He apologised for what he thought was an electrical fault, turned off the lamp and duly lit several candles. 'More romantic,' he said, with a generous smile. And he was right.

Cali's skin was golden honey against the lambent light. I knew, without doubt, that something of my own essence was already entwined with hers. More visions of us flitted before my mind's eye like a reminder of what had been or what was. I saw us in each other's arms beneath a white moon with a camp-fire glowing gold. Could I believe that the visions were of our future?

'I have so many questions,' I started, bringing my thoughts back to the present, 'like why is it happening to you? Why were you chosen?'

'I'm not the only one, Tom. There are many who have contact with beings from other realms and have been chosen for specific tasks. All I know is that I was brought up to be peaceful and to honour our earth mother and all living beings. I was gifted with the ability to heal from an early age, and raised to experience what you and the majority would find extraordinary or strange. I now realise it was never a question of why me, it was a question of when.'

'What do you mean?'

'Well, my grandmother was an esteemed healer, but she was much more. She was what some call a Light Weaver, someone who has the ability to control the light energy in a miraculous way. I believe I've inherited her skills and possibly some of her responsibilities.'

'You mentioned she died when you were eleven...'

'She passed over, yes.'

'Is that different to dying?'

'Yes, death in your view is final, whereas passing over is continuing life in our true energy form in another realm.'

'Okay, so she passed on, and was it naturally from old age?'

'Yes, it was her time to go.'

'So why aren't you allowed to fulfil your life on Earth, in this realm?'

'I can't answer that, Tom. All I know is that everything is as it should be.'

Our eyes focused on the dancing flame. Thoughts flitted like sparks.

'I'm not afraid of leaving this dimension,' she continued. 'It's not as if my physical life is ending. All I'm doing is travelling, continuing my work where it is needed. I know I have to go. It is expected of me... but I wish... I just wish it wasn't happening at this time. Meeting you, Tom Philips, changes everything.'

Her blue eyes watered with the threat of tears. She gazed into her wine glass as if scrying for a solution.

'And you're sure you can't stop... or even pause... what's being asked of you?'

'If only.'

A young couple melted into each other at the opposite side of the restaurant. Even from here, their love for one another was tangible, like a melody singing their plans for a long and full life together. Why couldn't we have a real-world relationship like them? Cali glanced over at the couple and lowered her eyes as if she knew what I was thinking.

'I meant to ask you about Jake's dream,' I said, distracting myself from self-pitying thoughts. 'You acknowledged it as if it made sense. What did he mean about you having to remember something?'

'Oh that,' she said, touching the shimmering crystal at her neck. 'To truly understand the journey ahead, I must remember the message of the past, from what my elders taught me.'

'What message?'

'Hmm, well, that's a slight problem. You see, my memory takes me back to the great meetings of the rainbow clans, gathering round the camp-fire in Avebury. I remember sitting with grandmother, watching the smoke curl upwards to form animal shapes in the sky. Her voice, which was neither wholly masculine nor wholly feminine, was speaking of the star-beings. I'm sure of it. Oh but I was too busy watching the smoke transform into horses, birds, and foxes, too busy dreaming to remember what was said. I was only eight at the time.'

'Remembering this message... It's important, right?'

'Yes,' she replied, twirling her crystal necklace round as if the very action might uncoil the memory she was searching for.

'You speak of rainbow clans and this healing community you were part of, and it's all strange to me. I mean, I know this country has a long association with the esoteric, spiritualism and paganism, but I thought that many of the rituals and associations were rooted in folklore and myth, and that anyone proclaiming to see little green elves, or anything out of the ordinary for that matter, had ingested too many of those magic mushrooms.'

She laughed. 'Well, there are many different paths, for sure. Mine is the path of love, and of peace and harmony. The rainbow clans exist all over our planet and beyond. Many of the indigenous people are of the rainbow clans. We share the common goal of healing and taking care of our earth mother. We are of one heart.'

I nodded, reclining into my Gothic chair, into the realms of the weird. 'I've been around for three decades, so how have I not noticed any of this?'

'The colour of the earth, the way the light touches it, all depends on where the observer stands,' she said, dabbing her sweet petal lips with a blood-red napkin. 'Everything is energy: us, this table, the world around us, the multiverse beyond. Thought is energy. What we choose to believe is energy. Whatever we give our energy to becomes our reality. You observed the world from a different place...'

'Aye, but I seem to have stumbled and now I'm seeing from somewhere new,' I said, 'although it's like looking at a Salvador Dali painting and thinking, what the hell is going on? And then, of course, there's all the uncertainty of what's to come...'

'I know,' she smiled, sympathetically. 'In many ways, it's best not to think too much... What's important is that we be in the moment together because that's all that really matters... let's make the most of what we have.'

I closed my hand round her tiny wrist, marvelling at how small and thin it was compared to mine, and I wondered if she's thinking what I was thinking. Out on the Lake, I imagined Arthur Ransome still sailing the dream that was *Swallows and Amazons*. I imagined Donald Campbell racing the Bluebird, racing to rapture's end. I even imagined alien spaceships diving in and out of the water. What was reality?

After a while, I shook my head, attempting to throw out all the meandering thoughts, and I asked the waiter for the bill.

'Let's go,' I said, more brightly. 'There's a place I want you to see.'

∞∞∞∞∞∞∞∞

'Light is more than what it seems.'

We drove west, chasing the day's fading colour, hoping to arrive at our destination before losing the light altogether. Cali sat beside me, her charisma so much larger than her petite figure, and she was part of me in a way that was all consuming and inexplicable. Despite all the weird stuff, despite knowing she would disappear at some point never to return, I was drunk on the moment, and that was all I could be.

The road weaved snake-like over the River Lickle, skirting south of the wooded knolls and howes and dense fern carpets of Duddon Valley. The engine roared in acceleration. The Dunnerdale Horseshoe of pikes and stickles and knots and crags loomed like giants, a playground of white quartz, stone cairns, and old copper mines for man and beast to roam. Over Duddon Bridge, and to the west, the sky was a pastel-pink wash, the colour deepening with each passing second. It was the time of day where light and shadow battled towards darkness, making more of the landscape than what was already there.

'Where are you taking me, Tom?' she asked, eyes filled with curiosity and a kind of child-like excitement.

'It's a surprise. You'll have to wait and see.'

'Will you give me a clue then?'

'No!'

She laughed, then thumbed through my eclectic music CDs and inserted a disc into the ageing player. Goldfrapp's 'Cologne Cerrone Houdini' filled the air, enveloping us, and I thought how apt the lyrics were.

Soon, we were there, off the main road and bumping along a secluded serpentine farm track.

'Close your eyes,' I said, 'and don't open them until I tell you.'

She did so without question, so trusting. The farm track was more potholed than when I was last here and the vehicle sprung along, rattling over cattle grids. Our destination came into view and the spectacular light astonished me. I'd never seen it like this before. It reminded me of a Turner painting. I parked up and turned off the engine.

There's something so mystifying about looking at a woman's face when her eyes are closed. It's like all her secrets are hidden beneath soft lids and long lashes. I lingered for a moment, mesmerised by her quiet expression, her petal lips, her anticipation.

'You can open your eyes now.'

She did so and her face lit up. She gasped. 'Magical! It's a stone circle. Oh, just look at the sunset. It's enchanting, Tom.'

'I thought you'd like it. I wish I could say I put on this incredible light show just for you, but then I really would be some kind of magician.'

'Well, maybe you are.' She unclipped her seatbelt. 'Some things are far more than coincidence.'

The Land Rover's doors closed with a thud. I grabbed hold of her hand as we entered the pasture. 'This is Swinside, although it's also known as Sunkenkirk in the archaeological field. It's one of the finest preserved Neolithic circles in Europe.'

She skipped, turned to me grinning furiously, then tugged at my arm to follow, and we ran together across the pasture, bathed in this melodic light. We stopped at the circle's edge.

'How many stones?' she asked, already counting.

'From memory fifty-five... originally sixty, but there are only thirty-two standing now. Those stones that have fallen all fell into the circle, which apparently baffled the experts. I'm sure there'll be a logical explanation for that.'

We entered the circle. She skipped from stone to stone, touching each weathered monolith. She twirled and danced, her blue dress spinning, and I saw the girl within the woman.

'This is perfect, Tom, being with you, here and now. Can you feel the energy?'

'Hmm... No.'

I stood perfectly still, as if it would make a difference, but I couldn't feel anything except the faintest dusk-scented zephyr.

'It's pulsing so strong, like it's a gateway between dimensions.'

She held her arms out, as if she could see the energy trickling over her.

'You're not going to disappear on me again?' I asked, frown furling my forehead.

'No, not now, don't worry... Oh but the energy... Yay!'

She laughed, she sang, she performed cartwheels in the apricot glow of sunset, and then she stood before me, unbuttoning her dress, and my eyebrows shot upwards.

'Take off your clothes, Tom,' she teased, giggling, mischief in her eyes.

'What?'

'It's okay; there's no one else around.'

'Well, you're here!'

'And so are you,' she replied, letting her dress fall around her feet. She hesitated with her underwear. 'Well?'

I didn't quite believe I was doing this. She watched as I took off my shirt, shoes, and socks, and unbuttoned and stepped out of my jeans, until I was down to my boxers.

'Everything!' she said, as she removed her underwear.

For a moment too many, I watched her break into a dance, like I'd watched her the first time I saw her, and I was mesmerised. Her naked skin was honey-bronzed and sunset-flushed; her river of dark hair teased her delicate shoulders and back; and something animal-like, raw and visceral, stirred within me, an energy I'd never felt before. 'I can't believe I'm doing this,' I said again as I stepped out of my boxers. I ran alongside her, and something wild and primitive took over my senses. Was I possessed? The energy soared inside me and around me and I forgot myself.

Many moments passed. We stopped dancing, and caught our breath. Our pulses settled. The first stars gathered in the east as darkness crept, as the night's canopy closed over us, and a half-moon glimmered pale cream and revealed the shadow of its fullness. Cali walked towards me, like a goddess in my dreams. The iridescent crystal pendant sparkled blue and silver like a temple of stars.

'Your necklace... is it a kind of talisman?'

'Yes, it belonged to my grandmother,' she said, drawing her hand towards it. 'It came into my possession when I attended a rainbow clan gathering. I don't remember what that particular ceremony was about, but it went on into the night.

What I do remember is afterwards. The sky was awash with meteors: green, blue, gold, and silver streaks streaming out of the spangled awning of night, and we stood there watching the spectacle. Grandmother said it was an omen, and she took off the necklace and placed it round my neck. I was so young and it was very cumbersome but grandmother bade me to wear it always. Even now, I hear her voice telling me to take care of it.'

'I've always liked labradorite. Your grandmother must have thought it was special.'

'It is known as a magician's stone, offering insight, wisdom, and protection. I don't know how the necklace came to be in grandmother's possession. There were rumours that she was found by pagan elders in Avebury circle when she was just a babe, and that the necklace was in a bag attached to her tiny body. I'm not sure if that story is true but I have no reason to doubt it.'

We tilted our heads to the stars.

'Is that where you're going,' I pointed randomly towards a constellation, 'somewhere out there?'

'Sort of, out there, somewhere,' she whispered, uncertain, 'but, really, I'll only be on the other side of wherever you are, just like stepping through an invisible door into another world... but I'm not going anywhere today.'

'You are human?' I asked, and then shook my head, laughing at the absurdity. 'Sorry, that's a ridiculous question. I mean, of course you are.'

'Yes, I'm a star child just like you and everyone else.'

She was certainly not like any woman I'd met or known. Physically, she was no different. Physically she was a pretty fine example of the female form. Still, there was something that set her apart, something profoundly rare like a fire rainbow, bio-luminescent sands or giant snowflakes.

'The only difference,' she said, as if reading my thoughts, 'is the way we embrace reality. We are all born as awakened beings. What we experience, how we are educated, and what we believe form our reality. My grandmother and my spirit guides taught me to live from the heart, to live with love for all life forms, and that is my reality.'

'Right now, I'm not sure what is real... whether this is real.'

'Oh but it is real.'

'How can you be sure?'

She stepped closer, the last light draining colour from her skin, leaving a more spectral lunar glow. Her beauty haunted me.

'You think too much, Tom Philips.'

She moved into me, and we were skin and sinew, merging as one. We stood in each other's arms in a timeless together-ness, just like a monolith, and I imagined us turning to stone, granite flesh, fashioned by the Cumbrian elements.

The evening held us in its breath. She rose on her tiptoes, reaching for my mouth, and I drew her to me, and we kissed beneath an audience of stars, those bright constellations like tea lights set out in the dark cloth of night. We kissed; our bodies blazed as we slipped deeper, and then we were on the cool earth, a bed of grass, with the stones standing sentinel, and we slid with each other, falling in wildly and rapidly, and I was inside her, listening to her sweetly taken breath. We were one. The world around us faded, leaving just us: nothing more. And her eyes never left mine.

Afterwards, we curled together silently star-gazing, se-cretly wishing, and I must have had a crazy awe-struck grin on my face. We stayed in each other's arms until the cold nipped at our naked bodies, then we dressed in silence and walked back to the Land Rover. A barn owl swooped by, and I was wondering if I was dreaming. Yet I knew that what had just happened between us was as real as real could be.

∞∞∞∞∞∞∞∞∞

'Thought is the light.'

There was nothing quite like waking up, realising the most amazing, arousing, satisfying dream wasn't actually a dream but reality. All morning, I'd been reliving every second spent with Cali at the stone circle and I was going about my work with a smile to beat all smiles. I never imagined that the first time we'd make love would be amidst the monoliths under the stars. I'd fantasised enough, daring to believe it would happen, ever since I first saw her, and I had imagined so many different scenarios, but not this. Thinking about it, with Cali it was never going to be conventional.

The day passed quickly. I had been in Kendal early to restock the van, sort book orders, and resolve queries. I also reorganised the shelves, making sure the books were placed in order of classification. It's a nuisance when customers don't put books back where they should be. It wouldn't be so bad if they'd put them on the right shelf. Instead, I found *1001 Greatest Inventions* placed upside down in the new fiction showcase and several romance books scattered amidst the poetry. Oh and there was a political biography placed in the horror section, which on reflection was probably the best place for it.

After I'd finished in Kendal, I completed six scheduled stops, ending in Staveley, and now I was parked up by the River Kent, taking a few moments to myself, looking forward to meeting Cali later. I checked my watch, which didn't seem to have suffered any lasting impact after she had worked her strange energy on it. I considered whether I'd have time to call at Verity Lait's to drop off her book orders. We're not supposed to make personal deliveries but I'd become quite fond of Verity, despite her obsession with angels, and I knew that she was also very fond of Cali.

My thoughts wandered back to last night. Had I really pranced around naked in the stone circle? On the way back, I had asked Cali if she'd ever been in love and her reply was 'always'. I wasn't quite sure what she meant by that. But then she had told me that she was in love because she 'is' love, and that made some kind of sense even though it wasn't really the answer I'd been looking for.

I checked my phone. There was a voice message from Tristian, confirming his arrival on Friday. I drank my coffee, captivated by the river, lost in its silver-lit transience. How I was drawn to water. Whether I was by river, sea, lake, or stream, or simply walking in the rain, water soothed me. I wasn't certain whether it was the sound or something beyond the senses' detection, but being by water brought clarity and stillness.

I recalled discussing the secrets of water with Tristian one evening in Blake's just off Edinburgh's Princes Street. It had been many years ago, before Trist completed his MSc in Frontier Physics followed by his PhD. His fascination with all things elemental had been – and still was – an unquestionable passion. That night, after bemoaning student loans, Trist had gazed into his lager with that vacant expression that meant he was churning some complex physics equation or considering some mad theory. After a time, he launched into conversation about water. Apart from being the essence of life itself, he had theorised that water was also significant in unlocking the universe's secrets. His mind had turned over much quicker than he could talk, and his thoughts spilled out into that then smoke-filled bar about how a simple combination of two atoms of hydrogen and one atom of oxygen had the power to create and sustain life. He had lost me when he rattled off numerous equations. I had never been that great at maths. I just recalled the crazy mind-bending thought he finished on: that, essentially, we were drinking the same water that dinosaurs drank millions of years ago; and that we were the essence of everything that came before us and of everything that would come to pass.

Tristian always had a knack of making you think beyond the remnants of the day. For a man of science, he had an incredible capacity for embracing even the most far-flung concepts. For example, he had once told me that he was open to the idea that ghosts exist. I remembered him saying that just because there was no empirical evidence of such apparitions being real didn't mean they were not. He was one of the few scientists I knew willing to take risks, willing to speak out even if it went against the collective grain. What's more, there was always some well-conceived logic to his theories and yet they always took you to the edge of reason, to the extremes of possibility. That was why I knew that my good friend would help make sense of what was happening to Cali.

∞∞∞∞∞∞∞∞

'Thought directs light.'

When Verity answered the door, I had to look and look again. She appeared at least twenty years younger, if not more.

'Tom! Oh, it's good to see you, young man. Cali was here earlier giving me a healing treatment. What a star she is. I feel absolutely wonderful.'

'Whoa, Verity... You look like you've discovered the fountain of youth.' I scratched my head in amazement. There was colour in her previously white hair, a kind of chestnut brown. And the deep lines and creases on her face had disappeared, leaving a healthy smooth pink glow.

'Isn't it incredible? Cali thought so too. She wasn't expecting the healing to have such a rejuvenating effect. Anyway, don't stand there on the doorstep. Come in... I see my angel books have arrived,' she said, taking them out of my hands. 'I'll put the kettle on and make us a nice cup of tea.'

'It's only a flying visit,' I said, as she showed me to the living room before disappearing in a flurry of activity into the kitchen.

An eclectic collection of angel and fairy ornaments littered cabinet shelves. Framed family photographs, documenting her life, took pride of place on a mahogany sideboard. Paintings, a curious collection of artistic influences as diverse as Rackham to Rothko, hung haphazardly on pastel-peach walls. And there were clocks, lots of them, all different styles and from several historical periods, on the mantelpiece, on the walls, on the dresser, and also two grandfather clocks standing opposite each other, proud like guards. Each clock displayed a different time, none of which was correct.

Verity returned with a tray containing a tea set, with winged cherubs painted on to white china cups and matching teapot, milk jug, and sugar bowl. This was completed with a plate of chocolate angel cookies. There were damn angels everywhere. I sank into the chintz sofa as she placed the loaded tray on the coffee table, and simply stared at her hypnotic transformation.

'I'm glad you've called, Tom,' she began, with that imposing principal's voice of hers. 'You see, I know you and Cali are in love because she told me, which is why you should know that I'm worried about her.'

'She told you we're in love?' I said, momentarily brightening, before the last part of her sentence hit home. 'Hang on, worried... What do you mean, Verity?'

'Well, she seemed to have a lot on her mind today. Usually, she's so joyful and carefree but she was terribly quiet. I just know when something isn't right. Do you think it has something to do with the angels?'

I wanted to tell her what was happening to Cali, tell her that these angels of hers were actually entities from other realms, but I couldn't. It wasn't because I didn't think she'd believe me. In fact, Verity was probably one of the few who would. It was just if I told her, she might inadvertently mention it to someone else and the whole thing would escalate. It was already risky that Cali was being seen to perform miracles in the way of healing and, now, youth restoration. It wouldn't take much for any investigator to find a link between Cali and all the strange phenomena that were occurring around the villages.

'She's just tired, Verity,' I chose to say. 'She's been really busy with her healing sessions. She needs to take a break.'

'Well, that's what's she's doing. She said she's cancelling her classes and going on her travels for a bit but,' Verity frowned, 'it's as if she was saying goodbye.'

I was suddenly reminded that I didn't have endless days, months or years with Cali at all. Time was short for us, so very short. I hid the sadness rising within me, and distracted myself by gulping down hot tea and listening to the jingling angel chimes hanging from trees in Verity's garden.

'You mustn't worry, Verity. Cali's fine.'

'Hmm,' she mumbled, 'so why the gloomy face? Why is every bone in that skinny body of yours telling me otherwise?'

'Because... because when she goes on her travels, I'll miss her.'

She considered this. 'Why don't you go with her then – a nice holiday together? How about Paris? I went there with my Timothy, oh, many moons ago... it was a surprise trip to celebrate the publication of my first illustrated children's book. I do so miss him. What a romantic he was.'

I really wished it were as simple as going on holiday. She drifted off, remembering moments in time. There was a photograph on the sideboard of an even younger Verity on the arm of a stout-looking man with slicked-back hair.

'Quite dashing, wasn't he?' She caught me looking at the photograph. 'I still feel his presence, sometimes. Cali says he often stands at my side, smiling like some early Hollywood movie star. When he makes an appearance, she says, "He's here again, Verity, checking up on you." It always makes me smile.'

I gazed through the large bay window, where whimsical topiary and stepping stone footpaths led into a walkway of slender pines. Beyond the wooded heights, a wave of hills lifted and fell, like the body of a sleeping beast. Clouds rolled in and a tide of dark shadows slithered across the landscape, stealing us from the light.

'When did you lose your husband?'

'Oh, some twenty years ago... boating accident... took me a long time to adjust. We were soul mates, you see.'

I considered the grief of losing someone you love. For me, the last time had been when my granddad passed. He'd been the guiding light in my life and I had wandered around like a lost boy for months after his funeral. Now, I was set to lose Cali... I drained my cup, turning off my thoughts to cease the pain.

Verity's now not-so-grey eyebrows knitted together. 'You will take care of her, won't you?'

'Of course I will, Verity.' I stood up, ready to leave. 'And you know she has angels looking after her, too.'

I couldn't believe I'd said that. Angels were still such an alien concept to me. I cringed.

Verity clasped her hands together, smiling. 'Wonderful! I see she's made progress opening your mind on the esoteric front. And to think you didn't believe.'

'Trust me, Verity, my mind is opening.'

∞∞∞∞∞∞∞∞

'Past, present, and future co-exist.'

I t had gone 4 p.m. and nerves crawled like ants in my stomach. Where was she? I leant against the mobile library door, craning my neck left and right. The high street was quieter now as locals made their way home to prepare dinners and give way to the respite of evening. There was no sign of Cali. No sign of her at all. Oh hell, what if she'd gone? What if she'd gone for good? I tried to erase the thought but it hovered like a wasp around sugar. I resolved to wait until 4.30 p.m. and then I'd go looking for her.

I checked my watch every few seconds, tapping the van's steering wheel, impatience growing. At 4.11 p.m., I waited no longer. I set off to find her. I drove less than a mile and, before turning into Damselfly Lane, my heart thumped against my chest. There, on the elevated slope by the roadside, another large circular pattern lay in tall green grass. I slammed on the brakes. Books clattered against their shelves. The formation was clearly visible, revealing three frosted spirals covering at least 200 feet. Two hours earlier, I had passed this field on my way to the village and it wasn't there then. Anxiety rushed through my blood and I tried eradicating a torrent of thoughts that threatened to drown me. Those thoughts you never want to consider: what if she was gone before we'd said all we wanted to say?

I wound the window down and listened. Bird song played on a strengthening westerly wind. I scanned the field. Trees fringed sky, teasing grey cloud, and there was a choking stillness in the hollow. I waited, disabled by the creeping catatonia brought on by the unknown. I was all and nothing in this moment. I was caught in a space between reality and dreams. Over and over, my thoughts whispered: please, bring her back to me. The wind dropped, and birds stopped singing. A low hum penetrated the air. It was the same noise I had heard when Cali disappeared in the mobile library. I opened the van door, in anticipation. Nothing. And then a figure stumbled from the top crag. It was Cali.

My heartbeat quickened. I scrambled over the wall and ran into the field. She stumbled into the formation, clearly disorientated and unsteady, and then she fell. I sprinted until I was at the edge of the main circle. She was sprawled on the frost-stiffened downed grass. Her long hair spread fan-like around her. Inside the circle there was stillness. Complete stillness. No breeze, not even the sound of birds, but there was a low electrical buzzing and a fine silvery blue mist rising from the ground, and it was freezing cold. The hairs on my arms stood upright. From nowhere, three glowing white balls of light appeared, just as Verity had described. My heart threatened to break out of my chest and yet I was not afraid. They hovered for a few seconds, curiously watching then, in an instance, they shot away, disappearing over the crag. I knelt beside Cali. She was conscious but drowsy and I pulled her to her feet, only her legs wouldn't hold her upright. She stumbled again. I picked her up and carried her back to the van. Inside, I placed her on the floor and held her to me.

'Cali... Are you okay?'

'I need water...'

I rolled my coat into a pillow, placing it under her head. I remembered I had a bottle of water in my bag so I reached for that, quickly taking off the bottle's lid with a shaking hand. I propped her up against me and put the bottle to her mouth. She gulped the water, drinking with an unquenchable thirst.

Her half-shuttered eyes searched mine and those sweet petal lips trembled.

'We need to go,' she said, 'quickly.'

'Why? What's happening?'

'It's Matt... he followed me, saw me disappear. I'm not sure what he'll do. We have to go, Tom – now.'

Adrenalin flooded my insides. Quickly, I made Cali comfortable and secure and then closed the van door. I stumbled into my driver's seat, fumbling with the ignition. The engine fired to life. I sped out of Ravenshead, and took the back road past Hawkdale. Just before I reached the crossroads, which connected to the main road, three blacked-out vehicles and a military Jeep roared past heading towards Ravenshead. I accelerated, silently counting to seven, adrenalin burning through me. I kept checking my rearview mirror. Cali was curled up by the bookshelves, her head still resting on my rolled-up coat.

Why was Matt Darker following her? Had he reported what he'd seen? Did those vehicles belong to the investigators that had been in the area? Other questions flooded my mind. What if they had already connected Cali to the phenomenon? What if it was Cali they now wanted? I pushed the ridiculous thoughts from my head because that was all they were. As I turned the corner, I hit the brakes, scarcely missing a black cow wandering on the road. It stopped and stared at the van with an odd fascination, and then trotted past. It seemed to know exactly where it was going. I was about to set off when I noticed figures in the adjacent field... figures of those seven strange men I'd recently seen in the pastures by Nevermore. This time, they were gathered round a single rock obelisk jutting out of the ground. They had their heads bowed as if in prayer, but why? What was it with this place?

Without warning, everything started to shake. The road rippled and a heavy rumble, like thunder, vibrated the ground. It was an earth tremor. The dashboard creaked. The whole van trembled. Tree branches shimmied and loose stone fell from the roadside wall. After a few seconds, the tremor passed. I looked behind me. Cali was still sleeping. Crows flooded the sky, amongst them a single white one calling out in a strange high pitch like a wailing woman. As for the seven strange men, they were nowhere to be seen.

The air seemed to twitch. Thump, thump, thump went my pulse. I pressed my foot to the accelerator, eager to be away. Instinctively, I drove south of the county to Silverdale, where my granddad used to have his holiday home. I'd spent many an hour there, happily searching those white shores. It always seemed a million miles away, as if the rest of the world didn't exist, and it would be an ideal place to lay low for a night, at least until Cali had come round and we'd worked out what to do.

First, I needed to call County Library to tell them a wee lie. Upon reaching Milnthorpe, I pulled into the car park and gave them a call on my mobile phone. The security guard answered.

'I won't be back at the depot this evening,' I began, trying to steady my voice to its usual deep pitch. 'Hmm... the battery's dead on the van.'

'Do you want me to send a mechanic out to you?'

'No... no, it's okay, Ted. Hmm... I'm at home now so I'll have the battery on charge overnight. The van is secure so I'll see you tomorrow. I just wanted to let you know so that you don't send out a search party.'

He laughed and we wished each other a good night, but I was still cringing at my little lie as I finished the call. Still, it had to be better than trying to explain the strange truth.

Before I set off, I spied the general store across the car park. I already had a few camping essentials in my rucksack, together with a first-aid kit, wind-up lantern, and travel blankets in the cab, but we would need some provisions to see us through the night. I quickly checked on Cali, locked the van, and raced round the store, picking up a large bottle of water, apples, a mixed salad, bread, a much-needed jar of coffee, Kendal mint cake, and a box of matches. The purple-haired girl at the counter slowly scanned each item through the till. As she did so, I looked through the window, anxious to return to Cali. Two other customers behind me chatted nervously about the latest earth tremor. My eyes were drawn to an alien-face necklace hung round the purple-haired girl's neck. The necklace twinkled beneath the strip lighting. I paid for my shopping and she winked a knowing wink. I twitched a smile in return.

'Bye', she said, as I made my way to the door, 'and don't worry. Everything will be fine.'

Our eyes connected. I might as well have been standing there naked. This purple-haired girl, who I'd never seen before in my life, seemed to know what was going on, but how could she? It was probably paranoia making me think this way. As I nodded a thank-you, she held the necklace between her fingers and simply watched me leave.

The strangeness of the situation began to hit me. Here I was: an ordinary guy, up until recently living an ordinary life with quite ordinary goals and expectations. Now I was caught up in some weird Twilight Zone type of episode with a woman who frequently disappeared into other worlds. How could life be so normal one minute and turn into something so astonishing the next?

Before long, I was off the main route and negotiating the maze of undulating roads that took us over the county boundary and into Silverdale's heart. I breathed. Already I felt more at ease as if nothing could touch us here – at least nothing I would term as paranormal. Little had changed in this coastal village since my childhood. I steered along the twisting woodland road and eventually reached a clearing where the sea, just a watery ribbon, glistened on the horizon. I turned left down a narrow lane, passing Lindeth Tower where Victorian novelist Elizabeth Gaskell used to stay on her escapes from the city. Further still, I passed granddad's old house. I half-expected him to be at the blue door, waving to me. And why not? Anything was possible now. The laws of the universe were no longer what I'd believed. Perhaps the dead could come back. Perhaps they did, regularly, and our eyes just weren't accustomed to seeing them. All the mad, extraordinary phenomena I'd previously denied were now rooted in probability.

I searched for the track that led to shore. I was certain it was on this quiet stretch, just past Jack Scout, one of the highest viewing points where I used to watch the tidal bore snaking its way inland. From here, the road dropped rapidly. I let the van stroll so that I didn't miss the turning. And, yes, there! The entrance was overgrown, forgotten, but there was just enough room to pass through. I slowly turned the van.

Brambles and hedgerow screeched their wooden claws against fibreglass. An overhanging tree branch clattered the van's roof-lights. I grimaced, hoping the paintwork wasn't scratched. The van descended just a short way along the tree-lined track, juddering over an uneven surface until the terrain flattened. I stopped on a rocky plateau, beneath a shielding canopy of green leaves and vines, and turned off the engine. Here was nature's domain, where sea and land kissed like lovers. At this moment, the sea was but a silver streak, miles away for now. Here was the perfect hide-away. Behind and to the sides, a rise of tender green woodland and silver stone curtained this secret shore, and beyond this limestone escarpment were mud-flats and gullies, clandestine channels and treacherous quicksand, constantly shaped by the ebb and flow of tidal waters.

Cali breathed steadily, eyelids shut, and mouth slightly open; she was still lost in the deepest sleep so I covered her with a travel rug and let her rest to regain her strength. I opened the van door and breathed in. The contrasting aroma of sea and land sweetened my lungs. No, nothing had changed here at all. Memories of past times lulled me. I squinted along the shore to Jenny Brown's Point, named after the nanny who had died trying to rescue her young charges caught out by rapid incoming tides. The chimney stack, once used for copper smelting, climbed out of the shore's edge as if it was a relic transported from some other time and place. My granddad had enjoyed walking here. He said it gave him space to think clearly. Together, we'd searched through broken limestone beds looking for curiosities given up by the sea.

It was good to be back, although I wished it was under different circumstances. With evening fast approaching, practicalities kept me busy. I gathered driftwood and made up a fire. There was no shortage of dry grass and twigs for kindling. After a short while, sparks spat and fire flared. I found sticks to make a spit and rummaged through my rucksack for the billy-can, which hadn't had much use these past years but would certainly earn its keep this night. I poured water into the can and hung it on the spit. The water fizzed and didn't take long to boil. I made black coffee and sat on this rocky plateau, watching the sea's silver thread spill into gullies as it slowly made its way inland. Blue skies were already tinged red and orange with the promise of another glorious sunset. I watched sea and sky, losing myself in the moment. I watched and tried to forget what was to come.

Another hour passed. My stomach churned. It seemed impossible that I could be hungry at a time like this. I stretched my legs. Bitterns boomed in the spreading dusk, their calls almost alien, and the crackling fire provided a welcome heat as day waned. The tide came in fast, stealthily filling hidden channels, and sea-birds screeched like the small screams of those drowned here.

'Tom?'

Cali's voice startled me. I turned round. She was leaning against the mobile library door. The travel rug draped her petite shoulders, and her face was stark and colourless.

'Where are we?' she asked.

∞∞∞∞∞∞∞∞∞

'Other realities co-exist.'

'How are you feeling?'

'A little fragile,' she replied.

I placed my arm round her, and led her to the rocky ledge poking out of the sand. She sat on the stone seat, draping the travel rug over her shoulders. The fire surged, snapping at the cooling air.

'Am I dreaming?' She rubbed her eyes and gazed at sea and sky: a wash of colour and light.

'No, as far as I can tell, this is all real, Cali. I didn't know where else to go, so I brought you here. We're in Silverdale, a little coastal village on the Cumbria and Lancashire border. Do you remember what happened earlier?'

She simply nodded. I tried to imagine what it must be like attempting to make sense of being in one world one moment and then in some other place the next. The exhaustion was possibly like jet-lag but probably a million-fold worse. I jabbed a spindled stick into the fire. Cinders flickered in a flurry, quickly extinguishing in the cooling air.

'You must be thirsty and hungry. I'll make some fresh coffee.' I refilled the can with bottled water. 'I bought some fruit, bread, and snacks. It's nothing fancy but should keep us going.'

The water boiled quickly and I spooned coffee into two metal cups and poured the hissing water into them. Carefully, I placed the cup in her hands. Coffee aroma lifted our senses and we ate and drank together on this ancient and ever-changing shore.

'Feeling better?'

She nodded and placed her hand on my shoulder, and I rested my hand on top of hers, but she was trembling. At first I thought it was probably the after-shock of her otherworldly travels, but then she looked at me with broken eyes.

Her words tumbled out. 'It can't be stopped... there isn't much time... they've told me, Tom... they've told me I have to go next time...'

'Shush,' I whispered, wrapping my arm around her, shutting off the words neither of us wanted to hear.

My heart gulped. Next time... next time the portal opened, she would be gone forever. I moved a strand of hair away from her face. Next time, my sweet little songbird would be gone. I tried to soothe her while also trying to stem the panic surging within me. I pressed her head against my chest. I didn't want her to see the tears pooling in my eyes although I was sure she knew. I was sure she sensed my fear. Her hair was like fine silk beneath my hand. I wondered if she was counting my heartbeat, reassured somehow by the rhythm beating out just for her. We stayed clinging together, clinging to the fading light, until the fire burned low, until our tears were sea-blown. After a while of unspoken thoughts, the late evening air settled us.

'This place has special meaning for you,' she said, calmer now as she gazed along the shore.

'Aye, this is where my granddad conducted some of his geology research.' I smiled, letting past memories surface. 'I spent many winter weekends on these shores, reading, looking for treasure, watching the bore sneak in rapidly as it does here.'

'It's beautiful, Tom, like it's on the edge of life... and I feel the connection you have. I'm glad you've brought me here.'

She slipped off her moccasins and wiggled her toes in the sand. I piled extra wood on the fire, which quickly caught alight, intensifying the blaze. She smiled at me and that usual sparkling energy of hers sizzled and snapped back to life like an inextinguishable flame.

'Do you want to tell me what happened?' I began, tentatively. 'You said that Matt Darker saw you disappear.'

'Yes, he did.' She drew her feet in and sat cross-legged. 'I'd been feeling unsettled all day so I went for a walk through Ravenshead woods and along the craggy rise. I stopped for five minutes or so by the boulder stone as I'd started to sense the energy... I knew the star-beings were coming for me. Just as the portal opened, I saw Matt. He was stood, just off the path, close enough for me to see the strange mix of horror and wonder on his face as I disappeared into the light.'

'I bet he got the shock of his life,' I said, not sure whether I should empathise with the guy or not. 'What was he doing following you? What do you think he'll do?'

She shook her head.

'Have you had any psychic insights about him? I mean, you've told me that you've seen a glimpse of Jake's future... you have visions... so you must know or maybe have a sense of something where Matt's concerned?'

'It doesn't work like that, Tom. I don't know everything.

I'm still learning... still working with these new energies, which are rapidly changing me on every level.'

'Okay,' I said, reaching for her hand. 'Well, let's think about this. As far as he knows, you've gone. If he reports you missing, what's he going to tell the police? That you disappeared in a beam of light on the side of Ravenshead? That you were taken by alien beings? I know things are weird around these parts right now, but who's going to believe that?'

She giggled and I laughed too. It seemed absurd, as true as it was. Another thought did come to my mind though, which sent a shiver through me. If Matt had reported it then I imagined the implications: the government or military or some secret authority would certainly want to know about it. Last thing we needed was Cali being taken away for questioning or something worse. I shook the thoughts away. It seemed pointless creating additional worries.

'Well, whatever action he takes,' I continued, 'he doesn't actually know that you've returned and that you're with me. If anything, it should give us more time before... well, you know... before you leave.'

She squeezed my hand. Her eyes twinkled in the firelight tessellating on this windless night. Neither of us wanted to think about the moment that was coming, and yet it was there and I knew, without doubt, that time for us was shortening by the day.

I stoked the fire, stirring bright red embers, sending spurs fizzing like meteors, burning to nothing.

'Can you see the fire spirits?' she asked.

'I see the fire... I see sparks and flames.'

'Yes, and there are spirits, too, dancing wild.'

I stared into the fire and looked really hard to see whatever it was she could see, but there were just bright embers, red and orange tongues, yellow glints burning to ash. It was just a physical process of elements reacting to their environment. Nothing more.

'I see visions of you and me,' she said, eyes focused on the flames. 'The mountains are behind us, trembling in a heat haze. And we are dressed in summer clothes, and you are smiling at me with those green-grey eyes of yours, and your hair is longer, your skin is golden-brown, and...' She paused, gasping, her face glowing. 'You have your hand resting upon my ripening belly... I'm carrying your child.'

I placed my arm round her thin shoulders, and drew her to me, kissing her forehead. 'What does it mean? Is it a dream?'

'I'm not sure whether I'm seeing past or future or another reality playing out in a different realm,' she said, cheeks fire-rouged. 'As I said, I'm still trying to make sense. All I do know is you're my twin flame, and we are here and now... here and now... and there is nowhere else I want to be.'

The shore sat snug around us. An errant streak of lucid light brushed the horizon, and the sea was a glimmer in this runaway darkness. I spread out a large tartan travel rug.

'My granddad used to say if you want to put your troubles in perspective, simply lose yourself in the stars... so come here.'

I settled on the rug, legs out-stretched, and pulled her towards me, and we lay side-by-side, taking in the starlit roof above.

'Isn't it breath-taking?'

Most of the sky above was now coal black and dotted with scintilla of stars and planets, and yes, we were here and now, here and now. Our fingers entwined and my heart was full of her.

The fire spat as it consumed dead wood. There was a laden hush for a long moment, and I squeezed her hand and rolled onto my side. I stroked her face with my fingertips.

'So, what happened? Where did you go?'

She turned her face towards me and her eyes glowed as she recounted her latest journey. 'I was taken to a planet, which showed me what Earth could become if we were to take greater care of her. There was no pollution there. The energy was so pure and vibrant. It's a remarkable place... miles upon miles of lovingly tended landscape... everything in harmonious arrangement. I was on a mountain of blue-speckled rock. It reminded me of azurite, and yet it has what I can only describe as magical qualities. In fact, wait a minute...' She delved into her rainbow-striped bag and pulled out a polished palm-sized pebble. She placed it into my hand. 'I brought this back for you.'

I sat up and studied it. The pebble shimmered in a remarkable way as if containing its own light source.

'It's almost translucent,' I said, tumbling it. 'My granddad had a collection of every rock and crystal known, as well as a few fragments of meteorite. I helped him catalogue them. There was nothing like this. I'd have remembered. It's beautiful... exquisite.' I turned the pebble again, enchanted by the flashing blue and silver lights within.

She held her hand against her heart. 'The guide took me to meet the Seon. They are a race of gentle beings, quite human in appearance although they are highly evolved and speak without words. They are very much in harmony with nature and live like we should live... in a sustainable and balanced way. Their technology is far superior to ours but there's no materialism, no egotism, no monetary system, no crime, no famine nor poverty. In fact, imagine the most beautiful place you could ever be.'

'It sounds like utopia.'

'It is, and that kind of helps because when I leave this dimension, I'll be staying with them for a while to provide healing. It is an exchange.'

'How do you mean?'

'The Seon are frequent visitors to Earth. They come peacefully, silently blending in, tending to nature, attempting to undo the damage humans are causing. Alas, such visits poison them. Our air is too impure for their delicate lungs. So, in exchange for their help...'

'You heal them?'

'Yes, me, and other Light Weavers like me.'

'Why do they come here, knowing our air is toxic to them?'

'They come because they love us, Tom. They care deeply about us and mother earth.'

I traced spirals in the sand with my finger, contemplating everything she was saying. My logical self was trying to convince me that it was an elaborate story, just make-believe, and yet other thoughts were awakening. As incredible as it all seemed, I knew she was saying the truth.

'Things are changing rapidly. The energy is strengthening. This morning, I gave healing to Verity and I'm sure I reversed her age by about twenty or more years.'

'I know,' I said, resting upon my forearm. 'I saw her this afternoon and couldn't believe my eyes... You know she's so worried about you. She told me you weren't your usual self. Is that because you knew the star-beings were coming for you today?'

'Yes, I knew. I sensed it as soon as I woke this morning. It's like having butterflies in your tummy but for no apparent reason. When I think about it, this is how I've felt each time they've come for me.'

'It's like an early warning,' I said.

'I guess it is.'

I rubbed my chin. I continued to tumble the alien pebble in my hand, dazzled by its light.

She laughed and her voice spooked the night air. 'I think you found me strange before you knew what was happening to me, and now...'

'Now, the strangeness doesn't matter,' I said, meeting her eyes. 'You can tell me that all this is an illusion and the moon is hollow and the stars aren't stars at all, and I promise not to bat an eyelid because, well, I think you know how I feel...'

Our hearts gave us both away. She held her finger to my lips. 'I know,' she whispered. 'I feel the same way, too.'

Our lips met, and we kissed like we might never kiss again, and I didn't want to be anywhere else but there. And, in the sparkling dark, on this silent shore, I fell into her, magically. We became as one, and as we moved together, slowly-slowly, heartbeats synchronised, energy rising, we lost ourselves in each other, rising and rising, eyes finding truth, until we reached that forever moment, the frenzied rapture. Afterwards I cradled her to me, and we drifted in the still bliss star-blazed night.

∞∞∞∞∞∞∞∞∞

'The world is as you dream it.'

Everything knitted together here: grasslands, ancient woods, salt marshes, and sea, enclosed by these low lime-stone hills and crags deposited some 360 million years ago. I tried to contemplate the passing of those years, but it was impossible. It simply wouldn't register. So I looked out to Humphrey Head, just a shadow in the dark, where it's said England's last lone wolf met its death. I imagined that wolf howling in the dark.

I made another hot drink and placed the cup in Cali's hands. We huddled together, breathing in the heady swooning aroma of coffee, wood smoke, and seashore. How easy it was in her presence, how easy and assured our lovemaking, as if we had been together forever. A thought teased a smile and I laughed, wondering if the madness of all this had started to affect me.

'Care to share?' she invited, with a curious smile.

'I was just wondering if our lovemaking will ever make it to a bedroom.'

She prodded my chest. I laughed, and I really didn't care because what was more perfect than making love under the stars?

We cuddled close with a blanket over our backs. Tired-ness crept over me. For a moment, uncertainties flitted like moths. I wanted to freeze time, push back those walls that were closing in.

'It's getting cold,' I said, watching orange embers turn to ashen dust. 'We should go into the van for the night and try to sleep.'

I helped her to her feet and shook sand from the travel rug. She straightened her flowery dress and eased her bare feet into her moccasins. The fire fizzled as cinders cooled. We took it in turns to pee behind the van's shelter, and then entered the mobile library's dark interior. I switched on the lantern. A token orange light cast shadows, closeting the van, making the space smaller than what it was. Although I didn't think I needed to, I locked the doors. I laid out the travel rugs by the shelves housing romantic fiction.

'I bet you've never slept in a mobile library before, in the company of so many authors.'

She settled on the rug. 'No, this is a first... and made special because I'm here with you. I've been waiting for you to come into my life for a long time, but I have to say that you're not what I expected.'

'Oh? A bit of a disappointment, am I?' I teased.

'Not at all. It's just that my boyfriends have tended to be spiritual and very much in tune with their chakras, whereas you're not. I thought my twin flame would be on a similar wavelength. I'm not comparing or complaining and I'm definitely *not* disappointed. It's simply an observation.'

'Are you sure I'm the one? I mean, what if there was some kind of glitch in the universe's programming? What if Cupid's arrow fired off course and you got me by accident when your real soul-mate could be just a mile away from here, searching for you, heartbroken.'

She gave me that look which said don't be ridiculous, and then said, 'You already know the answer, Tom.'

I stared into the lamplight's saffron glow. Yes, I did already know. 'I've never felt like this about anyone,' I admitted, 'and despite me being at odds with the way you see the world, I knew as soon as we met. I just knew I had to be with you.'

She linked her fingers with mine. 'I believe all the enlightened spirits in the universe conspired to bring us together. Our union covers many lifetimes.'

Those effervescent eyes of hers glistened in the lamplight, and although I hadn't previously believed in reincarnation, I began to wonder if she could be right. It had to be something powerful. I couldn't help thinking, though, that this force, whatever it was that had brought us together, would also tear us apart. I didn't understand. It made no sense.

'Be in the moment,' Cali whispered, as if reading my thoughts.

I drew the lantern near. 'Shall I read to you?'

'I'd like that.'

I moved along the shelves, lantern light picking out titles and authors' names, all those words, ideas, and imaginings captured on paper. I found the book I was looking for: *A Collection of English Poetry Classics.*

She settled her head on the mobile library floor upon coats rolled up as pillows and closed her eyes. I hung the lantern on the shelf behind me. It provided just enough reading light. I lay by her side, resting on my elbow, and she placed her hand on my thigh. I opened the book and recited Dylan Thomas' 'Do Not Go Gentle Into That Good Night' in my best poetic voice, and then thought it wasn't perhaps the best choice of poem because I, too, was raging – raging against losing her light. I turned a few pages and read Coleridge's 'Kubla Khan', imagining these other worlds, wondering if Coleridge had slipped through into other dimensions in a laudanum haze. Then I moved on quietly to Keats' 'Bright Star', which roused my emotions in such a way that I was in danger of swooning in an endless free-fall of despair. Enough! I abandoned the book, switched off the lantern, and settled beside her. She turned towards me. Her hand slid beneath my jumper and shirt, coming to rest upon my bare chest. Her touch was light, tantalising.

'I can hear the song of the sea,' she said, her voice sleepy.

'It's the tidal rush,' I whispered. I listened to the movement of water filling the gullies. ' Don't worry; the water can't reach us here.'

Soon, her mind and body surrendered to sleep. I considered how tides rise and fall as the Earth turns on its axis, influenced by forces of gravity as Earth, moon, and sun moved in relation to each other. The world was turning and I was like driftwood, constantly taken and given up by changing tides.

I listened to the shifting sea and sand murmuring soliloquies in the darkness. The hour was full of tomorrow. I held her in my arms, drowsed by her honeysuckle perfume, and eventually fell into some strange sleep, darting from dream to waking in a fitful unrest.

∞∞∞∞∞∞∞∞∞

'Everything is energy. Everything exists because of energy.'

I shifted onto my elbows, eyes half-shuttered. 'You're awake.'

'I am, and the sun isn't up yet, but I've lit the fire and made you coffee.'

I propped myself up, squinting beyond the windscreen at the day's beginnings. I checked my watch. It wasn't yet 5 a.m. She passed me the cup and the coffee aroma began working its own magic, waking me up in an instant.

'Thank you,' I said, taking a sip. 'How are you feeling?'

'Absolutely fine,' she said, smiling.

Even in the dullness, she looked better than fine. Colour had returned to her cheeks. Her eyes flashed brightly like the labradorite crystal round her neck. She looked far too fresh and awake for the morning hour.

'My love is like a red, red rose,' I said, dreamily thinking of Rabbie Burns' most famous love poem. I breathed deeply, inhaling her presence. 'I'm in awe of you.'

'Ha!' she laughed, 'even though I'm more than a little strange?'

'Just a minor issue,' I said, cheekily.

'And I bet you've never had a girlfriend who disappears into thin air?'

'True enough, but then I never loved anyone like I love you.'

There, I'd said it: the love word. It came so effortlessly and yet, in a way, the words weren't necessary. Her eyes locked with mine. She took my hand and held it to her heart. In that moment, past, present, and future seemed to co-exist. It was as if time ceased to mean anything.

'Listen, Tom... can you hear my heart singing?'

I closed my eyes and concentrated. At first, I heard nothing, and then something: something distant. And, yes, there was a faint sound as if a choir was singing. It reminded me of the time I was a boy, walking the fells one December eve, when I'd heard the most angelic voices rising and drifting in the wind: that weirding wind, the stealer of moments. For just a short time, I'd really thought the voices were from some divine source until I discovered it was a group of touring Carol singers giving a concert in the village. But there wasn't a choir outside the mobile library right now.

'Yes, I hear something,' I said, listening hard. 'It's like an aria, like the voices I heard when you were doing that healing thing with the crystal at Ravenshead.'

I opened my eyes to see hers brimming with tears, and she smiled and held me in her smile. And I knew that what I'd heard was her unconditional love for me.

We sank down beside each other and I kissed her forehead, her neck, her hands, and then her lips, and we cradled together, watching the strengthening light. Gulls gathered, crying out overhead. I wanted to stay here and hold on to her, but the clock was ticking again. The world continued to turn as sure as the beat of my heart. There was no other choice than to face the day and decide what to do. I stood up, stretched and pressed the night out of my body, and rubbed my bristled chin.

'C'mon,' I said, attempting to be upbeat. 'Let's meet the morning together and grab some fresh sea air.'

I opened the mobile library door. A bleached sky hung like an untouched canvas, waiting for its first brush-stroke or a splash of colour. The morning promised little but it was still too early to say how the day would evolve. There was something so beautiful here even in the murky light. The sea sat on the horizon like a string of pearls. We ventured out along the edge of this white rock-strewn shore, walking hand-in-hand as if this was the way it had always been. In the distance, sea birds gathered where the water had ebbed, feasting on what they could find. The light was certainly shy this morning and the gloom wrapped around me as if suffocating hope. Cali seemed to sense this because she turned towards me, poking her finger into the hole of my jumper just beneath my ribs, and then ran away from me, teasing me to follow. And although the light was slow to wake the day, Cali was definitely back to her usual radiant self. I ran after her, stepping precariously over a jumble of broken rocks: rocks that had formed from the sediment of tropical marine waters that were here long, long ago. She bounded, cat-like, onto the limestone embankment, and there she let me catch her. We rocked in each other's arms, giddy with love and longing, intoxicated with the sharp sea air.

'There's so little time,' I sighed, watching a flock of sea birds fly on hungry wings, swooping to land further down shore.

'Yet every moment shared is a gift. Every moment lived fully in love is forever.' She looked up at me, her hands on my chest, and commanded my attention. 'Some people spend their life taking such moments for granted, not loving completely, procrastinating, promising themselves and their loved ones happiness tomorrow, and yet all we ever have is now. It is in the moment where all things begin and end. It is the moment we must fully embrace in love.'

She was right, but how do you go about holding on to a moment so that it was always forever?

We returned to the mobile library perched oddly on the limestone shelf as if it had just materialised. We sat by the fire and used the last of the water for coffee. Marine fossils, of brachiopods and trilobites, coated the tabular clints, reminding me of a very different world that was once here. It left me thinking how fleeting our lives were, that we only sparkle for such a minuscule moment. The fire twitched in the fickle light. We would have to leave soon.

'Okay,' I began, shaking sand out of my shoes. 'As much as I'd like to, we can't stay here so I guess we need some kind of plan. Obviously, you can't go back to Starfell Cottage. It's far too risky. So, if you like, I thought you could stay with me up at the farm for as long as... well, for as long as needed.'

'Are you sure?'

'Surer than I've ever been.'

'I'd like that, Tom. Thank you.'

'As for today, I have four scheduled stops to make then I need to return the mobile library to HQ. I'd already booked some time off... starting from tomorrow.'

'You have?'

'Yes, I meant to tell you earlier,' I continued, hesitantly. 'You see, I have an old friend from the university arriving tomorrow afternoon. He's a theoretical physicist. Now I'm not saying he can help, but he may be able to throw some light on what's happening. What do you think?'

'Is he a good friend?'

'He is.'

'Can you trust him?'

'I always have.'

'Okay,' she smiled, completely unconcerned.

We listened to the morning song of birds and insects. In the distance, herons stood silent in the channels, fishing for flukes.

'C'mon; let's go,' I said.

We tidied up and she began to sing. Her song was hypnotic, holding me in the moment, chasing away all the dark emotion lurking within. Ragged skies turned blue. We made ready to leave, ensuring the fire was out. All that was left of us being here was charcoal and ash. She sat in the passenger seat and I switched on the ignition. The engine shuddered to life. Slowly, ever so slowly, I reversed the van through the narrow gap in the hedgerows back onto the road, back into an uncertain world and, reluctantly, we left Silverdale's sanctuary behind.

∞∞∞∞∞∞∞∞

'Move without moving to reach your destination.'

When life was at its most surreal, the best way forward was to pretend everything was normal. Being immersed in the everyday stuff would keep me grounded even though I was untethering like a ship that had slipped its anchor. So, I kept my mind pre-occupied and went about the day's schedule as per usual with the only difference being that Cali was by my side. There were moments where we forgot the crazy elements. There were moments where I was so in tune with her – anticipating her next word, silently reading her expressions, knowing what she'd do next – that, yes, I truly believed I'd already spent a lifetime with her. I couldn't explain the synchronicity between us. I couldn't explain the intensity of what I felt. At times, it was as though we shared one heart-beat.

The day passed swiftly and, much to my relief, without event. My scheduled stops were in the east of the county on the Yorkshire border – away from all the strange phenomena and away from people we knew. Only a few readers returned books and browsed the mobile library's shelves. There were no strange queries about UFOs or ETs and no episodes of miraculous healing. In fact, it was probably the most normal day I'd had since I started the job. Upon returning to Kendal, Cali visited the bustling high street market so she could buy provisions and a few items of clothing for her unanticipated stay with me, while I checked in at County Library. I was expecting a barrage of questions concerning the little lie I'd told about the van's drained battery, but it wasn't mentioned. Everyone was too busy, too wrapped up in their day's activities, which was good as I didn't want anyone to notice my slightly wild, unshaven appearance.

Before long, we were in my Land Rover driving back to the farm. Although we would be a few miles from Ravenshead as the bird flies, I was consumed by a growing unease. I turned the radio on to listen to the local news bulletin, just in case Matt Darker had reported Cali missing. I held my breath as the newsreader mentioned paranormal investigators were still examining the latest field anomalies. He talked about it in a jokey way as the media often did when dealing with paranormal subjects. I reasoned that the media's ridicule was to make light of the ridiculous, or that the matter was serious and they were attempting to stop locals from descending into panic and paranoia. Thankfully, there were no reports of a woman disappearing into thin air. Cali switched the radio to the classic pop and rock channel as a way of distraction. It seemed like a good idea at first, even though it was music my folks used to play, and then it seemed as though every song was about lovers leaving, or life's unquestionable transience, and the lyrics held me captive and I felt a slow meltdown into melancholy.

Soon, we were driving through the heart of Crowdale village, which was nothing more than two long rows of wind-weathered cottages, a patiently manicured village green with a pretty display of flower borders, the pub curiously slanting towards a crooked tree, a grocery shop, and a redundant chapel. The fells surrounded the village like an amphitheatre. It seemed an unchangeable place unaffected by time, and yet there wasn't a soul about. It was as if everyone had turned their backs on this drab and dreary parish. I felt it needed new life... a bit of Cali magic. A curious red balloon floated along the empty street, offering a flash of colour to an otherwise colourless place. It was funny that although I'd grown up here, I didn't feel any sense of connection.

The road was shadow-dappled. The cottages sat squat in the valley, and smoke oozed from their chimneys creating sky-etched messages. We drove straight through and, within less than half a mile, reached the winding private road leading to the farm. My father's sheep grazed the rocky pasture with little care in the world. The Land Rover rattled over the cattle grid, past the ruined barn to our right, and past the track weaving up the side of Tarn Fell to our left. The climbing base of the fell curtained the road. Ahead, the farm nestled in sunshine.

'Here we are,' I said, and with a flourish, I added, 'welcome to the lands of my ancestors.'

'It looks so familiar, Tom... as if I've been here before.'

Perhaps she had been here on one of her astral trips or skipped through while travelling to some other dimension. Nothing seemed that strange or impossible any more.

I parked up in my usual place near the tearoom. The last song on the radio was an oldie that my father used to play when I was young. It was a real old weepy to further wither the mood, and the lyric that tormented me: 'I'll be leaving here any day soon.' Oh hell, what should I do? What could I do? I turned off the ignition and the radio died almost along with my will to live.

The double-thud of the Land Rover's doors must have piqued my mother's curiosity because she suddenly appeared at the tearoom door. She put her hand to her finely arched eyebrows, and squinted at us through the light.

'Mum!' I exclaimed. I shouldn't have been surprised. Nothing escaped her attention so I didn't know why I thought I could sneak Cali into my lodge unnoticed. I felt sheepish, like I'd been caught doing something I shouldn't be doing. 'Hmm, this is Cali.'

'It's a pleasure to meet you, Mrs Philips,' Cali beamed.

'Call me, Fay, dear,' my mother replied, with a generous smile.

There was an awkward pause, a mesmerising pause. I'm not sure whether it was the quality of the afternoon light but Cali appeared haloed by rainbow-coloured sun-sprites, which made her shimmer even more than usual. My mother seemed transfixed.

'Cali will be staying with me for a while,' I said, a little unsure of my mother's response. 'I'd have mentioned sooner...'

'That's fine, son, and you're very welcome, Cali.' She smiled. 'Actually, Tom, I've just finished preparing next door's lodge ready for your friend's arrival tomorrow. Did you say his train arrives late afternoon?'

'Aye, he's on the 4.11. We'll be there to meet him.'

'Very good,' she said, tidying her hair with her nimble fingers. 'Now then, would you both like to join us for dinner, try some of my lovely home-grown organic fruit and veg?'

'That would be lovely,' Cali replied, giving me no time to answer. She squeezed my hand, reassuringly.

My mother hurried back to the house, giving me an approving smile as she went.

I shook my head, and grinned. 'You know, she will be choosing her outfit for our wedding as we speak.'

Cali giggled and then silence followed. The prospect of a wedding and a long life together was never going to be. We gazed at each other, knowingly, and there was no room for words. I opened the lodge door and we went inside.

In truth, I didn't know how much time we had before Cali left this world for good, but I had a sense it would be soon. And I wanted to make the most of every moment with her, hoping this brief time we shared would always keep us connected and together in a way that would transcend time and space. We kissed. Her lips still tasted of Silverdale's sea.

'Are you sure you want to spend dinner with my family?' I asked. 'We don't have to.'

'It'll be nice, Tom. Remember, we must carry on as normal for as long as possible.'

'I can't promise it'll be normal, especially if my father's there, but you're right... Anyway, welcome to my humble home.' I straightened the Monet print, which was askew again, probably as a result of the latest earth tremor.

She read the spines on a small tower of books leaning, precariously, on my desk. Three other piles of books teetered in a corner, waiting for shelves.

'I'm usually tidier than this,' I apologised. 'I haven't had chance to buy the shelving I need. Everything is in order, though. I know exactly where to find what I want.'

'Have you read all these?'

'Yes, all except that pile on my desk. There are about three hundred of my favourites here and the rest of my books are currently in storage.'

'The rest?'

'Aye, I have about a thousand or more, which I've picked up over the years.'

She raised her eyebrows but I wasn't sure whether she was surprised, impressed or simply thought I had far too many. Pete didn't understand my hoard, especially when I could borrow books from the library or read digital editions on a book reader. I'd never questioned it before. I loved books – simple. It was inevitable that I'd keep hold of a few titles along the way. Yet I'd never regarded myself as a collector of anything.

'I don't know how I've accumulated so many. I guess I'll sort them out before I buy my own place...' My voice trailed off, and I averted my eyes, staring through the front window, beyond the porch and into the meadow. I imagined what it would be like, tried to will the vision to life of us buying and setting up our first home together, but there was nothing but a void. I shuffled, awkwardly. 'Anyway, make yourself at home.'

I disappeared into the kitchen and took a few seconds to compose myself, letting go of a future that would never be. I breathed and counted to seven. As I did so, Cali started singing, a bright and happy tune to drown out the sadness. Her song anchored me in the present moment, and that was where I needed to be.

'Have I told you that you sing beautifully?'

She turned her head from side to side, continuing with her song as she danced round the living room, teasing me to catch her. She swirled past, and I grabbed her tiny waist and drew her to me. As I did so, we tripped and fell backwards onto the sofa. We lay there, just staring at each other again with love and longing.

'Well, we have an hour before dinner, so how would you like to spend it?'

My question hovered more seductively than I'd intended.
'I could do with a shower, if that's okay?'
'So could I.'

A smile curved our lips simultaneously. The next thing I knew, I was leading her upstairs. I turned on the shower and we kissed, littering the floor with our clothes as we quickly undressed. Naked, we stood beneath the sobering spray, holding each other, letting the water, this secret element that is water, wash away all thoughts of days to come. We embraced like marbled statues in a fountain, our mouths full of unspoken words, and we clung to the present moment.

∞∞∞∞∞∞∞∞∞∞

'It begins with consciousness.'

My father loomed at the head of the dining room table. His bulky arms were crossed in that defiant way as he quietly assessed Cali and me. My mother, Pete, and Ellie were exchanging small talk, joking and laughing, which deflected my father's stone-faced mood and made the atmosphere friendly and warm. I gently squeezed Cali's hand under the table, and she grinned back at me, quite at ease.

The inevitable questions came at Cali, mostly from my mother and Ellie, about what she did, where she lived, where she came from, and so on, and Cali answered as truthfully as she could, and with humour and poise and joy that energised the room with such beguiling force. She talked candidly about her healing work (although thankfully choosing to leave out the otherworldly aspects) without any embarrassment or fear of ridicule and, I had to say, my family listened with minds that appeared more open than mine was when I'd first met her. Even my father was melting in her presence. Was that a smile I saw on his lips? Crikey! I hadn't seen one of those from him since I was ten years old. And I wasn't surprised. She was special. There was something about her that set her apart, that lifted people's spirits, made them laugh, made them forget about their troubles. Her very presence was like a powerful tonic.

'Can you heal animals?' Pete asked, after scoffing the last of the home-made apple crumble.

'Yes,' she said. 'In fact, animals are more receptive to healing than humans. Their brains don't question or doubt the effectiveness of energy medicine. They are very much in tune with the energy and they heal quickly.'

'Right,' he nodded. 'So, is there any chance you could look at our new stallion tomorrow morning? He's lame.'

'Pete, don't be so cheeky.' Ellie nudged him with her elbow, and rolled her eyes. 'I do apologise for my husband, Cali.'

'I'd be more than happy to help,' Cali said, checking with me as if to make sure it would be okay. I nodded.

'Thanks,' Pete replied. 'I've more faith in natural medicine than all those Frankenstein drugs they dish out these days. And it'll save me calling the vet,' he added, with a wide grin.

Dinner passed more pleasantly than anticipated, and although my father didn't give me the time of day, it was clear he was enchanted by Cali. They talked enthusiastically over dinner. Apparently, Cali's uncle had worked on a farm in Wiltshire. She had helped at harvest time and had also been responsible for looking after her grandmother's hens. Of course, all this was new to me. There was so much I didn't know about her. And she talked to my father about the importance of bees, and organic farming the way it used to be and should be, and about living in harmony. He listened with an enthusiasm I hadn't seen for a long time.

'We don't weave life's web, we are merely a strand,' Cali said. 'We are nature's guests, first and foremost. Most traditional farmers, those who work on the land and with the land, know that more than most.'

'Very true, lass,' my father replied, nodding energetically.

And so I wondered what my father would think of this surreal situation that I found myself in. Would he regard it as the work of God or some demonic force? Did it even matter what he thought? He had his beliefs and I had mine, or at least I did have beliefs. Now, I wasn't really sure what they were. My whole perception of the universe, and life as we knew it, had been altered beyond recognition. For all I knew, there could even be a tooth fairy flying around.

Pete nudged me with his elbow. 'So, this is your naked lady,' he whispered to me, winking. He put up his thumb, approvingly.

We moved through to the guest lounge for tea and mint chocolates, which had been an after-dinner custom in our family from way back. Ellie and Cali chatted about the healing dance and what it involved. My father, who seemed unusually relaxed as though he'd been taking happy pills, sat in his usual armchair. Had Cali miraculously healed his bad mood? I wondered.

Mother was in the kitchen and I helped her prepare the teas.

'Well, I never,' she spoke quietly, waiting for the kettle to boil on the stove, 'your father's certainly taken a shine to your girlfriend. And it's not surprising, as she's lovely. She's a breath of fresh air.'

I smiled and tried not to let her see the pain in my eyes, the knowledge that Cali, the bright light that she was, would soon be gone from here. At some point, I would have to tell them she'd gone, and invent another little lie that she'd chosen to work and live in some far-flung country, which I guess wouldn't be far from the truth. I'd have to pretend it hadn't worked out between us, and the thought of it twisted my insides.

She straightened my collar like she used to do. 'You know, I'm so happy everything is going well and I'm proud of you for sticking to your chosen path in life. And, although your father won't admit it, I know that somewhere in that thick skull of his, he's proud of you too.'

My throat tightened and I swallowed back the emotion. She hugged me and although I now towered over her, I was still her wee boy. I breathed in her aroma: a beguiling mix of apples, freshly baked bread, and strawberry shampoo.

'We'd better deliver these drinks before they go cold,' she said.

Raucous laughter filled the guest lounge. Pete was telling one of his stories about the time he rescued a tourist from a flock of sheep.

'... a city gent, he was. He'd never set foot in the country-side and this was his first experience, and probably his last,' Pete roared. 'Those sheep herded him into a corner of the field and he was whimpering like a puppy when I found him. Poor bloke.'

I placed the tray of teacups on the table and settled next to Cali. Her arm pressed warm against mine, like she'd always been at my side. She turned to me, sneaking a quick kiss with those pink petal lips of hers. And we chatted; we laughed; we forgot, and life teetered on. We enjoyed the evening together, basking in the strange normality of family life, defending ourselves for as long as possible from uncertainties to come.

Daylight faded and my father switched on the light. Within seconds, the bulb started to flicker, buzzing and flaring wildly as if it might blow a fuse.

'That's odd,' he mumbled, flicking the switch on and off, curiously.

Cali and I looked at each other and she nodded at me, reading my thoughts. It was time to call it a day.

'Well, we'll be getting back to the lodge,' I said, as my father searched through a drawer, looking for a replacement bulb.

Pete grabbed his coat. 'I think I'll grab a quick pint while the pub's still open.'

Ellie folded her arms, obviously disgruntled.

'I won't be late,' he attempted to reassure her. 'Anyway, someone's got to support the local hostelry.'

'Well, don't get drunk... otherwise you'll be sleeping on the couch again.'

Ellie kind of smiled but it was clear she meant what she said.

'It's lovely to meet you all,' Cali beamed, hugging everyone in turn. 'And thank you for dinner, Fay. It was delicious. I know you've made everything with love.'

'C'mon, Cali,' I said, eager to leave before my father changed the light bulb and realised the electrical fault wasn't as simple as he'd thought.

We said our good-nights and Pete walked with us across the cobbled farm yard. It wasn't fully dark yet but the moon was up, playing peek-a-boo through rolling layers of white cloud, chequering the landscape below.

'Everything okay, Pete?'

'Yeah, sure,' he answered, a little too quickly.

I knew there was something on his mind, but like Philips senior, he had a tendency to bury certain emotions and the problem simply simmered beneath the surface like a pan of soup threatening to spill over.

'Well, have a good night, bro,' I said, knowing now wasn't the time to dig for answers.

'You, too.' He winked, suggestively. He started to walk away and then stopped. 'Oh yeah, I've been thinking about that question you asked me... about whether all this is real.'

He threw up his arms to take in the immensity of everything around us, just as I did that day I'd asked him the question. I felt Cali's eyes flash from him to me.

'Aye... and what's your conclusion?'

'It's all a dream, Tom. It's just a big fecking dream and, one day, we'll wake up.'

He stood there for a second more, allowing his answer to sink in, and then he took a bow, waved, and set off on his way.

Cali settled her head against my chest, and we watched him go. It was only when he was out of earshot that Cali spoke. 'He's frightened, Tom.'

'What do you mean, frightened? What of?'

'He's frightened of losing something – something important – but he's not going to lose what he thinks he's going to lose.'

I studied her with a confused expression and she shrugged her shoulders. She couldn't explain what she'd said or why she'd said it, and I was none the wiser. I shivered. A dark shape darted across the deepening turquoise sky. I blinked and it was gone. Pale stars grew more radiant with the evening's advance and the landscape seemed ever more alive. We entered the lodge, drank hot chocolate, talked for a wee while, and finally I took her to my bed. Soon, we fell asleep in each other's arms.

Although exhausted from thinking, I woke startled in the middle of the night, not sure where I was at first, until I heard Cali softly breathing at my side, her arm resting on my naked chest. Through the skylight, stars pulsated in that rectangle of liquorice black. I considered that she belonged to the stars and it was inevitable she'd return to them. In the fizzing darkness, that sickening sense of her leaving, of never being able to see her again, surged within, knotting my throat. I started sinking into the quicksand of helplessness. I shook the thoughts from my head because they were too painful, too raw. I wrapped my body round hers, protectively. Everything about her: those gentle curves, her silken hair, the sweet warmth of her skin, was all so new to me and yet, oddly, not new at all. An owl called out somewhere in the darkness and, as I slipped back to sleep, I thought I heard a man's anguished cry followed by a soothing song. I listened again but only heard the strengthening wind whipping round the eaves.

∞∞∞∞∞∞∞∞

'What you think expands the universe.'

We woke early to a twitching dawn. Cali lay still in my bed, gazing through the skylight as if recalling a dream. I waited, unsure of the moment, and then a smile curled her lips. 'Don't worry,' she said, 'I'm still here. It's not going to happen today.'

I sighed in relief but couldn't help feel this waiting was like Russian roulette. Soon, time would be up, and she'd be gone, and it would hit me like a bullet.

While Cali showered and dressed and sang, I made coffee. I turned the radio on, quietly checking the news bulletin again to see if there'd been any reports of her disappearance. There was an interview with a man who claimed to have seen fairies while walking by Coniston Water, but that was all. Once more, the news reader made light of the story, hinting that the man must have been enchanted after stepping into a fairy toadstool ring; either that or he'd partaken in the green fairy drink also known as absinthe. I turned the radio off. It looked as though Matt Darker had decided to keep what he'd seen to himself. It made sense. After all, what could he gain from reporting it except a barrage of ridicule?

Cali breezed into the room wearing a pastel-blue summer dress, which she'd bought at Kendal market the day before. There was no fussiness about her appearance.

Fresh-faced, she exuded a natural glow. As ever, she looked beautiful and I told her so and she kissed me in appreciation. We sat by the window and watched a kestrel hovering in the powdery blue sky, sharp eyes focused on catching its morning meal. Cali munched on an apple. She didn't want anything else and never seemed to be hungry. I, on the other hand, had a healthy appetite and although, like Cali, I didn't eat meat, I seemed to need plenty of calories. After several rounds of marmalade on toast, washed down by several cups of tea, we went to the stables as arranged.

'Morning, Pete,' I hollered.

'Shush,' he moaned, holding his head. 'I'm feeling fragile this morning... had one too many beers, and I didn't sleep too well.'

I shook my head at him, disapprovingly.

'I know... I know,' he said. 'I've already had an earful off Ellie so let's leave it there.'

He gave me that look which said, 'argue with me at your peril', and so I said no more. He beckoned us to the end stall. We heard the stallion before we saw him. He snorted restlessly and the stable door rattled violently with his kicking.

'I'd better warn you, Cali, he has a fiery temper.' Pete did little to reassure me that this was a good idea. Cali seemed unconcerned, though, which made me feel strangely easier.

The stallion was blacker than polished obsidian, with feverish dark eyes. Strong muscles rippled his sweat-soaked shoulder. He pawed at the ground and threw his head up, nostrils flaring. Undeterred, Cali approached him. He quietened instantly. She stroked his neck and something unspoken passed between them.

'Can you open the door, Pete?' Cali asked, 'I need to see him in the paddock... in the light.'

'I'll get his head collar.'

'There's no need,' Cali said. 'He'll follow me.'

Pete looked at Cali and then at me. 'Are you serious? I mean, he's temperamental... needs a firm hand.'

'Do as she says, Pete,' I said.

Pete opened the door and his face glazed in astonishment as the stallion obediently followed her out of the stalls and into the outdoor paddock. She walked the stallion to the far side of the enclosure, soothing him with her gentle song. He moved stiffly and with some discomfort. She stroked his neck and moved her hand along the curve of his back to his hindquarters. He flinched as she touched the injured leg. Cali had her back to us, which was probably a good thing, as how would I have explained to Pete the healing light emanating from her hands? Instead, there was just a brief flash, which Pete didn't appear to notice in the blinding sun. Cali stepped away. The stallion hesitated and then walked towards her, pressing his soft muzzle into her open palms as if in gratitude, and then he trotted round the paddock, head held high, mane and tail flaring. There was no sign of lameness. No sign that he'd ever been lame.

'Blimey!' Pete's mouth was agape. 'What did you do?'

'I'm a healer,' she said, closing the paddock gate. 'I found out what was wrong and then I put it right.'

'Will he be okay?'

'Yes. Apparently, he'd hurt his leg on his way here.'

'That's right, he did. The previous owners had trouble loading him into the horse-box and he slipped off the ramp and stumbled... Hang on a moment, how do you know?'

'He told me,' Cali said, smiling as she watched the stallion canter playfully.

Pete's eyes widened in amazement and he laughed. 'I've never seen or heard anything like it. I know about horse whisperers, but what you've just done is pretty astonishing. Thanks, Cali. Now, what do I owe you for your services?'

'Nothing,' she said, and then she paused, twirling dark strands of her hair around her fingers. 'Well, actually, there is something.' She turned to me. 'Tom, please can you give me a few moments to speak with Pete?'

'Aye, sure,' I replied, more than a bit curious. 'I'll meet you back at the lodge.'

I sat on the porch bench. Sparrows argued, lost in their own small world, defending territory and searching for their next meal. Four cyclists pedalled along the farm track heading towards the tearoom. A heat haze hung like a watery curtain, distorting their movement. Above them, on the sharp slope of Tarn Fell, orbs of light glimmered, moving rapidly, and then disappeared. I couldn't be certain if it was a trick of the light or something otherworldly. At the end of the far pasture, the ruined barn sat in the land, wrecked and roofless, slowly sinking into the earth, reminding me that everything changes. Nothing's constant.

I panned east and my heart jolted. Through the haze in the furthest corner, dark figures stood motionless like monoliths, forming a human circle. Even before I counted, I knew it was the seven strange men. Curious, I got up, shielding out the sun with my hand. What were they doing here? A hand touched my shoulder and I virtually leapt out of my shoes.

'Are you okay?' asked Cali. 'You seem on edge.'

I breathed away the cold sensation rattling in my bones. 'No more than expected under the circumstances. No, I'm just wondering what those guys are doing.'

'What guys?'

I turned round. The field still quivered in the morning's haze but there was no one there. The men had vanished. I shook my head. 'They've gone.'

She studied me for a second or two and then she led me away into the lodge for a cold drink of lemonade. She didn't tell me what she'd said to Pete so I didn't ask. Whatever it had been was obviously meant for his ears only. There were still a few hours before we met Tristian so I suggested we go for a walk around the farmland. I wanted to show her this little paradise, this contrasting patchwork fabric of pasture, fells, woodland, and streams, where I'd spent my early childhood. I also needed to keep moving, as if moving would shake loose this coiling uncertainty and stop me from dwelling. And so we walked.

The days were lengthening as summer solstice approached and the meadows and fells carried the song of bees. We ascended the back fell, walking against the flow of the stream. The gradient was easier than neighbouring Tarn Fell and there was abundant tree cover along the route, but even though the green canopy afforded some shade, it did little to protect us from the day's rasping heat. I wondered if the walk had been such a good idea. It was more humid than I realised and my shirt began sticking to my skin. On the fell-top, the land flattened to a wide girth of green, punctuated with lichen-stained rocks, yellow gorse, and the occasional flurry of hart's tongue fern rising from vertical grikes. We rested on a green knoll, which offered sweeping southerly views down into the valley unfolding to the estuary beyond.

'When I had a row with my father, I used to come here', I said, wiping the sweat off my brow, 'and I'd dream of finding a boat down by the estuary and sailing across the Irish Sea. I even set off one day and got as far as Broughton in Furness.'

'What happened?'

'I found my granddad waiting for me at the bus stop. He took me back to the farm, but not before we had a good chat.' I laughed, unfurling the memory.

'I had my little spot sat beneath a great oak in the middle of a field near Avebury. I spent hours there, head full of song and story. Sometimes, I'd fall asleep and wake to find rabbits nestling by my feet. Sometimes, I'd have visions or journey into the astral realm. If I stayed out too long, grandmother always turned up to bring me back, but I never felt alone or in danger.'

She sat cross-legged, breathing in the view. I drew my knees into my chest, thoughts brooding in the day's heat.

'Sometimes, in the quiet moments of night, I wonder if this is really happening. I keep thinking I'll wake up and everything will be normal. In my most desperate moments, I've even considered praying.' I stifled a sarcastic laugh.

'Praying isn't such a bad thing, Tom. It's transformational. It sends out a ripple into fields of conscious energy. Sometimes, the universe listens...'

'Next you'll tell me there's a god... and that there's karmic justice for all those ignored by their god in their hour of need. Please don't go there, Cali. I'm still getting my head round you travelling into other worlds.'

215

We sat in hot silence. I fanned my shirt to stay cool. I closed my eyes and saw all the weirdness playing out on the back of my eyelids.

'I think I'm seeing things, too,' I said, straightening my shirt collar.

'What things?'

'Strange figures appearing and then vanishing; lights flashing; dark shapes – that sort of thing.'

She nodded in understanding. 'The fabric of space-time is splintering right now, creating what are known as crossing places. It happens where worlds collide, causing other realms to leak through, and it's a side effect of what's happening to me. It's nothing to worry about. It will stop when I'm gone.'

'You're going and it's nothing to worry about?' A knot of frustration tightened inside me. My mood tilted, changing like the sudden rush of air riding ahead of a storm. She squeezed my hand but I brushed her away. I stood up, my long thin shadow marking the ground like a sundial.

'I've known you for a few short weeks and yet I love you like we've always been together, so why the hell is this happening?'

My voice searched furiously for answers that wouldn't come. She lowered her head, eyes penetrating the earth. It irritated me that despite her power of insight, she knew so little about what mattered.

I paced up and down, attempting to diffuse the frustration, anger, or whatever it was raging inside me but I couldn't stop it, and a torrent of words and feelings sprang forth, spluttering out of my mouth like poor orphans: 'Life was fine before we met... I never asked for this... I don't want to feel this way... I don't think I can face losing you... in fact, let's stop this now...'

The words and feelings were unrelenting, and inexcusably self-pitying. I stomped over to her like an angry child, pulled her up to face me, and I was not myself. I knew I wasn't myself as I grabbed her fragile shoulders. 'I can't stand this. Every moment I'm with you, I fall deeper... Don't you understand, it hurts, the thought of losing you is killing me.'

A rush of air blew in from nowhere, capturing my breath, my words, my pain, and I let go of her and turned away. I strode to the edge of the fell. The estuary called to me and I wanted to sail away. Something deep, monstrous and primordial shuddered through me like an express train and I yelled out: '*Why?*'

My voice thundered over the valley, permeating everything, threatening to break the sky in two, and I was shaking as all the energy drained from me. Moments passed. I turned to Cali, feeling withered and ashamed by my outburst. Tears rolled down her face like tiny star-sparkling crystals, which seemed alien and out of place in the afternoon sun. I took her into my trembling arms, and we held each other like we'd never let go.

'I'm sorry, Cali... I love you; I just can't bear the thought of losing you. I want to be strong for both of us, but I'm struggling.'

'I know,' she soothed, 'you don't have to apologise. I understand, and I love you. I love you with all that I am.'

We held each other until the rawness slowly eased. A firm breeze sneaked in from the west, pilfering the stifling heat. It ruffled our hair and cooled our skin. It rushed through the hawthorns behind us.

'Tom, do you hear the trees talking?'

'I hear the wind, and the leaves rustling, that's all.'

'They speak from wisdom and have a message for us... They say our love transcends time and space. They say our true selves will always be together because we are one.'

'I want to believe,' I said, holding her heart-shaped face in my eyes. 'I so want to believe that we'll always be together.' I cradled her to my chest. 'If you find a way, you will come back to me?'

'You know I will, Tom. I promise.'

∞∞∞∞∞∞∞∞

'What you know is not constant.'

What could I tell you about Professor Tristian Neeble? Well, he was an ordinary guy with an extraordinary mind. Like most thinkers, he certainly had his quirks. For starters, he wore gaudy-coloured shirts and had even less fashion sense than I did. He loved spicy food (chilli peppers had no impact on him whatsoever), and he could play saxophone a damn site better than I played guitar. He was shy but became incredibly vocal when discussing physics. He preferred *Star Trek* to *Star Wars*. The word 'possessed' would adequately describe his approach to work and the word 'imaginative' perfectly summed up his theoretical reasoning. There was definitely a little madness there, too. He had once lived in a caravan in his early student days and had a lucky escape when a little fuel cell experiment went wrong and blew up that same caravan. Oh but he had genius streaking through him, had published many thought-provoking physics papers, was working on ground-breaking science projects often at CERN in Geneva, and was well respected by students and peers alike. But most of all, genius and idiosyncrasies aside, he was a fine friend.

And here we were at Oxenholme station waiting for his arrival. We leant back on the platform bench. Cali rested her head on my shoulder and I breathed in her all now-too-familiar honeysuckle perfume. All the earlier angst had burnt away, consumed by the day's heat. I was present again but still clinging to the hope that we'd have a future together. I'd even gone as far as sending out a quiet wish to the universe – just in case some force was listening. After all, what harm could it do?

The platform was surprisingly quiet. The station clock dragged out time and there was expectation in the air. Being here reminded me of past adventures, of emotional departures and uncertain arrivals. Travelling through the landscape by train had a particular romanticism unequalled by other forms of travel. Maybe it was that sense of moving without moving; quietly observing the rush of life passing by; travelling along steel arteries to gain momentary glimpses of villages, towns, and cities stitched together by a patchwork of green. I imagined what it would be like to travel freely between different planets. I guessed all travel – whether a few miles down the road or billions and billions of miles away – afforded the same sense of anticipation and wonder.

A funnel of warm air raced along the rail track as if an invisible train was passing through. An inaudible announcement came over the speaker and pigeons scattered. I stood up as Tristian's train rolled in, right on time. It shuddered to a stop. Doors opened and several people stepped onto the platform: two Japanese women; an elderly couple; a boy with a guitar case on his back; and a couple of men wearing identical suits. Tristian, however, was nowhere to be seen. I looked up and down the platform, then raced alongside each carriage, gawking through each window until I saw his familiar hunched outline. He had his head pressed between the pages of a science book, hair spiralling in all directions, oblivious to where he was. I knocked on the window, urgently, and he glanced up with intense brown eyes, somewhat surprised to see me. He checked his watch as if he'd lost all sense of time.

'C'mon, Trist,' I shouted, 'the train is about to leave.'

He reached for his weekend bag from the luggage rack, picked up his coat, and rushed to the door. He leapt off the train onto the platform just in time. A moment later, the train lurched forwards and departed.

'Close call,' I said, and then gave him a manly hug.

'It's not the first time I've almost missed my stop,' he said, patting me on the back. 'Good to see you, my friend.'

He was wearing one of his trademark shirts, something resembling a painting by Jackson Pollock. His jacket and trousers were not of the same suit nor did they co-ordinate, but it didn't matter because this was the very recognisable and unique style of Tristian Neeble.

Cali was at my side, all bright and sunny in her summery dress.

'Tristian, I'd like to introduce you to Cali Silverthorn.'

'Hello. A pleasure to meet you,' he said, awkwardly shaking her hand. His eyes shot at us both curiously. 'Are you both, err, together, as in a couple?'

'Aye,' I said, feeling as though we'd never been anything else.

'Twin flames,' Cali added.

'Well, well... It seems I have some news to catch up on.'

'Oh, there's much more than news, Trist, much more.'

We drove to a country pub outside of town, and although I wanted to jump right in and tell him everything that was happening, I decided we'd have dinner first because I knew it would be the only ordinary part of the weekend. We ordered food and Tristian told me what I'd been missing from the Edinburgh scene. I discovered that he was now a senior lecturer at the university and had been working on a new research project in an attempt to discover the impact of dark energy and why the universe was accelerating. He said that Blake's, where we used to socialise and drink the best beer, was now an Indian restaurant, albeit a good one. The most surprising news was the mention of a girlfriend. Tristian, the consummate bachelor boy, was in love with a scientist from the astronomical research department.

'We've been together a couple of months and it's working out rather well,' he announced, expressing surprise at his own admission. 'We spend our time together mulling over theories. It's incredibly stimulating.'

'You always were a romantic,' I teased. 'Seriously, it's good you've met someone on the same wavelength and I'm happy for you.'

Trist finished his coffee. 'Well, I've talked enough,' he said, adjusting his spectacles. 'So, tell me, what's going on here?'

Cali's eyes sparkled, and the air seemed full of possibility.

'Let's go back to the farm first.' I stood up, eager to go. 'You can settle in and we'll talk there.'

And that's exactly what we did.

Once unpacked and freshened up, Tristian joined us in my lodge. He sat in the armchair, plumped the cushions, and tapped his fingers together as if drumming out a Morse code message. Cali quietly studied him and he returned a shy grin.

'You have a problem with your neck, Tristian,' she said. 'You have pain radiating into your right shoulder.'

'Yes, how do you know that?'

'Cali's a healer. She can see your energy field.'

Tristian held my gaze with some initial bemusement then shot his intrigued eyes at Cali. 'Interesting,' he began, fidgeting with the edge of his collar, 'very interesting! I didn't think you believed in this stuff, Tom.'

'No, I didn't but you could say I've seen the light.'

Cali and I shared a knowing smile.

'Would you like me to give you healing?'

Early evening sunlight streamed through the window, and Cali's necklace flashed blue and silver.

'Well, I've been having physio for months and conventional treatment hasn't helped so, yes, why not? I'm willing to give it a go.'

She moved to his side. 'Just close your eyes and relax,' she said, as she positioned her hands just above my friend's head.

Tristian visibly tried to relax by letting his shoulders droop, but all it seemed to do was exaggerate the tension. Cali's hands hovered a few inches from his unwieldy frame. Her bare arms were slender, toned, and honey-bronzed. Her dark hair tumbled over her small shoulders. She closed her eyes, as if meditating, and waves of light radiated from her as if she had powerful torches embedded in her palms. I stared in astonishment. It was the first time I'd seen the healing take place at such close range. The light was golden, like a gaseous stream of solar energy surging from her hands. She seemed to master it, making it move in the way she wanted, and I understood now what she meant by being a Light Weaver. The energy appeared to penetrate Tristian's shoulder and back while surrounding him in an aura.

'There,' she said, after only several seconds. 'You won't have any more trouble.'

He turned his head to one side and then the other and lifted his shoulder. He rotated his arm back and forth and then spun it round like a wind turbine. He looked at me, and then at Cali, with the most amazed expression on his face. 'Goodness!' he proclaimed. 'The pain has gone. It's completely gone. I can move my shoulder with ease. Look!' He spun his arm round again just to be sure it had worked. 'How did you do that?'

She smiled. 'I'm a healer, but really it has nothing to do with me. It's universal energy working through me. You had an energy blockage in the side of your neck and I was able to move the energy on.'

'Tom?'

'It's just as she says. She moved the energy on.'

'That's incredible,' he said. 'I'm not exactly sure how you actually did that, but thank you.'

'You're welcome,' Cali replied, blushed cheeks aglow as she giggled.

'I've seen spiritual healing at work but the results have never been so quick and as effective as this,' he pondered, scratching his head, causing a tuft of dark wiry hair to stick up at a funny angle.

There was a moment of simmering silence. He tapped his fingers against his bristled chin.

'So, tell me,' he began, sitting closer to the edge of his chair, curiosity heightened, 'has this got something to do with what's going on?'

Cali curled herself into the corner of the sofa like a kitten settling for the night. Her eyes fixed on mine and she nodded a silent approval.

'First of all, let me take your mind back to a conversation we had in Blake's about eight years ago,' I began. 'We were talking about the possibility of time travel and there being other dimensions. I think I said that if other dimensions were proven to exist, I'd buy the most expensive bottle of cognac to celebrate.'

'Yes, I vaguely remember that conversation.'

I reached into the cupboard and pulled out a bottle of vintage cognac, which we'd bought from the wine and spirits store before Trist arrived. I placed the bottle on the coffee table in front of him.

Tristian stared at the bottle and then at me, his thick eyebrows askew. 'I don't understand. Are you saying you've found evidence of other dimensions?'

I placed three glasses on the table, opened the bottle, and poured the golden liquid into each one. A floral aroma filled my nostrils and perfumed the air.

I smiled at my good friend. 'Aye, you could say that.'

Tristian perched right on the edge of his seat, pupils darkening in anticipation. 'I'm all ears,' he said.

'Well, sit comfortably, my friend. We're in for a long night.'

∞∞∞∞∞∞∞∞

'You are more than your physical journey.'

Slowly, I explained what had been happening to Cali, giving Tristian time to digest each weird little detail. His eyes grew wider and his face fashioned a permanent look of astonishment. On several occasions, he jumped to his feet and marched up and down the room, grasping at details and trying to sort, assimilate and juggle each potent revelation as if it was a hot coal. Mostly, he sat with his chin resting in his cupped palm, listening intently and absorbing what had been only conjecture, his greatest imaginings or simply the works of fiction or dreams.

'This is, indeed, a wow moment,' he said, his voice almost spectral in its excited pitch. And he paced some more and then paused. 'You wouldn't jest with me? This isn't *let's fool Tristian Neeble day*?'

'I wouldn't do that to you, my friend,' I replied, solemn-faced. 'I only wish it was something made-up but it's definitely real. I've seen Cali disappear and then return in front of my eyes. There's no trickery involved. She's travelling between worlds and communicating with other entities.'

Tristian regarded Cali, seeking confirmation, searching for truth. 'I know it seems incredible,' she said, 'but it is really happening.'

Once again, there was silence for a long moment and Tristian downed a shot of cognac. He blinked, brown eyes watering as the warm liquid hit the back of his throat, and then he took a long slow breath.

'It's a lot to take in,' I added, turning a glass of cognac round in my hand as if it was a compass. 'I'm still struggling. As you know, Trist, I'm a grounded kind of guy. My life is built on the foundation blocks of logic and order. I turn to science for answers, not religion or divination or beings from other dimensions. This kind of stuff doesn't exist in my world. I've never had a William Blake moment. Until now, I've never had to question reality. In my eyes, the miraculous is found in nature and the evolution of life... processes that can be scientifically proven. Everything that's happening to Cali is... is...'

'... is rooted in possibility.'

Tristian finished my sentence with an answer I wasn't expecting.

'So you believe?'

'Believing isn't the issue,' he replied, tapping his jaw with his index finger. 'I'm more concerned with the "hows" and the "whys". And, you know, reality *is* a questionable thing. Your reality worked well for you, Tom. It tends to work well for us all until something comes along and throws a pretty hefty spanner in the works. If you think about it, some pretty big spanners have been thrown in the past. You only have to consider that once upon a time, black holes, the slowing of time at high speeds, even the Earth being round were the stuff of fiction, often ridiculed or rejected as heresy before being scientifically proven.'

I nodded, relieved in many ways to be finally talking about this with someone other than Cali, someone who had the mind to delve far deeper than me.

'What's happening to Cali is weird... at least, I find it weird.'

'Weird stuff happens out there every single moment,' he said, pointing upwards. 'Did you know that the energy of *nothing* appears to be taking over the universe... that dark energy has magical properties? I live with weird every day. And, you know there are already many multiverse theories suggesting that there is at least one other universe close to our own.'

'Really? How close?'

'How does a millimetre away sound?'

'Crazy?'

'Yes but completely possible. Some would go as far as saying probable. If all this is true then Cali appears to have gone beyond the theoretical and is the one who could say definitely. And, yes, there are plenty of theories that support what appears to be taking place. Although hypothetical, what's happening could involve some kind of wormhole, which is allowing superluminal travel. Is it possible to travel through a traversable wormhole?' He paused, pondering on his own question. 'Hmm, it would require some extraordinary propulsion vessel, something that allows return to a point of origin. There would be an incredible amount of energy involved.'

The evening began to wane, poaching the natural light, so I switched on the wall lamps in a moment of forgetfulness. Within seconds, they flickered violently, on and off, on and off. I rolled my eyes and Cali grinned, shrugging her shoulders.

'Cali, or some aspect of the energy associated with what's happening to her, seems to have an effect on the lights, too.'

Tristian observed the flickering, stroking his chin. 'It's not an electrical fault?'

'No, it happens wherever she goes.'

I found some candles in the cupboard and Cali helped me light them. I then switched off the electric wall lights. The flames shot tall, their sprightly shadows dancing on the walls.

'Are there any other side effects of these events?'

'Do the thing with the watch, Cali,' I said.

She asked for Tristian's arm and he rolled up his brightly coloured shirt sleeve. He was wearing an old-fashioned watch with a star constellation on its face. She placed her hand close to the watch and the hands whizzed round at great speed. Tristian's face was alight with amused amazement.

'How?' he asked.

'I don't know,' she said. 'I believe it is part of my preparation, as if I'm being tuned into a certain energy frequency.'

'Preparation... for what, exactly?'

'For when I leave this realm for good.'

Tristian stared at Cali and then at me.

'The problem with what's happening,' I said, picking at the hole in my jumper, 'is that Cali has no control of this. At some point soon, she will leave and she won't be able to return. The next time will be the last time. There's no coming back.'

'How intriguing,' he said, scratching his head, and then realising the gravity of the situation for Cali and me. 'Oh but I mean that's not good for you two. No, it's not good at all.'

Cali held my hand. Her eyes met mine with that familiar reassuring gaze.

Tristian delved in his pocket and took out an electronic notebook, and then changed his mind. 'Tom, do you have paper and pen? In light of Cali's talents, I think it'll be a more reliable medium.'

I rooted through my desk drawer and found him a new blank notebook and one of my silver poetry pens.

'Let's start from the beginning,' he said, with pen poised. 'I'm not sure how – or even if – I'll be able to help, but the more information I have, the more chance there is of trying to make sense of it all. You see, if what you say is really happening, and it's not some illusionary episode, which as you can under-stand, I need to eliminate, then this will be significant for physics... Earth-shatteringly significant.'

He streamed question after question and Cali answered as best she could: questions such as: when and how often does it happen? What do you see and experience? Why do you think it's happening to you? Have you noticed any distortion of time? What do the star-beings want? What are they like? What are their worlds like? He asked her to explain exactly what happened when she travelled, to describe the light, the noise, the sensations she felt. He noted every tiny detail. And she shared what she could remember of her upbringing, about the rainbow clans' prophecies, about her vague childhood memories of the star-beings, and how she believed she had been chosen for this role. She told him that there were others chosen: that she wasn't the only one on Earth being taken out of this dimension to be of service. It made me think of all those people who go missing under mysterious circumstances: the unsolved disappearances. Had they had contact with the star-beings? Questions led to more questions, as was the way, and we talked late into the darkening night.

I made coffee for us all and stood for a while, watching the steam rise from my cup and from Tristian's head. He read through his notes, feverishly. Every now and again, he stared blindly at the ceiling cornice, his mind computing and considering every extraordinary detail.

'Do you have an idea when you're about to travel?' he asked, sipping at the still-too-hot coffee.

'Yes,' she said, placing her hand just under her ribs. 'I have an unsettled butterfly feeling in my solar plexus... usually when I wake up in the morning. It's like a premonition.'

'When you experience this, approximately how long is it before you go on your travels?'

'I'd say several hours later. At least, that has been my experience so far.'

I drew the curtains, shutting out the uncertain darkness, and Tristian twirled the pen between his fingers. The candle flames burnt brightly and a cosy orange glow chased shadows into corners.

'So, what do you think of it all, Trist?' I asked.

'I'm flabbergasted. I mean, I haven't seen Cali disappear, and I haven't experienced these other realms she's described so, right now, I have to be open-minded. That's all I can be until I know more. It's a kind of a Schrödinger's cat conundrum. Once Cali disappears into another dimension of space, we can't possibly know what's happening unless we observe it and experience it for ourselves. Of course, the difference is that Cali can tell us about her travels but, even so, it is still only her experience. It's purely subjective. Oh but then that's the curious thing about the nature of reality.'

I reached into my trouser pocket for the blue pebble Cali had given me and I passed it to Tristian.

'Cali brought this back from one of her trips. Many years ago, I helped my granddad catalogue every known gem and mineral on Earth, and there was nothing like this.'

Tristian tumbled the stone in his hand.

'What a remarkable piece,' he said, studying it closely. 'It appears to have a light source within. Well, this could certainly be sent for analysis, if that's what you want?'

I stared at the red spirals in the rug covering the wooden floor.

'I don't know,' I replied. 'I don't think it matters right now in the grand scheme of things.'

Cali's eyes shuttered with the call of sleep. She stifled a yawn, and apologised.

'You look tired,' I said. 'Why don't you grab some sleep?'

'I think I will, if you don't mind. Do you have all you need, Tristian?' she asked, uncurling from the armchair.

'Yes, thank you, for the moment at least,' he said. 'Right now, my mind has blown a fuse. As you can imagine, after years of chasing equations round a blackboard, which incidentally is now a white screen and involves a click of the mouse rather than the scratch of chalk, but that's by the by... Where was I? Oh yes, after years contemplating the existence of other dimensions and such quandaries, coming to terms with what you're actually experiencing is just... well, just mind-blowing.'

I cleared the cups away. While I was in the kitchen, voices faded to whispers, and I returned to the lounge to find Cali hugging Tristian, her head buried in his multi-coloured shirt. He simply patted her back and then awkwardly stepped away, clearing his throat. I knew, from his empathic expression, the way he avoided my eyes, that she'd asked him to look out for me after she'd gone. I just knew. My heart jolted and panic raged inside me.

'Well, good night,' he said, with a reverent bow of his head. 'We'll talk more tomorrow.'

I kissed Cali and gave her a hug, breathing her in, reluctant to let her go. 'I'll be up in a short while.'

She said goodnight and my little songbird sang her way up the wooden staircase.

∞∞∞∞∞∞∞∞

'You are more than your Earthly experience.'

Tristian perched on the edge of his seat with his head resting in his hand, doing a damn good impression of Rodin's *Thinker*, albeit a clothed version. He gazed at his watch but realised it was still displaying the wrong time courtesy of Cali's earlier demonstration.

'It's 2.21 a.m.'

'Still early then,' he replied, and he wasn't joking. Tristian didn't seem to need much sleep. Instead, he took regular catnaps and drank plenty of coffee to keep his mind ticking.

I rubbed my hands over my face to wash away the accelerating tiredness. My thoughts jogged over everything we'd talked about this evening. There was still more to mention and it seemed that every tiny thread of weird further unravelled the world I'd known.

'Something I forgot to mention earlier is that whatever is going on appears to have an impact locally.'

'How do you mean?'

'Paranormal activity: light anomalies, UFOs, and the appearance of strange figures. There are also frequent small earth tremors... and crop formations, although nothing quite like the kind you see in Wiltshire.'

'Does anyone else know about Cali's other-worldly travels?'

'No although Matt Darker, an astronomer who owns the

house where Cali's staying, actually saw her disappear a few days ago.'

'He did? How's he taken it?'

'Don't know... We haven't been back to find out.'

'Do you think he'll report what he'd seen?'

'Can't be certain.'

'Well, he's bound to be curious. Any scientist would be, whether he's reported her disappearance or not.'

Tristian hunched his shoulders and drummed his fingertips against his chin: one, two, three; one, two, three. He rubbed his forehead. 'My head's bursting with questions and equations... I could do with some fresh air.'

'Grab your jacket,' I said, topping up the glasses with an extra shot of cognac. 'Let's sit on the porch for a while.'

Apart from a skittish breeze rustling the leaves of the barely visible trees in the night-coated meadow, it was eerily silent and the sky was abundant with stars. We sat together on the bench by the door, clinging to the cognac. The cooler air wakened us.

'All this must be a shock,' I began. 'I know it was for me – and still is.'

'It's phenomenal, Tom. I don't even know where to start. If Cali really is travelling into other dimensions and it's not simply some psychological or other unusual episode, which you know I can't rule out at this stage without empirical evidence, then can you imagine the implications?'

'It will change everything.'

'Yes, it really will.'

'That's what I'm scared of... that and the fact I'm going to lose her.'

I downed a swig of cognac. Tentatively, he placed his hand on my shoulder and there was an awkward pause. Tristian didn't find it easy dealing with emotional situations. He'd once said that our greatest downfall and time-waster was our inability to let go of difficulties or, more accurately, the emotions that cause them. It's not that he didn't care. He just didn't dwell on things, didn't allow himself to fester over anything he couldn't control. What was the point, he'd said. Life was too short. It seemed an abrupt way of dealing with stuff, although I could understand the logic.

'I'm sorry,' he said. 'Realistically I don't think there's anything I can do to help. I mean we're only just beginning to really understand what's going on in the universe, and if Cali is travelling into other dimensions and meeting other entities, then that's going to add an incredible amount of spice to the mix. However, working out exactly what is happening is going to take time, and I understand that you and Cali don't have that luxury.'

'No, we don't,' I said, solemnly, still feeling the cognac's warmth in my throat. 'To be honest, I'm just happy you're here, Trist. I'm hoping you'll be able to see what I've seen.'

We absorbed the strange hush of the night, aware of the pulse of all that was. Somewhere in the distance, a dog howled. Tristian was contemplating and I was trying not to.

'I've always dared to believe we live in a complex multiverse teeming with other intelligent life,' he mused. 'I've spent a good portion of my life looking to prove it. Up until now, all I've had are theories, just mere possibilities of other worlds through the vein-like splinters of reality.'

'Reality, hey? What's real, Trist, as I'm damned if I know.'

'Now, there's a question,' he boomed, his voice echoing in the darkness. 'As for the answer, you could say it depends upon whom you ask. From a quantum mechanics viewpoint, reality only exists if you interact with it. Many modern physicists believe there is no deep objective reality. Life, as we experience it, consists of potentials and actualities. The bottom line is that we create the world we perceive through our senses and beliefs.'

'Cali says that the nature of reality is that we think we exist, and so we do, creating and co-creating every single moment. She says thoughts have power behind them, that everything is part of a collective conscious energy.'

'Yes, possibly! Life – everything you see and everything you can't see – is made up of a multitude of energy signatures.' He tapped the side of his glass. 'Cali is fundamentally right. We influence reality. There are a growing number of scientists researching what Cali believes... that consciousness is the programming language of the universe, and that we effectively transmit the reality. At sub-atomic level, reality can behave in accordance with the expectations of the observer. This is fundamental in the Heisenberg Uncertainty Principle. When we observe something, we affect it in some way. Oh but who knows why that is so? Frankly, the jury is still out on the nature of reality.'

He craned his neck towards the stars, and I followed his gaze.

'Bloody good views of the night sky,' he enthused. 'Just look at the Milky Way... and there, just above Pegasus, can you see that fuzzy oval? That's the Andromeda galaxy, some 2.5 million light years away.'

Slack-jawed, I focused on the clusters of stars and planets, trying to assimilate the distance from Earth. It felt like all my dreams were coiling and then disintegrating into that heavy, potent sky. A tiger moth flapped towards the solar lantern hanging in the porch. It scurried around the weak beam of light, hitting the lantern several times, and I considered the absurdity of its folly, just as I considered the madness of my own.

'I'd go with her, if I could.'

Even in the feeble yellow glow of the porch light, I saw his eyebrows lift. He was silent for a few moments, his mind churning, and then he turned to me, and said, 'Well, if that's what you both want, then why don't you?'

Tristian's response blazed like a meteor through my mind.

'I didn't think I could.'

'Well, you're both made of the same stuff. If Cali can safely travel through to other dimensions, I don't see why you can't too... unless you need a specific kind of alien passport. Of course, you'd have to be with her at the exact point of travel.'

The thought of being able to go with her sobered me, made me giddy, and gave me a slice of hope. I sat bolt upright, remembering how way led to way. 'I never looked at it like that. Now you mention it...'

'Of course, there are un-quantifiable dangers,' he considered, see-sawing his finger against his chin. 'Until we know what we're dealing with, then it's risky. Alas, like I've already said, research takes a long time – I mean just applying for funds to carry out research would take a long time. Oh, but don't get me going on the subject of measly government budgets.'

'If I try to go with her, what's the worst that can happen?'

'It's difficult to answer. Your molecules may be flung into all dimensions; you could die; but I'm thinking that the way you feel, the worst that can happen is if she goes and you're left behind.'

He was right. I took another swig of cognac, and gazed at the stars, letting go of my fear in their beautiful perfection. Dreams started coiling again but instead of fading into oblivion, they burst into life, expanding with each crazy thought.

'What would you do, Trist?'

'I'd go. I'd take the risk – but that's me. Science does strange things to a man.'

'You could say the same about love,' I replied.

He nodded, silently. We drained our glasses, and surrendered to the night.

∞∞∞∞∞∞∞∞

'You are of the stars.'

I curled myself round her body like an extra skin, and kissed her neck. She whispered, 'I love you,' and drifted back to sleep. I lay awake, watching the remains of the night, reflecting whether I was mad to even consider going with her. Like Tristian said, there'd be unknown risks. It would certainly be a one-way ticket. Could I leave all that I knew behind? What about my career, my aspirations, the normal stuff like settling down, buying my own place? What about family and friends? How would they feel? If I went, and survived the journey, what would I do there? After all, Cali had been chosen for her role, probably from birth. She was a healer. She had a natural empathy and a special gift. She had a part to play. What if I ended up doing something I hated, or couldn't do anything at all? And were there any books in these other realms? What about poetry and music? In the starkness of night, the idea was starting to sound untenable and ridiculous, rattling around in my head like a coin spinning in a tin box. I breathed and then returned my focus to what mattered: I loved her, unconditionally. I wanted to be with her, unconditionally. I'd fly to the end of the universe to be at her side. Really, what else could be more important than love?

Before long, dawn streamed white through the skylight, brimming with the day's promise. I savoured her sleeping face, committing every detail: the soft pink curves of her cheek-bones, the long dark arches of her brows, the perfection of her Cupid's bow, the smooth line of her nose, that determined and yet fragile chin, those petal lips, and closed eyelids hiding worlds within. She was beautiful and yet ordinarily human in light of her quest. I stretched my limbs and tightened my arms around her.

'I'm not letting you go,' I whispered in her ear.

She stretched and giggled, softly. 'Not even for a yummy Cali-cooked breakfast?'

'Tempting,' I teased, loosening my grip.

She snuggled against my bare chest, watching my heart-beat quiver beneath my skin.

'How are you feeling today?'

'Fine,' she reassured. 'I'm not going anywhere.'

'Good!'

I breathed relief. She stroked my arm and kissed my brandy lips.

'So, what do you think of Tristian?'

'I like him,' she said, grinning. 'He has a peculiar nature – a bit intense – but he's charming and kind and I trust him. Oh but what a busy mind. I gained a glimpse of all those neurons sparking. What a clever man he is.'

The room brightened with the strengthening light, and my thoughts swooned and spiralled with possibilities.

'I don't think there's anything he can do to help, Cali, but...'

I shifted onto my elbow, hesitant.

'But what?'

'Well, we talked a while last night and... to cut a long

story... I was left with a question: what's actually stopping me from going with you?'

The moment hovered and seemed to drift like seedlings in the wind. She slowly sat up, and the light quivered over her soft skin. Her eyebrows puckered as the question strayed over them. I sat up too, my chest like moonstone in the morning's miasma.

'Nothing,' she replied, her eyes flashing with realisation. 'Nothing is stopping you. I mean, I can't think of anything. If the star-beings objected then I'm sure it would be made known in some way. But...'

'Yes?'

'Would you leave all this behind... your family, friends, career, Earth... all that you know?'

'I love you. I'd follow you to the end of time to be with you.'

'But... but what if you grow tired of me?'

'Never!'

'The lifestyle will be very different to what you know. You might hate it.'

'I'm willing to take that risk.'

'What does Tristian think?'

'He says there are unknowns, and that it's risky because of those unknowns, but he understands why I would do this. He understands completely.'

She lowered her head and traced her finger round her chin, creating imaginary spirals.

'I don't know; it could be risky, Tom. I wouldn't be able to forgive myself if anything happened to you.'

I gently brushed back her hair. A blackbird whistled its morning song, and I heard hope in its cheerful melody.

'Didn't you tell me that belief is everything – that what we think creates our reality? If so, then we can make it happen. We can be together. We can travel together.'

She smiled, and her cornflower-blue eyes sparkled with love, with what could be. She touched the side of my face. 'I couldn't wish for anything more.'

'Then somehow we'll make it happen,' I reassured.

We kissed and slipped back under the duvet.

And the day had a new energy about it, radiating with possibilities, and after a while she sang and we teased each other out of bed.

∞∞∞∞∞∞∞∞∞

'When you shift your perception, other dimensions become visible.'

Confident that Cali wasn't going to disappear into another dimension any time today, I left her at the lodge with my mother and Ellie, while I drove Tristian to Ravenshead to see the strange anomaly in the fields. After a bright start, the sky had taken on a dull wash. Thick grey clouds smudged the fell-tops with the threat of rain but, as we travelled, a brisk wind sent them into retreat and, soon after, the sun burnt through. We parked at the village hall and decided to walk to the field, which was less than half a mile away.

While Tristian tied his shoelaces, I noticed Cali's hand-written poster, which she'd put up on the village news-board a little over a week ago. It declared that her healing dance classes were now cancelled. I imagined there would be a fair number of disappointed people and that she was already dearly missed. And yet she had done more good in the short time she'd been here than most people were able to do in a lifetime.

Tristian peered over my shoulder at the poster. 'So, this was Cali's healing venue. If her classes helped people as effectively as she fixed my funny shoulder then I imagine her being exceedingly popular here.'

'I've heard local people talk about what she's done for them, how she's cured conditions that were thought untreatable and restored their health and vitality. She's even made people young again... and I don't just mean 'feel' young but look decades younger. I've seen it. Just being around her is a tonic.'

Within a minute, we were walking out of the village and into nature's domain. Birds trilled in the thick hedgerows, busy with their young. Trees shimmered in their sea-green mossy coats. Life was blooming all around us, spilling over onto the footpath and then, when the footpath stopped, nature spilled into the road: a crowd of green spears; thorny stems; yellow, white, and blue blossoms. Such diversity of life in such small spaces made me dizzy with the thought of what more there could be.

'Don't take this the wrong way, Tom,' Tristian continued, 'but it's probably as well she's, for want of a better phrase, moving on. If she's curing people, that's going to impact big pharma's profits. And you can't expect to perform miracles without attracting the wrong kind of people. Sooner or later, those with little conscience will approach her. Do you understand what I'm saying?'

'Aye, I know. This has been on my mind for a while.'

'Over the years, some of our greatest minds have been employed, often dubiously and occasionally by force, to satisfy the needs of the few rather than the needs of the whole, to make those with wealth, power and influence have even more wealth, power and influence. Imagine having an amazing gift or making a fabulous discovery only for it to be used in a destructive way. Many have battled with the fruits of their knowledge. Oppenheimer, Einstein, Russell, and many others before and since, warned about the dangers of scientific discovery and about managing the power of knowledge. It's a burden.'

'Aye, it is indeed. Cali says the human race as a whole just isn't spiritually evolved enough to use what we have in a smart way, and I tend to agree. We're like kids running around with loaded guns. We must be a major embarrassment from the viewpoint of other intelligent entities.'

'Intellectually, we've been advancing rapidly, particularly over the past one hundred years.'

'Aye, but are we advancing from the heart – on an emotional level? I know most decent people don't want to kill, destroy, go to war or ruin the planet we live on, but you only have to look at our historical time-line to see that we don't have an impressive track record for taking care of the Earth or each other. Despite all our intellectual and scientific advancement, our planet is in more of a sorry state now than it's ever been.'

'That's true enough,' Tristian said, suddenly ducking to tie his loosened shoelace again.

'Cali said there are star-beings who travel here at great risk to their own well-being to help put things right, and she says they do it simply because they care about us and our planet. What would our great leaders do if they travelled to other worlds? Before you know it, they'd be bleeding some other poor planet dry and be warring about who owns what. Can't say I'm proud to be human. If I'm able to go with Cali, I think I'll spend all my time apologising to ET on behalf of our kind for the terrible mess we've inflicted here.'

Tristian stood up again, eyes intensely studying. 'So, you've spoken to Cali... about going with her?'

'I have, and she's unsure... mostly because she thinks I'm making a big sacrifice leaving everything behind, and partly because of the unknown risks.'

'Does she think there'll be any physical problems travelling with her?'

'She said if it's not possible for me to go, the star-beings would intervene – hopefully without risk to life or limb, although I don't know about soul. If I can't be with her, my soul will be crushed in any case. Anyway, I don't want to think about it. I've made my decision. I'm going with her and that's that.'

We turned a corner and the field containing the anomaly came into view. There were cars parked on the grass verge and several people were in the formation, researchers it seemed, taking photos and gathering data. From here, the anomaly appeared like three large Ferris wheels. We entered the field and reached the edge of the first circle. The ground was marked out like a crime scene.

'It's okay to enter,' one of the men shouted.

The researchers were all wearing black t-shirts with the ubiquitous grey alien face incorporated into the design. Tristian stepped into the circle first and I followed.

'It's noticeably cooler inside the formation,' he said. He stepped out of the circle and then back in to feel the distinct temperature difference.

'This is nothing,' I said quietly so as not to be overheard. 'It was completely frosted over when it first appeared, even though it was a hot day. In fact, we're standing almost where Cali was when I found her.'

There was no longer any frost. In fact, the grass appeared to be growing again, seeking the sun instinctively and doing what nature had intended. Tristian knelt to examine the ground.

'This is different to the anomalies I've seen in Wiltshire,' he said as he studied the smooth stems. 'See... there is no damage, which is highly unusual.'

'Blimey, I didn't realise you've researched crop circles, especially after that lecture we went to years back. Remember?'

'It was that very lecture that sparked my curiosity, Tom. I know there was a great deal of ridicule at the time, but I couldn't resist doing a little independent study of my own.'

'And what conclusions did you come to?'

'That a large percentage of crop circles are man-made, but there are one or two that defy current explanation – and a number that seem to attract other unusual phenomena.'

'And this?'

'I haven't seen anything quite like this one, Tom. Let me have a word with the research team, see if they know anything.'

The researcher who appeared to be in charge took a long studious look at Tristian. It was difficult not to notice my friend's eclectic clothing ensemble: a shirt resembling a Mondrian painting (all geometric shapes and bold colours), a tweed jacket patched at the elbows, grey trousers, and tan shoes. As per usual, nothing matched.

'Professor Tristian Neeble,' he introduced himself.

'I'm Dom F. Luxer, BSc, head of Cumbria Paranormal Investigations,' the man replied, stating his full title and straightening his back rigidly as if reinforcing his authority or importance.

The two stiffly shook hands. So, this was the local X-Files squad. For some reason, this made me feel a little easier.

'Do you have a special interest in crop circles, professor?'

'No, just a passing curiosity, that's all. I've visited one or two in Wiltshire but this is the first time I've seen them in this part of the world. How's the research going?'

'Good, thanks. Like the other recent formations around here, this is something a little different to the usual crop circle phenomenon,' Mr Luxer replied, scratching his balding head. 'This one's a few days old yet we're still picking up heavy electro-magnetic frequency readings and, as you've probably noticed, odd temperature fluctuations. And, whatever is happening here, it's draining batteries in the cameras and equipment and yet everything works fine just outside the formation. Strange, don't you think?'

'Any thoughts about what's caused this?'

'That's the million-dollar question. There are plenty of suggestions going round but, to be honest, I wouldn't like to commit myself. There are just too many unknowns.'

'It's ET,' a young blond guy shouted. 'Ask the locals. They've seen unexplained lights and UFOs. One guy said he'd seen a Vulcan, like out of *Star Trek*.'

A couple of the researchers laughed.

'Seriously, man,' he replied, 'there's some freaky shit going on. The other day, I saw seven dudes meditating in a field. They were just sat there, middle of nowhere, like in a trance. An old woman passed on her bike. I asked her what they were doing, and she said they were receiving downloads. What the hell?'

'Downloads... as in information?' Tristian asked.

'I haven't the foggiest. All I know is that there's something happening round here and it's not just the crop circles. It's mental.'

Tristian scratched his chin, and then he turned to me. 'Hmm... interesting.'

'I've also seen those seven men,' I mentioned. 'I thought I was seeing things. Like he said, they appeared to be meditating. They'd be there one moment and gone the next.'

Tristian's eyebrows lifted in the peculiar way they did when he was surprised or contemplative. 'Okay, I think I've seen enough here, Tom.'

We thanked the researchers and then we stepped out of the crop circle to the noticeably warmer air. It was like going from a fridge into a hot house, as if there was an invisible wall surrounding the anomaly.

'Very interesting indeed,' Tristian said again, as we walked back to the village. 'Has Cali mentioned anything about the associated phenomena?'

'Only that the energy used to journey back and forth was creating what she called crossing places, where elements from different realms and also various time periods sort of leak through into ours.'

'Hmm. Well, there are theories suggesting that energy displacement or fluctuation creates such conditions. Of course, some argue that when people admit to seeing ghosts or monsters or encountering alien abductions, that it's a psycho-logical issue... that the mind is experiencing a waking dream or hallucination. If enough stories are circulated, more people feed into the collective perspective, and also start experienc-ing the unusual. Strange things can happen. The power of the mind – consciousness – is often seriously underestimated.'

'But you don't think this is what's happening here... It's not just all in the mind?'

'Who knows for sure? Isn't life but a dream?' he replied, eyes glinting.

The thought hovered over me and then flew away. I wasn't sure what to think, whether what was happening was a product of the imagination. It all seemed very real.

'And what about science? Do you think it will discover the truth about what's happening?'

'Science is a continuous process of truth-finding, but know this, my friend,' he said, as we marched back to the village, 'when you find truth you can never claim you have the whole truth.'

Before we realised, we were back at the village hall. Tristian knelt down to tie his shoelaces again, virtually in the same spot he'd tied them before. Two elderly ladies were pulling shopping trolleys along the main street. Rainbow reflections danced on the shop window opposite, but I couldn't make out where the light was coming from. The pub at the top of the road opened its doors. I considered we could go there for a quick bite to eat. A man breezed out of the post office store and my eyes did a double take. It was Matt Darker. He recognised me straight away, too, and even though he was across the road, our eyes locked long enough to read that Cali was on both our minds. His face was drawn and greyish, as though he hadn't slept properly in some time. Grey flecks streaked through his black hair. I'd assumed he was in his forties but today he appeared older. Neither of us exchanged any greeting. We just stared at each other for longer than considered polite. It made me think of two male stags, weighing each other up before fighting over territory or a female. Tristian stood up.

'I need to get some new laces,' he said, holding a broken piece of brown cord between his fingers. He saw my face. 'You okay, Tom?'

Matt Darker lowered his eyes and walked away, back in the direction of Starfell Cottage. Tristian followed my gaze.

'That was Matt Darker, the astronomer who saw Cali disappear.' I watched him stride purposefully away. I kept on watching until he was out of sight. 'Look, I was going to suggest lunch at the pub, but would you mind if we get back to Cali? We can eat in the farm tearoom.'

'If that means sampling your mother's home cooking, then let's go. I'm quite hungry, actually. Thinking gives me an appetite.'

We drove away. Tristian rubbed his chin and then his forehead as if the very act might summon answers. Of course, we already knew far more than the researchers, and yet still so little.

'So, what do you think?' I asked.

'About the crop circle anomaly?'

'About everything, I guess.'

'There's something strange going on, for sure, and it's a compelling strangeness. Where the anomaly is concerned, I'm not certain how it correlates with inter-dimensional travel. I can't say if the formation appeared as a consequence of the energy used or whether it's simply a calling card or something else. Maybe that's something Cali could ask the ETs? Finding out what's happening to her shakes up physics in a way that is mind-blowing, but the phenomena appears to be impacting on the locality, too. Now, it's possible the locals are reacting to what they've seen or heard, but receiving 'downloads', which is an odd term for an old lady to use, suggests that some are tuned into what's going on.'

'Like they're picking up a radio signal, you mean?'

'Yes, something on those lines. Some, who are particularly sensitive, may be experiencing shifts in their perception. It sounds a bit goofy and not very scientific but, hey, I'm a theoretical physicist. Sometimes, I have to stray into goofy territory. That said, the difference in temperature in and out of the crop formations, and all the anomalies, add up to measurable energy fluctuations that aren't at all natural – at least not natural in the presiding conditions here on Earth.'

'And Cali's right at the heart of it,' I said.

'So it seems.'

I took the road back through Hawkdale. Tristian was silent although I could clearly hear his mind churning, trying to grasp answers, trying to hold on to logic. I drove past the field where the other crop formation had appeared. Although it wasn't visible, you could just make out the edges where the grass dipped. At the top end, the row of old crone oaks seemed to taunt the sky with their spindled late-to-green branches. There was a glimmer of light. Something was moving in the woods.

'Did you see that?' I asked Tristian, who was already looking in that direction.

'Yes – stop!' he shouted.

I slammed on the brakes and we lurched forwards. I let the engine idle. There it was again: a strong pulsating light, at least the size of a football, moving between the trees. For several moments, we watched it without daring to mutter a word. Even though we were some 300 feet away, it was clearly something out of the ordinary. After a minute or two, it brightened intensely, changing shape from a circle to a diamond to something unrecognisable, and then in a flash it seemed to implode and completely disappear.

Tristian gawked with an impressed grin on his face. 'Well, I haven't seen anything like that before... at least not outside laboratory conditions.'

'Aye, well stick around. I promise you haven't seen any-thing yet.'

I stepped hard on the accelerator and only slowed down as we reached the outskirts of Hawkdale. We passed the village green and the pond littered with moorhens and ducks before reaching the main thoroughfare. Cottages in their uniform grey graced the approach to the high street and then gave way to a more colourful assembly of historical and fake historical buildings with eclectic facades, all competing for the consumer's attention. On the surface everything was normal. People were going about their daily activities as they'd always done. And yet something had changed here. Something ex-traordinary was rippling through the core, awakening possi-bilities. There was a growing awareness, a quiet knowing, a glimmer in the eyes and a meaning behind the wink of people on the streets. In fact, everywhere, people were winking at one another as if they were sharing a secret. Tristian seemed to notice, too.

'Perhaps Jack Kerouac was right when he said, "Maybe that's what life is... a wink of the eye and winking stars,"' I mused. 'There appears to be a lot of winking going on around here today.'

'Is it not one of those strange parochial rituals you often stumble across? It seems like every little English town of note has some quirky custom.'

'Hawkdale is known for its wool sack racing... there's the summer green-man parade... but I'm not aware of a "winking day".'

A stretch of charcoal cloud slivered snake-like along the peeping fell-top. It was busier than usual on the main street, and I had to give way to an oncoming stream of cars. As we idled towards the memorial cross, two parked military vehicles captured our attention. A tall thickset man with cropped hair and wearing a black suit and dark sunglasses was talking to a similarly attired man beside a Jeep with tinted windows.

'What do you think, Trist? Military or Special Ops?'

'I'd say both. Don't look at them, Tom. Keep driving.'

These were the same vehicles I'd seen racing towards Ravenshead after Cali's last trip. My jaw tightened. I guess it would be natural that the military or government scientists would catch up with what was going on round here. We were soon out of the town centre. A little further on and we were upon Verity's detached house set back from the road. She was in the front garden amidst a flamboyant display of flowers. I stopped a little too abruptly outside her gate and Tristian lurched forwards in his seat. She marched down the garden path and I wound the window down.

'Oh, it's you, Tom,' she said, and her expression fell serious and bloated with concern. 'Oh dear, are you all right?'

'Yes, thank you, Verity. What's going on with all the strangers in the village?'

'You don't know? Oh I'm so sorry, Tom. It's Cali. Her landlord reported her missing. They say it's something to do with all the goings-on. Oh dear, I thought you knew.'

I glanced at Tristian, wondering what to say.

'Hmm... I've been away for a few days, Verity.'

'I'm so upset,' she continued, clearly agitated. 'I know the angels wouldn't do her any harm. I just know they won't. To be honest, I'm far more afraid of these military people hanging about. They tramp about like they own the place... don't give a damn about anything or anyone.'

'Angels?' Tristian interjected.

'I'll explain later.'

Verity dabbed her now-youthful brow with a chequered handkerchief. 'I'm so worried, Tom, and what a shock it must be to you.'

I so wanted to tell her the truth, that Cali was okay, but I couldn't take the chance. 'Don't worry, Verity,' I said. 'I'm sure she'll be fine. The angels... the angels will protect her. I'm positive of that.'

'I'm so glad you think so, Tom. That fair puts my heart at ease. Of course, I didn't mention the angels to the military people as I don't want them to know.'

'They've been to see you?'

'Yes, they've questioned most people in the town. I told them that Cali isn't missing, that she's just gone on holiday because that's exactly what she told me the last time I saw her. Do you think there's been a mix-up, that they've mistaken her for someone else? She said she'd try to send me a postcard, but I haven't received anything so far. Anyway, I didn't tell those military people anything. Would you believe that one of them trampled all over my begonias? The fairies aren't at all pleased.'

'Fairies?' whispered Tristian.

He prodded me in my side and all I could do was flash that resigned look that said 'hey, the world has gone crazy. Get used to it.'

'You will let me know when she comes back from her travels. You're most likely to hear from her first.'

'Did you mention to the investigators that Cali and I are, you know, together?'

'No, I didn't, but mark my words, they'll find out sooner or later. They're questioning everyone.'

I nodded, and reassured Verity that everything would be fine.

'Angels? Fairies?' Tristian repeated, as I drove away. He gripped onto his seat as I flew round the corners.

'Verity actually saw one of the crop circles being made. She thinks angels create them.'

'Incredible!'

'And would you believe me if I said she's in her seventies?'

'Really? She doesn't look a day over forty... I take it Cali has something to do with that.'

I didn't need to answer. Right then, all I wanted to do was return to the farm, and return to Cali.

∞∞∞∞∞∞∞∞

'Life is a magical manifestation.'

Anxiety surged through my veins and I had this sense that time was running out. Even though my thoughts were spinning, I had to pretend everything was normal, particularly in front of my folks because I couldn't contemplate the drama that would ensue if they found out what was really going on. So, we had lunch in my mother's tearoom. Cali was particularly fond of the fresh herb salad, which I had too, and Tristian enjoyed an all-day breakfast, with double of everything, followed by my mother's home-made organic rhubarb pie. My mother loved chatting with Tristian. She'd heard so much about him in my letters over the years and, with both of them having PhDs, albeit in different sciences, there was already a respectful connection between them.

So, in this questionable reality, I sat there, pretending that everything was fine. I smiled – probably more than I normally did. I listened to the chatter about everyday stuff, trying to stem this sense of time and reason racing away from me. I only half-listened, really, because I was too busy fielding crazy internal questions such as: what do they eat where Cali and I are going? And, should I tell my folks I'm leaving? If so, what do I tell them exactly? Then I thought this could easily be the last time I saw my mother. At this point, I gulped and nearly choked on my coffee. I promptly pushed the thought away because it was too painful to contemplate. Granted, I hadn't seen much of my family for over ten years, but the thought of never seeing them again – ever – added to the creeping morbidity. Leaving would be like a death of sorts.

Lunch over, we returned to my lodge. I made coffee and then perched on the desk near the window so I could keep an eye on the road leading to the farm. As much as I tried to be in the moment, let go of the nightmare scenarios, Verity was right. The investigators would catch up with me and it would lead them to Cali. I wondered if we should go somewhere else, leave the county, find a better hide-away. I thought of Silverdale again. Perhaps we could camp there. It would give us more time...

Cali caressed my shoulder. 'Relax, Tom,' she whispered into my ear. 'It's okay. What will be, will be.'

She smiled into my eyes and all my worries seemed to fragment and disappear. And that was just a typical effect of being in the presence of Cali Silverthorn. She had this way about her that could dissolve angst and fear. I sat on the sofa and she curled beside me.

Tristian slurped his coffee while reading through his notes. He peered over his spectacles. 'Cali, can you describe how it feels when you travel?' he said, continuing to eke out as much information as he could gather.

Cali stretched out on the sofa, using my lap as a pillow, and recalled the experience as if she was reliving it. 'There's intense light... it engulfs me... and then there's a moment, just a moment of absolute stillness, then *whoosh* and I'm moving without moving, as if I'm in a craft hurtling through a tunnel of spiralling light. I look down, up, and around. There's nothing but light. Even for me, simple logic tells me if I'm standing, then surely there must be something to stand on, but there doesn't appear to be anything solid beneath my feet. It's just sparkling light. Occasionally, I see through the sides, as if there's a viewing window in the otherwise seamless bubble. I see stars and planets and nebulas. I see glimpses of other worlds passing by. After a while – I'm not really sure how long – everything slows and this invisible treadmill stops and I find I'm no longer on Earth but somewhere else... somewhere in another world.'

Tristian had a momentary faraway look on his face as if he'd just taken this fantastic voyage, and then he slipped back into his usual searching mode. 'Do they register the passing of time in these other dimensions?'

'I don't think so; not in the way we do. You see, I'd said to the guide that I needed more time to adjust to what was happening to me, that it was all too quick, and he told me that time was immaterial, that I am girl, woman, and wise elder. I am past, present, and future. I am all that was, and all that will be, right now. He said that consciousness is always present.'

'Interesting,' he said, scribbling into the notebook.

'And, this guide you mentioned... are we talking about a guardian angel, some form of higher being?'

'No, the guide is human... there are many humans on the planet with two moons. They are ones that have crossed over from Earth, the ones who know the way.'

Tristian's eyebrows shot upwards. 'Human? You mean others, like you, who are chosen?'

'The first guides were invited by star-beings, many centuries ago. Those that followed were chosen... and my guide said there are some who found themselves there by accident or curiosity.'

'Don't suppose he explained in scientific terms exactly how they got there?'

'No,' she said, 'and if he had, I'm not sure I'd have remembered the details.'

Tristian got up and gazed through the window. He turned round and leant against my desk. 'As far back as the 1940s right through to the present, there have been rumours of military experiments... where people have simply vanished. Perhaps some discovered the way through to these other dimensions. There were claims that Einstein and Tesla had completed papers on the Unified Field Theory, although they were never published. It was rumoured that Einstein said that the world wasn't ready for it. I've always been wary about such rebutted claims but maybe, just maybe there's some truth in it.'

'Ha! Conspiracy theorists would love it,' I said. 'And I guess that would explain what happened to Flight 19 and the search crew that went looking for them over Bermuda... perhaps they all passed through into another realm.'

'By accident or curiosity, the guide told Cali so, yes, perhaps.'

Tristian tapped the pen against his chest. Cali sat up and sipped her coffee, staring thoughtfully into the rich brown liquid.

'I once read there are more stars out there than there are grains of sand,' I mused, 'so I can't begin to imagine how many dimensions there are.'

'It's mind-blowing, isn't it,' Tristian said, 'and that's why I love physics. We think we know what's going on and, it's true, we've unravelled some of the great mysteries of our time, but there are worlds out there... realities waiting to be discovered.

I mean, an aspect of quantum theory predicts that a single classical reality will gradually split into separate simultaneously existing realms. Imagine that? If the universe is infinite, then all things are possible. Everything that could occur has happened, is happening, or will happen. Doesn't that just freak you out? I have to say, Cali, I'm somewhat envious of your position even though it must seem like a burden.'

The air throbbed with uncertainty, or perhaps the throbbing was in my head. Either way the afternoon had grown humid. The lodge walls closeted, hemming us in.

'Fancy a walk?' I asked, keen to be outside and moving.

Tristian rolled up his colourful shirtsleeves. 'Good idea,' he said. 'But, first of all, can anyone spare a shoelace?'

We looked down at Tristian's lace-less shoe and laughed.

'Perhaps it's a sign that everything is coming undone,' I joked. 'No doubt someone could attach some kind of symbolism to it, and even create a whole new philosophical debate: the lace-less shoe; the great unravelling.'

Tristian's eyes spun. 'It wouldn't surprise me in the slightest.'

Overhead, plumes of white cloud passed over us like great sailing ships in the bluest ocean. We walked together along the gradual incline. Fields, either side of us, were carpeted green and yellow. Uncountable insects with flashing wings tripped the airspace seemingly in a haphazard way and yet knowing exactly what they were here to do. Tristian now had a black lace in his brown shoe, but it didn't really look too odd considering his lively dress sense. Cali went on ahead of us, skipping and dancing and weaving around the scattered trees. I laughed at her playfulness, and Tristian smiled.

'She's an absolute delight,' Tristian said. 'I can see why you fell for her.'

'It all happened so quickly, Trist. I didn't believe in love at first sight until I saw her. Then again, there are quite a number of things I didn't believe in until she entered my life.'

'"Expect the unexpected" is my motto,' he said, patting me on the back. 'One thing I've learnt over the years of scientific exploration is that things are never quite how they appear. There are always surprises, and our understanding of the world around us is still an open chapter waiting to be written. And then, of course, there are some chapters that need to be re-written to take into account new discoveries. So, yes, expect the unexpected and the transition won't hit you in the face as hard.'

Tristian grinned. He then duly tripped over a piece of limestone jutting out of the grassy ascent. He looked at me, and then laughed. I laughed, too, and I remembered the times we'd shared, the countless discussions over a pint in Blake's, eating lunch in Princes Street Gardens, our summer cycling and walking tours through Scotland with the rest of the gang. Good times. Different times.

'Cheers, Trist, for being here.'

'I'm just sorry there isn't more I can do. Given time, well...'

'I understand, my friend. And there's no need to apologise. What's important is that you know... that you have the information that Cali has given you... that you're here to witness what takes place. Once we're gone, I think, perhaps, it will open new doors of enquiry for you.'

'I'm envious that you're going, that you get to be on what is probably the greatest adventure known to man, and with the girl you love. And I understand why you would leave everything behind to be with her, Tom. As I've lately come to realise myself, love is a powerful emotion.'

'The crazy thing is, out of all the weird stuff, falling in love with her has been the most extraordinary happening. Nothing prepared me for the force of that, how it hit me so quickly and so completely.'

Cali danced in and out of the trees, touching the tangled boughs. Sun-sprites caught and played with her dark river of hair. Love was in everything she did, in everything she touched. With every movement she made, my pulse raced towards her.

'Are you going to tell your family, Tom?'

'No... I mean, where would I begin?'

He picked up a blade of grass, examining it closely. I watched my friend: a man I'd known for more than a decade; a man who I'd journeyed with in search of inspiration, knowledge, and truth; a man who had been there through the highs and lows; and I was suddenly overwhelmed, realising that the next goodbye would be the last.

'Trist,' I began, searching for words, 'I want you to know that you're the best mate a guy can have and, well, whatever happens...'

'Likewise, Tom, and I know. No need for words or goodbyes.'

I placed my arm round his shoulder and he gave me a self-conscious hug, followed by a feeble prod at my chest, and there was a stupid grin on his face. Then he walked on ahead, and that was that. I rubbed my eyes, taking a moment to compose myself.

We walked the route round the top end of the farm and began making our way back. Cali skipped by my side. She had a string of daisies crowning her head.

'The queen of summer,' I said, and she grabbed hold of my hand.

'I saw you as a boy earlier today,' she smiled. 'You were sat on the fence by the apple orchard, reading a book. You were wearing a purple jumper, and it had a hole in it.'

'My primary school jumper was purple,' I recalled, 'and, it probably did have a hole in it. Most of my jumpers end up that way. I'm never quite sure how or why they appear.'

'You were reading *The Time Machine* by H. G. Wells.'

She skipped, and she grinned, and the changing light flitted over her. She ran towards Tristian, and she put her thin arm round his waist, and she seemed so petite by his side. And I thought back. Yes, I remembered reading *The Time Machine*, one summer, sat on the fence by the apple orchard. What's more, and this was strange, I vaguely recall looking up, just for a split second, and seeing a beautiful woman giggling at me. I always thought I'd imagined her but, no, the memory rushed back to me... It was Cali who I'd seen. I shook my head, and smiled at the strangeness of it all.

After a while, we strolled into the farmyard, feeling sun-drunk and drowsed by the potent aromatics of summer blooms. My mother waited at the farmhouse gate, face taut. Instantly, I knew something was wrong. My stomach bowled.

'Come into the house,' she said. 'Your father needs to have a word.'

I stared at Cali and Tristian. 'I'll meet you back in the lodge.'

'No,' she said, 'it's best you all come.'

We entered the house and my father was standing at the kitchen table with his arms folded. The mood was sober. Pete and Ellie sat silent in the grimness, eyes seeking answers.

'What's going on?' I asked.

'I should ask you the same thing,' my father replied, ashen-faced.

He threw the local newspaper on the table. The lead story headline read: 'Hunt for Missing Local Woman' and went on to mention how military investigators were keen to speak with anyone who knew the whereabouts of Cali Silverthorn, who was recently reported missing following unexplained phenomena in Ravenshead.

Cali silently read the report, her hand placed over her labradorite necklace.

'They mustn't find her,' Tristian said, quietly. 'There's no telling what they'll do.'

'Are you going to tell us what's going on?' my father asked, impatiently.

My eyes flashed quickly at Tristian and at Cali. I breathed deeply and said, 'I'm not sure you'd believe us. In fact, I'm not even sure you'd want to know.'

'Try me,' he replied, pulling up a chair and sitting down. He crossed his arms again in that stubborn way I was accustomed to, and I knew that we weren't going to leave here until we'd explained.

So, my mother brewed the tea and we gathered round the table, and together we told the most incredible story that my family would ever likely hear.

∞∞∞∞∞∞∞∞

'Embrace the moment; it is where all things begin and end.'

I f Tristian hadn't been there to verify everything, my family wouldn't have believed me. They respected him as the eminent scientist he was. Apart from the gasps, and the wide eyes, and Pete occasionally saying 'oh feck', they took in the incredible account better than anticipated. Of course, I was economical with the truth – very economical. I couldn't tell them that Cali was leaving for good. Nor could I tell them I was going with her. What we did say was that the military mustn't find her at any cost because of what they might do, and I was touched, in fact completely astounded, when my father said, 'don't worry, son; we'll not let them anywhere near her.' In that moment, I met my father's eyes, and all past hurts began to lift away.

It was gone midnight before we left the farmhouse. Surprisingly, I'd slept well but there was a sense of foreboding flickering in my solar plexus and I realised why. I opened my eyes to the morning's vulnerable shadows. Cali was already awake, sitting up in bed, knees tucked urchin-like under her chin. I slowly pulled myself up and placed my hand on her shoulder. She turned to me, her face damp with tears. She didn't have to say anything. I knew that today would be the day. I gathered her to me.

'Don't worry,' I reassured. 'Everything will be fine. We're going together. We just need to stay close so I'm with you at the right moment.'

'I know, Tom. I'm just... overwhelmed, that's all.'

I brushed her hair away from her tear-dewed face and held her to me. There was a lull where we said nothing but understood everything.

'Are you still absolutely sure you want to come with me?' she asked. 'There's so much we don't know.'

I held my finger over her lips.

'I've never been more certain about anything.'

We stayed in each other's arms, bodies entwined, embracing love and hope.

'Are you frightened?' I asked.

She hesitated, searching out her feelings in a rare moment of self-analysis. 'I think I'm more nervous and unsure than afraid. I'll be happier when we make it to the other side, together.' Her eyes searched mine. 'How about you? Are you afraid?'

'Truthfully? I've never been so scared. I guess that means I'm alive – madly alive.' I sort of laughed, curling her fingers round mine, contemplating the madness. 'It's crazy, isn't it? Maybe life is just an illusion, and we're all rowing imaginary boats gently down the stream.'

'My grandmother used to tell me that we are the dreamers and the dream and that everything unfolds exactly as it should.'

I sighed. If it was all a dream, it was certainly a convincing one.

I threw back the duvet. 'I guess we should get dressed and let Tristian know that today's the day.'

The light remained shy as we stepped onto the porch. The morning was slow to wake and the only noise was the creaking of timber beneath our feet as we walked the few steps to Tristian's lodge. I knocked at the door. No answer. So, I knocked again. When he finally appeared, he had a toothbrush sticking out of his mouth and a pile of papers with scribbled equations in his hands. When he saw us there, side-by-side, hand-in-hand, he scratched his head, and realisation followed.

'It's today?' he garbled, before removing the toothbrush from his mouth. 'It's happening today!'

I nodded and felt a shiver creep through me.

'Wait,' he said, and scuttled back inside to grab his shoes and jacket. His hair was sticking up at funny angles, and he was wearing another one of his brightly coloured shirts, with distorted patterns that made my eyes go funny. He followed us back to my lodge in his socks, attempting to undo a knot in his shoelaces.

Time seemed to crawl and we spent the morning drinking coffee. There was little else to do but wait. I stared out the window. Jagged clouds trailed the fell-tops like grey sombre notes, and the sky was darkening rapidly. Thunder rumbled in the distance. A solitary flash of lightning cut through the valley, catching me by surprise, and the energy pulsed through me, teasing the fine hairs on the back of my arms. I laughed, and Tristian breathed a sigh.

'The approaching storm... it's a bit clichéd, isn't it?' I said, pulling a face. 'I mean, if this was a film or a novel, it would be considered just a wee bit dramatic.'

Black cloud stole the light, and the atmosphere felt weighted.

'Aha... and here we have the theatrical rain,' Tristian announced with a flourish.

The rain did come and it seemed as though the sky had caved in. Silver splinters ricocheted off baked earth, driven by a coarse wind. Horses stood motionless in the field and simply endured it. It was as if a month's worth of rain was falling at once. It drummed the rooftops and pelted the ground, quickly filling the ruts and gullies. It overwhelmed the gutters, cascading like a waterfall from the drainpipe. It raged for twenty minutes and then it stopped as suddenly as it started, leaving just a drip, drip, drip. A brief glimmer of sunlight cut through a gap in the dense cloud, catching the raindrops on the window and shadow stippling the sill.

'Nice weather for the middle of summer,' Tristian said, sipping black coffee.

'Summer solstice,' I realised, and then remembered. 'Cali, didn't you say you were born on summer solstice?'

She nodded and smiled.

'So, it's your birthday!'

I kissed her, and I wondered whether there was such thing as coincidence. She came to Earth on 21 June and she was leaving Earth on 21 June, albeit twenty-six years later, and there seemed something so perfect about that and yet so eerily orchestrated.

'Is there any cognac left?' Tristian asked. 'We should toast Cali's birthday.'

There was less than a quarter of the amber liquid in the bottle and, although it was far too early for alcohol, it seemed fitting.

'Happy Birthday, Cali,' we both cheered, raising our glasses.

'And to you both... happy travels,' Tristian added.

Cali beamed and gave each of us a hug.

I knocked back the cognac, savouring the aroma and the swift heat as it hit my throat. I contemplated my travels with Cali into other worlds. It still seemed odd, crazily unreal. There hadn't been enough time to prepare or consider. That was probably a good thing. If time had been a luxury, maybe I'd have ended up talking myself out of going. Maybe fear would have grounded me. I wondered if this was how astronauts felt in the countdown to lift-off. There was a strange sense of excitement, the thrill of adventure that I'd always felt when going on a journey, but there was fear of the unknown, too. There was fear that I might not survive the actual lift-off as I travelled on this vessel of light. As for the realisation that I would never return, I just couldn't even begin to think about it. No, there wasn't enough time to dwell, and I didn't want to as dwelling might just lead to rational thinking and uncertainty. That would be a dangerous place to be. So, I remained focused. I wanted to be with Cali for the rest of my life. That was the one thing I was sure of.

'I know it's good to travel lightly,' I pondered, 'but do you think I should take anything with me?'

'Is there anything you need?' Cali replied.

I rubbed my chin. I'd never really been materialistic or attached to objects. I'd always travelled light in the past, but how could I possibly know what I'd need in another world? I guess money wasn't necessary. I suppose a change of clothes would be useful, but then Cali wasn't taking anything other than what she was wearing: her flowery dress, an emerald-green cardigan, her moccasins, and her labradorite necklace. In my coat pocket, I had my mobile phone, keys, wallet, notebook, pencil, and a packet of mints. I certainly wouldn't need the phone. I couldn't get a signal at the best of times, let alone light years away. I took it out of my pocket and let it spin on the coffee table, and then I had a desert-island thought. Urgently, I rooted through my pile of books, sending several of them scattering, and found one of my favourites. It contained my most-loved poems, from S. T. Coleridge to Dylan Thomas, and it fitted neatly in my jacket's inside pocket. I opened the desk drawer, rifled through, and found my grandfather's pocket watch, allowing myself one item of sentimentality. I thought of taking a few family photos but decided not to. Everything I really needed was in my mind and in my heart. I would remember them perfectly well without the need for pictures.

Tristian checked his watch and then skipped through the pages of his notebook.

'Is there anything else you need to know, Trist?'

He scratched his head, thoughtfully. 'No, I don't think so. Cali's been very helpful. There are interesting equations already buzzing around my head, but they'll likely be buzzing around for some time. It's going to take some strange thinking to work out inter-dimensional travel and, even then, I'm still not certain the human race is ready for it. I guess all I ask is that if you find a couple of travel tickets then save them for me, and if you find any way of sending a message, to let me know you're safe and well, then that would be appreciated.'

'Will do, my friend,' I replied, taking a deep, settling breath.

As the morning lengthened on this longest of days, the anticipation, fear, excitement, and uncertainty seemed to gather on the edge of my thoughts, distracted only by Cali's smile, her knowing glance, the soft movement of her fingers entwined with mine. There were so many emotions gathering, breaking occasionally like giant waves on a wild and unpredictable sea. I tried not to think about the things that could go wrong, about being left behind. Instead, I clung tightly to the positive, of being with the girl I loved, of travelling together albeit to places that you wouldn't find on the books of your local travel agent. In fact, that's what it'd be like. We were going on our travels but with a one-way ticket.

∞∞∞∞∞∞∞∞

'What you see is of your own creation.'

'It's like waiting for a birth,' Tristian said, tapping his fingers together.

'Aye, I guess it is, in a way.'

'I remember when my mother went into labour with my youngest sister,' he said, stretching his entwined fingers. 'Sixteen hours, it took. I was nine years old, and sixteen hours felt like forever.'

I squeezed Cali's hand, reassuringly, and joked, 'I hope it's not going to take that long.'

The cattle grid rattled and the noise of approaching vehicles sent me to my feet. I peered out the window and my heart darted into my mouth.

'No... this can't be happening,' I said, adrenalin flooding my veins. 'It's them!'

Two black Jeeps sped along the track, water and dirt spraying up from their tyres. Cali and Tristian were now at my side. The Jeeps stormed into the yard and stopped abruptly. Cautiously, we stepped away from the window, being careful not to be seen. Rainwater trickled from the slates, drip, drip, dripping into the gutters. For a moment, nothing happened. Then the doors of the first Jeep opened. A man in a suit stepped out of the passenger side. It was the man Tristian and I had seen in Hawkdale. He was still sporting sunglasses, despite the morning's gloom. The rear doors opened and two other men appeared. One was wearing a military uniform and was armed, and the other...

'It's Matt Darker,' Cali whispered.

My stomach did somersaults, crude realisation surfacing. 'I think it's pretty clear he has a deeper involvement. He wouldn't be here otherwise.'

At that moment, Pete swaggered into the yard like a cowboy ready for a showdown.

'Hey!' my brother shouted. 'What the hell do you think you're doing, racing in here?'

Unconcerned by their armed presence, Pete continued to rant, confronting the suited man who had his hands up in a kind of apology. My brother stood with arms crossed and quieter words were exchanged. Matt and the military officer scanned round them, and we quickly retreated from the window.

'We have to go now before they start searching. The Land Rover is at the back. We can sneak round without them noticing.'

'I don't think we'll get far,' said Tristian, frowning with uncertainty.

'We have to try. We can't just sit here and let them find us.'

I hovered by the window, keeping my eyes on Pete. He was pointing up towards the woodland trail, a little-used road beyond the farmhouse and tearoom, which passed through a thick avenue of trees and provided a back route out of Crowdale. Immediately, I knew what he was doing.

'Pete is sending them on a wild goose chase.'

'Good man!' Tristian exclaimed.

The men returned to the vehicle and, for a moment, just to be sure, we watched the black Jeeps speed away.

'Right, let's go.'

We flung open the lodge door, ran to the Land Rover, and jumped in. I turned the ignition and the engine fired to life. We idled forwards, enough to see the Jeeps racing away from the farm. Pete ran over to us and I rolled the window down.

He was flushed and breathing fast. 'I've told them that you've gone walking and sent them up the back road, but–'

Before he could finish his sentence, the Jeeps skidded to a halt. They began a hasty three-point turn on the narrow track.

'They're turning round,' Tristian said. 'We have to go.'

'Take care, bro,' Pete said. 'And look after each other.'

He winked, and I realised then that he knew. He knew I was going with her. I smiled with brimming eyes. Even if I could have found my voice, there wasn't enough time to say anything.

'Go!' he shouted, hitting the side panel. 'Go, go, go!'

I accelerated through the yard as fast as it was possible, and the engine roared in protest. Through my wing mirror, I saw my mother outside the tearoom. Her hands were clutched at her heart and that image of her was imprinted on my own. But there wasn't time for emotion. No time to feel anything except the flood of adrenalin. We rattled along the road, over the cattle grid, bouncing violently over muddy potholes. Water splashed up at the windows. Crows scattered and cawed.

'They're catching up,' Tristian shouted, competing with the engine's roar.

We skidded round the hem of the fell and reached the second cattle grid, where my father was waiting in his tractor. He quickly waved us past and then promptly moved the tractor across the narrow road, blocking the way through. He summoned us to go, and our eyes met. I nodded a thank-you and he nodded back. In that single moment, I knew my father's love.

'Keep going, Tom,' Tristian bellowed. 'We need to gain some distance.'

My foot pounced hard on the accelerator and water sprayed up behind us as we hurtled down the track to the main road. It was only as we approached the junction that we spotted two other military Jeeps flying along the main road.

'Damn! They must have called for assistance,' he said, hitting his seat with frustration.

'Hang on!' I shouted, 'We're going off-road.'

The Land Rover tilted and swerved as I turned too quickly. I shifted gears as the tyres negotiated the rutted ground. After several jolts driving over a brief ridge of limestone outcrop, I was able to reach the track that climbed the side of Tarn Fell. The two black Jeeps must have moved my father on because they were catching up again. I went as fast as I dared, avoiding the worst of the potholes in the undulating ground and, more importantly, avoiding slipping off the edge to a sheer drop.

It was obvious they weren't for giving up. I knew we were running out of road and that we'd have to continue on foot. There was a steep incline and the vehicle began to labour. I willed the engine on, pedal to the floor, and steered round the next bend.

'Okay,' I shouted. 'We're going to have to make a run for it. We'll head for the tarn. Beyond, there's a series of knolls... some dense foliage. We'll... we'll find somewhere to hide.'

Hiding seemed like a feeble idea, but I couldn't think of anything else. I knew we couldn't outrun them and if playing hide and seek gave us more time – the time we needed – then that was all that mattered.

Cali's eyes stared wild but I wasn't sure if it was just my own fear reflecting back at me. Then I noticed her white knuckles as she clung on to my shirt and I knew her heart was racing as fast as mine.

It started to rain again. I accelerated along the final stretch and brought the vehicle to an abrupt halt where the road terminated on a slanting ridge. We jumped out, leaving the doors swung open. Hand-in-hand, Cali and I scurried over the rocky knolls beneath a devil sky. Tristian followed. Rain pelted us and within minutes we were soaking wet. The sheer force and volume of water quickly formed pools and streams, feeling its way as it ran off the rock-strewn terrain, creating slippery vein-like rivers under our feet.

We heard other vehicles screeching to a halt. We heard doors open, angry shouts, and the thud of heavy footsteps following. I didn't dare look back. I tightened my grip on Cali's hand. For several seconds, my thoughts slipped back to the night we'd run naked at Swinside Stone Circle. I'd felt an energy flood through me, something raw and wild, and it was with me again now, and I realised... it was the rush of life, the rhythm of enduring love. I was running like the lone wolf, the last wolf.

'I can't keep up,' Tristian shouted, breathing haphazardly. 'Don't wait for me. Keep going!'

The thud of boots hit the ground. The hunters were closing in and my wolf-heart clattered against my chest. Breathless now, legs like jelly, we clambered over a low ridge and dipped down to the tarn. The tarn water was deathly black, mirroring the dark sky. We continued running together, hands clasped tight. Our breaths laboured in tune, throats burning, muscles aching, blood rushing. Cali's eyes were wide and dark. We kept on running towards the edge of the tarn, aiming for the path beyond, where the fell thickened with ferns and bushes. At that moment, I did what you should never do when you're running for your life. I looked over my shoulder. The men were closing in, running alongside Tristian now. They weren't interested in him or me, though. It was Cali they wanted. I looked round again and, as I did so, I tripped. My hand slipped from Cali's, and I fell hard, hitting the wet ground with a thump. She hesitated and reached out for me, but the men were closing in fast.

'Keep going,' I shouted. 'I'll catch up.'

She kept on running and I scrambled to my feet. A rush of air swept across the tarn, rippling the dark water. Then a low, familiar humming filled my ears. Just ahead, a spiral of light sparkled into being. It was time. But Cali was ahead of me. I had to catch up. I pushed on, but my legs were floundering. She stopped and turned, now haloed by the light.

'Tom!' she screamed.

A sparkling mist billowed around her. I tried running but everything seemed slow and heavy, as if I was running through treacle, and then I felt a hand grip my shoulder, pulling me back down. The man fell with me. I kicked out. I think I caught the side of his face but everything was a blur. I clambered back up, sliding on the wet grass, my energy waning. Somehow, I slipped loose, found my feet, and started running again, but the light began to warp and Cali was fading from view. Our eyes locked for a moment, a moment long enough to register love – and loss – and then the light engulfed her, pulsated, and swiftly vanished, taking her with it. I dropped to my knees. She was gone. I was still here. We were apart.

Tristian had overtaken me now along with the others, and they were searching the ground where they'd witnessed the portal appear. One of the investigators held out a device, which clicked, whistled, and whined as it detected high-energy frequencies. Excited voices filled the air outside the void I was in. Then there was a blinding flash, which knocked some of the men off their feet. At first it seemed like a lightning strike, but three small spheres of white light emerged from a large rotating silver disc hovering over us. The men were now crouching, uncertain. From the east of the fell, hundreds of owls appeared, their silent wings gently beating the air. Their haunting faces filled the sky above us and it was so unexpected, so apocalyptic, that some of the men cowered with fear in their eyes. The owls swooped towards the rotating disc, purposeful, and every last one of them passed through into an intense white light. A low hum filled the air. The orbs danced over the black waters of the tarn and, in seconds, it turned to thick ice. A series of spirals began to appear on the frozen tarn, as if being etched by an invisible hand. The light orbs hovered for several moments and then, in a flash, the orbs and rotating disc were gone. A fickle mist hung in the air, glistening in the now-fine drizzle, and there was a strange silence.

Slowly, the dark cloud drifted away and the rain stopped. There was quiet activity around me: muffled voices. The light lifted as the sun tried to force its way through the viscous cloud. It was fresher but still warm. My hair and clothes were rain-soaked. My ankle throbbed. My pulse continued racing. These were the small details I remembered. I remained on my knees for some time, heart as frozen as the tarn waters. Then I saw Matt Darker with the suited man. They were talking, high-spirited, oblivious, and cold-eyed. I didn't know what it was, perhaps an indifferent grin on Matt's face, or the mention of Cali's name, but I scrambled to my feet, rage rising from some hidden depth, and I lashed out at him, punching him once, twice, and again and again until I felt hands restraining me, pulling me away.

'Why?' I shouted.

He crouched, hands on his knees, spitting blood from a cut on his mouth. He slowly straightened up, sweeping his hand through his greying hair, pushing his tongue round his teeth to check they were still in place.

'I was trying to help,' he spat.

I looked at the suited men with their empty eyes and those in combat uniform with guns holstered. 'And you thought involving the military would help? She's a healer, not some fugitive to be hunted down.'

'She knows things, Mr Philips,' said the suited man. He spoke with an American accent. 'She knows classified things – of international security importance. So, you see, it is imperative we speak with her.'

'Well, that's impossible,' I snapped. 'She isn't coming back.'

'What do you mean?'

'She's gone... she's gone for good.'

The men exchanged urgent looks with a mix of disappointment and frustration.

'She's gone.' My voice faded. My own words lacerated, cutting me to ribbons. Numbness settled over me like fog on a winter's morning, and I dropped back down to my mud-stained knees. I could still smell her sweet honeysuckle perfume on me.

'We need to speak to you,' a military officer said, but I knelt there, eyes fixated on the spot where she had disappeared.

'He's in no fit state, officer,' Tristian said, placing a hand on my shoulder.

'And you are?'

'Professor Tristian Neeble.'

'Well, professor, perhaps you can help us with our investigations.'

The two walked away. I heard muted conversations around me. I was aware that eyes were flicking my way, some curious, some sympathetic. After a while, a hand rested on my shoulder. It was my father.

'Come home, son,' he said.

Tears swelled in my eyes, blurring everything to oblivion.

'I want to stay here a while.'

Tristian was by my side now. 'She's gone, Tom. There's no point staying.'

Emotional numbness was a strange sensation, like a natural anaesthetic to block the pain. All feeling drained away from me. I was detached, cut loose from the world and drifting like a boat that had lost its anchor.

'I'm okay,' I said, calmly. 'I just need to stay here for a while... on my own.'

Tristian squeezed my shoulder and then moved away, and soon everyone dispersed, everyone except my father. He gave me my space but waited for me. He waited four hours before guiding me back to the farm.

∞∞∞∞∞∞∞∞∞

'There is no beginning or end: just motion.'

For the best part of a week, life went on around me. I went through the mechanics of living. I drank, ate, and I even slept, and yet I was not here at all. The world played out its hollow tune but I was detached, as if my soul was light years away. I heard snatched comments: 'you're in shock' and 'it's going to take time' and 'I understand how you're feeling' and so on. I didn't have the presence of mind to react to anything that was said. The words floated away like autumn leaves.

My colleagues at County Library were very understanding and supportive. They had been told I was suffering from grief following bereavement. Well, I guess that was easier than trying to explain the truth. Tristian and my family were there for me. And I had a new understanding with my father, which had wiped out all past hurts between us. But the numbness persisted, like all sensation had permanently deserted me.

The military investigators did question me, but I wasn't in the right state of mind to help them with their enquiries even if I'd wanted to. They realised that. They realised I didn't know anything they weren't already aware of. What I did notice, though, was that they seemed to take a keen interest in Tristian, and he was visited several times for questioning. I could understand it, him being a theoretical physicist. After a few days though, they let us be.

'I have to return to Edinburgh,' Tristian announced one morning sometime during the second week. 'And as much as I love your mother's cooking, I'm needed at the university.'

'It's okay, Trist. I'll be fine and you should get back.'

'Are you sure? It's just that I promised Cali I'd look after you.'

'I know... and you have, Trist. You've done all you can for me and I'm grateful you've been here, but there's nothing else that can be done... not now.'

He placed his hand on my shoulder. 'You know where I'll be, if you need me?'

I nodded, and he placed the rest of his clothes and books in his overnight bag.

'I'm going to set up a new research project,' he said, fumbling with the zip on his bag. 'After looking into the eye of infinity, I think it's time we cracked this conundrum with hard physics. What do you think?'

'Are you planning on working with the military?' I asked.

Tristian stared straight into my eyes as if I'd delivered him a severe blow.

'You should know me better, Tom. I have no plans whatsoever of working with or for the military.'

'I had to ask. I know they talked to you.'

'They did, but only to see if I knew anything more than them, and I don't – at least not yet.' He grinned.

I nodded my head, satisfied.

'Look, you could always come back up to Edinburgh... take some time out or, better still, keep yourself busy.'

'I need to stay here, Trist, just in case–'

'In case she finds a way to return?' he said, swinging his

bag over his shoulder. 'Yes, I understand. Well, you know where I'll be.'

He patted me on the back, and then I drove him to the train station.

'Are you absolutely sure you'll be all right, Tom?' he asked again, as we stood on the platform.

'Trist, you're beginning to sound like a mother hen,' I said, half-joking, half-serious. 'Honestly, I just need time. After all, isn't that the greatest healer?'

'I'm not rightly sure any more, Tom. I'm not rightly sure time is relevant. At least, not as we've perceived it.'

He had that look on his face, as if equations were buzzing around in front of his eyes. Perhaps one day, my friend would find the answers, or perhaps the young boy I'd met in the mobile library just a few weeks ago. Maybe, just maybe, he'd be the one to unravel life's greatest mysteries.

The train eased in to the station. Three pigeons and a lone white dove scattered in a flap of wings.

'Take care, my friend,' he said, smiling kindly.

'You, too, Trist.'

He gave me a self-conscious hug and then slung his bag over his shoulder. He looked like he'd raided a charity shop and was wearing the first items of clothing he'd found: as per usual, a complete mish-mash of colours and patterns.

'Wait!' I shouted, as he boarded the train. He turned and I said, 'If some day you find I'm no longer here, you'll know...'

'Yes,' he said. 'I'll know she found a way of coming back for you.'

His eyes were full of sympathy and I knew what he was thinking: she wasn't coming back. I didn't want to believe it but it was probably true.

The train moved out of the station and I waited until the carriage was out of sight. The platform was empty again and the pigeons settled back in the rafters. The lone white dove, however, was nowhere to be seen. June was shifting into July but there was an unseasonably cold air blowing: a cold air that penetrated me, shaking me free of numbness.

Now alone, I drove through the afternoon into the night, in a trance, trying not to think, but the deadness was thawing, giving way to raw and uncertain emotions. The road curled serpentine, flanked by a legion of trees on either side. The headlights clung to tarmac, the only light beneath the dense wooded black. A fox scurried into the woods, turning round once, eyes glimmering eerily. A sharp incline and the road narrowed. Trees crowded in a suffocating embrace, and all I wanted was to be out of here. Eventually, the road started to open out, and the billowing branches fell away as if they'd never been. I breathed.

I kept driving and eventually found the road to Silverdale, and I returned to the shores by Jenny Brown's Point, where Cali and I had made love, and I was back, hoping she'd be here, that some part of her essence still lingered.

The air was still and suffused with the contrasting aroma of earth and sea. A dull moon strung in the sky like a misplaced pearl provided but a frail light, and I looked, and I looked again, all around me, and realised that I was lost, lost, completely lost without her. Emotion crashed through like waves on an unforgiving sea, rising from the depths of me, and I cried out into the night. I cried like I'd never cried before, howling like the last wolf, the lone wolf, and I dropped to my knees, the pain of her loss searing my stomach, my heart, my mind, my spirit. In this moment, I couldn't imagine how life, without her, would ever be the same again. I rolled onto my side and curled up on the silver slab of rock, and grief consumed me into a haunting state of exhausted sleep. And, in the lucidity of my dreams, I saw her. Over and over, I was running to her, trying to reach her, trying to grab hold of her hand so I could go with her, but I wasn't quick enough, and she faded away before me, gone forever, and I knew that this wasn't a dream but a living nightmare, playing out in dreamscape.

The pain of loss was an emotion like no other. Here, beneath this shriek of sky, my mind raged, shifting from grief to anger to fear to dwelling on how alone she must feel, how I had failed her, and each thought sliced me open. All I wanted to do was wake and find her beside me, with her river of dark hair stroking my face, skin against skin, spirits merging as one. Several times, I opened my eyes to an uncertain light pulsing from the sea, and to the dark figures of seven strange men rising from the cold waters. I closed my eyes and then opened them again. This time, the featureless figures were circled round me, demon black against the grey grating emptiness. I tightly shut my eyes, put my arms over my head and curled up like some pitiful creature waiting for death. As the night gave way to a faint stream of dawn light, I sank into oblivion, clinging only to memories of the brief but beautiful time we'd spent together.

When I finally emerged from this darkest night, spent of feeling and stiff from cold, I watched the morning dance on the tidal bore. I listened to the day's awakening. Tears slipped on the salt breeze, undressing my soul, but I had no more energy inside me. Soon the tears ran dry. I crouched on this silver rock slab, as if I was a jagged slice of the rock itself, fragmented and weather-weary as I surrendered to stillness. After some time, my thoughts turned to rationality. Deep within, I knew that wasting away here served little purpose. She would not be impressed by my self-pity. The thought that she could be watching me now, from another dimension, through the thin veils, made me sit up, made me realise that I had to carry on. So, I did just that. I carried on, in a fashion, chasing that loose ribbon of hope that she'd return some day.

∞∞∞∞∞∞∞∞

'The ultimate truth is within you.'

How long do you hold on to hope: a few months, years, or until the end of your days? It was almost six months since Cali had disappeared from my life – from this reality – and I was still burning away for her. She was constantly in my thoughts, both waking and sleeping. Sometimes, I thought I heard the sweet melody of her voice calling me, or I'd catch the aroma of her honeysuckle-perfumed hair on the breeze. Those moments were always unexpected, dragging me into a melancholic abyss.

All around me, life assumed some kind of normality. The weird stuff simply disappeared as if it had never been. People began discussing ordinary everyday affairs again such as the rising price of food and who to vote for in the next election. And yet something here was different. Those who had come into contact with either Cali or the phenomena had a special light in their eyes and a new perspective. Many were planting trees, campaigning for the well-being of our earth mother, and living with more love and gratitude. The experience had opened their hearts and liberated their minds. I called it the Silverthorn Effect. It was as if these people were tuned into a new frequency, one that resonated in an Earth-nurturing way.

And life continued. Jake Quake became a rock star, just as Cali said he would. He was currently preparing for a tour and promoting his new album, which was all about peace and love and living in harmony. One of his songs was called 'We are the ones we've been waiting for' and there was something about the melody that reminded me of Cali. I played it a lot in the evenings after I'd finished work. Life went on. The seasons played out their drama, constantly fighting for harmony. Soon, swallows gathered and took to the cooling sky, flying off to warmer climes. In the autumn, I travelled up to Edinburgh to see Tristian and meet his girlfriend, Lucy. She was a female version of him although, fortunately, she had a more conservative dress sense. We ate at the new Indian restaurant that used to be Blake's and he told me about the progress he was making in unlocking the secrets of the universe. I'd enjoyed being in Scotland again. I'd laughed a little, too. Yet I still felt displaced, as though I was far away from home. Not long after I returned from Edinburgh, Pete and Ellie's son, Alex, was born and I became Uncle Tom. The experience of fatherhood seemed to change my brother in a positive way. He was happier and settled.

As for me, I buried my head in books. I read about energy healing, reincarnation, astral travel, and all those subjects I once ignored. I enrolled in tai chi lessons. I bought crystals, too, and returned them to the earth. I began writing poetry again, channelling the dirge of feeling through words. Of course, the mobile library kept me occupied although the days were now very normal and strangely mundane. Mostly, I spent time at places Cali and I had visited. I ambled along the Coffin Path at Rydal. I meditated within Swinside Stone Circle. I'd go to her favourite spots on the fells and by the mother tree. I found myself in Silverdale, often, wandering the shores, listening to the sea's song, watching the changing light, and knowing that she was out there, just on the other side of here.

Sometimes, I'd swear she was calling out: 'I'm here, Tom!' but I couldn't see. Only a thin veil separated our worlds, just a wall of energy. It gave me some comfort, at least, to know she was still there, not far away at all. Many times, I'd say 'I love you', letting the words carry on the ether, hoping she could hear, and I waited for the reply that did not come.

I couldn't explain the intensity of what I was feeling. I had loved and lost loved ones before – family and girlfriends – and yet managed to work myself through the emotions and return to some kind of normality. Not so now. Losing her was like a wound to the heart that would not heal. It was a wound that wept and wept.

December was proving to be the coldest month on record, and there'd been a few scary moments in the mobile library. Fortunately, I'd had no more off-road incidents, although there'd been a close call just a week ago when the rear of the van shot across the road, skating on invisible black ice. I'm really not sure how I'd avoided catastrophe on that occasion. It was as if some invisible force – a guardian angel, perhaps – had kept me safe. I was telling this to Verity while sitting in her living room, warming my hands by the fire. She had invited me round for tea on her last visit to the mobile library, the time when I'd told her the truth about Cali, and she wouldn't take no for an answer. It's not that I hadn't wanted to visit; it was just I hadn't felt at all sociable these past months. Verity poured me a cup of tea from her angel cups. She smiled with her still-youthful glow.

'You're looking well, Verity,' I said, clasping the teacup so that it warmed my icy fingers.

'I feel fabulous, dear. Hmm, but you're not looking too great... See, you're far too thin. And pale... Yes, far too pale.

And you need to start smiling again, go out more, and make new friends.'

'I know, Verity, but it's difficult.'

'Only as difficult as you make it. Now, what will Cali think? She'd want you to get on with your life, wouldn't she?'

My head dropped. Even now, the mere mention of her and it was like no time had passed at all.

'I'm sorry, Tom, but it has to be said. She will be watching, mark my words. Even those who have passed – those who've let go of their physical bodies – are still around. My departed husband still visits, as you know. He likes to move my ornaments from one place to another, which is a trifle annoying.'

I found this funny, and started to laugh. Verity laughed too.

'Well, that's a start,' she said. 'Now, tell me, have you had any news on the investigation?'

'All they were able to do was report Cali as missing.' For a moment, I thought of all those other people on the missing list and wondered just how many of them had physically crossed over into other realms. 'As for the military investigators, I haven't heard anything else. My friend says they wouldn't have been able to glean enough information from what took place to use it in any way.'

'Good!' Verity snapped. 'After all, what do those psychopaths in power do with our best discoveries? You only have to look back in history to see. They use it to destroy, to gain power, to run amok, and blow things up. Oh, but don't get me going on that topic.' She frowned and sipped her tea. 'What about that horrible man, the one who shopped her to the military?'

'Matt Darker? Well, he seems to have disappeared as well. Nobody knows where he is. It's as if he's fallen into a black hole.'

'Crawled into one, more like. Well, good riddance! I reckon the investigators signed him up from the start, to keep an eye on her. Somehow, they must have known she was special even before she moved up here.'

'That's what my friend, Tristian, thinks.'

'Dear oh dear,' she sighed. 'You know everyone in the villages misses her dreadfully. She brought sunshine into our lives, more than we've seen in years. For the time she was here, she did a lot of good, Tom – much more than we probably know. You should take some comfort from that.'

I smiled at Verity, and drank the last of my tea. We talked for a while. We sat quietly for a while, too. Eventually, I stood up. 'It's time I was getting back,' I said.

She gave me a motherly hug. 'Now promise me you'll look after yourself,' she said, firmly.

I nodded, and she smiled a wrinkle-free smile. At the front door, she wrapped her thick cardigan around her, and waved her white hanky at me, and it filled me with a sense of surrender. I fastened the scarf round my neck to keep out the biting wind. I waved and drove away.

Hawkdale was busy with festive shoppers. I found myself in a queue of vehicles waiting for others to steal what available car parking there was on the high street. A mackerel sky stretched overhead, its rivulets turning pink and crimson. The day was fast losing light and crows flecked the sky as they returned to their roosts. The shops were lit with flashing fairy lights. Carol singers huddled in the square, seeking warmth while singing 'Silent Night'. I wound down my window to listen, while waiting for the traffic to start moving again. And that's when I saw the singing psychic. He was dancing around on those spindly crow legs of his, clapping his hands in tune to his own song as he weaved along the pavement. The last time I'd seen him was that afternoon with Cali outside Ravenshead village hall, so it seemed strange to see him again and oddly comforting. He danced around and then his eyes caught mine and he jigged towards the vehicle. As he came closer, his song became more audible…'Ta da, ta da, ta da, she comes from afar; the sky will open, and she'll steal your heart, ta da, ta da, ta da…' It was exactly the same tune he'd sung to me that first time. How strange that he even remembered. He kept on singing the tune again and again before he became distracted by someone else further up the road, and he moved on. It was the first bit of oddness I'd experienced these past months. The traffic began moving again and, soon, I was home.

The farm settled into stillness and the evening began to wane. I shivered. There'd be a heavy frost tonight, a heavy frost that would bring in winter solstice, the shortest day. Maybe I should start thinking about moving on in the new year, perhaps return to Edinburgh for a while, or somewhere new. Aye, perhaps that's what I'll do.

A sulphur glow emanated from the barn housing the stalls. It made me think of nativity stories. All that was missing was the bright star directly overhead, three kings, and a token donkey. I strolled over and found Pete checking the horses, making sure they had enough hay.

'It'll be a cold one tonight,' he said, rubbing his hands together, and then added, 'You're late back.'

'I visited Verity and then I was caught up in festive shopping traffic on the way back. It's a nightmare out there.'

He laughed. 'Consumer madness: never did understand it.'

He tied up the last hay net. The horses were sleepy-eyed and comfortable in their stalls layered thick with straw: a warm bed to keep out the frost, which was silently creeping, suspending everything it touched.

'Bet you can't guess who I saw on the way back,' I said.

'Santa Claus? Tree fairy? Snow White and the seven dwarfs? Okay, I give up.'

'The singing psychic!'

'Oh,' he simply said.

He swept the yard brush over the concrete floor: three pointless sweeps.

'The last time I saw him was when I was with Cali,' I continued. 'It was just odd. He sang that tune again, the same one he sang to me in the pub that night.'

'Don't pay any attention – there's nothing in what he says. I was wrong. And, if you dwell on what he says, you'll end up going mental.'

'What do you mean?'

He leant the yard brush against the whitewashed wall and then hesitated before speaking, as if wondering whether to say anything at all.

'Well, I started drinking a lot, didn't I?'

'Aye, it didn't go unnoticed.'

'Well, it's because I was worried about my son. You see, the singing psychic had approached me one night and he had a tune for me. It was something like, 'he will come, and he will go, and there will be sorrow,' or words to that effect. Of course, as Ellie had just found out we were expecting our boy I put two and two together and arrived at ten. The whole thing multiplied and I got it into my head that I'd lose him.'

'That's crazy... but you don't think that now, do you?'

'No, I don't, thanks to Cali.'

My eyes quizzed him. As always, my heart flitted with the mere mention of her name.

'Okay, do you remember that afternoon when Cali healed the lame stallion?' he began, standing with his hands in his pockets. 'Well, afterwards, she had that quiet word with me... told me she knew what I was worrying about. She said I'd not to worry as my son would be healthy and live a long life. She reassured me everything would be fine, and I believed her... and I believed her because I'd seen what she'd done with the horse. You thought I hadn't noticed that supernatural light coming from her hands, but I did. That moment changed everything for me because I knew your girl was gifted in ways I'd never imagined.'

I smiled. 'She was – is – gifted, Pete. Even now, I'm still discovering how much good she did while she was here.'

'Anyway, that singing psychic doesn't get it right every time.'

'No, just 99.9 per cent of the time,' I said, raising my eyebrows. 'Maybe he was referring to something or someone else.'

'Well, that did cross my mind, and actually I thought that someone was you... and you very nearly did go with Cali.'

'Aye, that's true. And you know if I had the opportunity, I'd go with her tomorrow if I could.'

'I know you would, bro. I know.'

He placed his heavy hand on my shoulder and then switched off the main lights and closed the door behind us as we stepped out into the night's sharp air. Above us, stars glowed like tea lights bobbing in a black sea.

'I used to think of heaven when I looked up at the stars,' Pete said, his face turned to the canopy above. 'Now, I think of other worlds, of other beings like us, and of other beings not like us... and of your girl travelling between those stars, doing her job.' He laughed. 'Still seems fecking mad!'

I shook my head and laughed. My icy breath billowed ghostly into the night's air. He gave me a brotherly thump on my shoulder, and strode back towards the farmhouse.

'What's real, hey?'

'Who the hell knows,' he said, as he strolled back to the farmhouse.

The sky was indeed alive, and full of worlds upon worlds, and Cali was out there dancing between those stars, doing her job as Pete said. In some ways, it was only as if she was living in some other country. Oh but how I missed her. The empty winter fields slept, with spring just a mere dream. Everything around me was ice-glazed and the fells glistened white. An owl hooted and then flew across the low pasture, startling me for a moment although, after everything I'd seen and experienced, nothing much startled me any more. I followed the owl's swooping flight, wondering if it was Cali's grandmother checking up on me. In my heartbeat's runaway quickening, some other beat raged, one that I had tried to bury and forget. I shivered again, surrendering all that I was to all that I was yet to become, and a new acceptance sailed into harbour. I went into the lodge and closed the door.

∞∞∞∞∞∞∞∞

'So begins the silent counting.'

The date was 21 December. As I turned a page of my desk journal to begin a new entry, my heart stuttered. There, between the thick cream sheets, was a folded slip of crisp white paper. I trembled. It had my name on the front written in Cali's flamboyant scrawl.

I hesitated, staring at it, a thousand thoughts flocking in my head. I picked up the piece of paper and held it to my face, breathing in as if some essence of her was trapped in paper or ink.

Slowly, I unfolded the paper to reveal a poem...

A Forbidden Moment

A blue wash overhead
matches my dress, and I am
sky this day:
ethereal and vibrant.
And you see it with knowing eyes
as you fall into me, carelessly
sipping a forbidden moment
and savouring it as if our last.
You unfold me
freeing the petals of my soul
sensing our time is uncertain

as we stand in nature's brightness
by solitary tree and stream
listening to teasing whispers
stroking these Lakeland hills.
We moved stars that day
and still it haunts me. Sometimes
I'm breathless with the thought
... what if?

At the end, she'd written: 'Whatever happens, Tom, know that our love is always now. I love you. Cali x'

I read the words over and over and over again. I read each line, looking for meaning, until I really was breathless with the thought... what if?

For a long time, I froze at my desk, gazing out of the window to the frost-draped world outside. I drank coffee, lost in the rising steaming swirls, while something feverish stirred within. Had she known that I'd be left behind? Was that why she had cried that final morning? Thoughts spat and I knew that they were questions that couldn't be answered. Maybe she'd put the poem there just in case. She'd said herself that she couldn't be sure of the outcome, and how close... how close I'd been to going with her.

My granddad used to say that there was a time for everything and everything had its time. It seemed obvious now that I wasn't meant to go with her that day.

I made a new entry in my journal:

Winter has settled in the Lakes. The fells are ice-kissed and the valley is resplendent in its white frosted gown. Today, I found a poem Cali wrote for me, tucked between these pages of my journal. I don't know what it means, if it means anything at all, but I'm feeling something swoon inside me... like a promise of tomorrow. I'm going up to Tarn Fell on Crow Howe today, which I've renamed Silverthorn Howe after Cali. It's exactly six months since she disappeared from there and I just need to return, to sit by the tarn for a while. I don't know why. It's simply where I have to be. I'm not expecting her to return but I haven't given up hope. I don't think I ever will. For the short time I knew her, she turned my entire world upside down. I never believed that love could hit me so forcibly or as complete-ly as it did. I know now that what we had – what we still have – is a bond that shatters the very concept of time and space. Love is infinite. Love is everything. No matter where we are, we are only a breath away from each other. I feel her so close. So, I just know that, at some point, we will be together again... Mean-while, I guess I need to make plans... perhaps move back up to Edinburgh in the New Year... apply for a lecturing job in the literature department... or maybe I'll spend my days writing poetry. Who knows? What I do know is that something is shifting within me... and it's time to move on.

I closed my journal and peered through the window. Silverthorn Howe loomed uncertain in the still, early hours. A weak sun began its lazy rise. The hoar-frosted fields, hedge-rows and trees sparkled in this half-light, beckoning me out of the warmth. I put on my walking boots, followed by my knee-length overcoat, grey scarf, gloves, and grey cord cap – not exactly conventional walking attire, although I reckoned that S. T. Coleridge wouldn't have blinked an eye – and I took my shoulder bag, filled with notebook, pencil, my favourite poet-ry book, flask, and Kendal mint cake. I checked my granddad's pocket watch was keeping time and slipped it back in my jacket pocket. I left the sparse shell of my lodgings as I always did, gazing back into a space that had always felt temporary. Yes, perhaps soon I'd move on again. I should give Tristian a call later.

The walk up Silverthorn Howe was exhilarating. On a slow sunlit morning like this, the frosted ground made for challenging terrain. Much of the rutted earth was dotted with frozen water-filled potholes, ice glazed in various degrees of thickness. I skirted the slopes, finding a ghost-path – just a mere hint of previous footfall – and zig-zagged my way along the bracing ascent. As I walked, the morning brightened as the feeble sun peered through the mist-bitten horizon. It was a perfect winter solstice and I felt improved by what would be the gradual return of the light.

I climbed higher, remembering the day when I was last with Cali and Tristian, still hopeful at this point that I would always be with her. This time, I paused to look back. The family farm stooped in the hollow, smoke oozing from its chimney, which slowly joined other smoke trails from the village beyond, creating an eerie eddying white mist. Life was going on as it always had, and I knew that I was from it but no longer part of it. I was just like a drop of water in this icy stream next to me, the stream that wound its way down past the farm, the same stream where Dorothy Wordsworth had once bathed her feet and where I had dipped my own toes while reading my books in summers past. I was like a drop of water, this age-old secret that is water, that was only ever passing through, that was part of the whole but never still, and that was why I couldn't settle. Something inside me was travelling and I felt as though I was always in motion.

A few more feet, and I was at the place where we had abandoned the Land Rover that day. There were still tyre tracks in the ground where the vehicles had been. It was as if no time had passed as I relived those moments, the sense of breathless urgency as we had tried to outrun our hunters. My lungs burned. I had to stop a couple of times to shake the thoughts loose. Further on, over the rise, I reached the plateau by the tarn where the light portal had appeared, taking Cali in what seemed like an instant. The tarn water was iced over now, all a shimmer like frosted glass, but this time the ice was a result of the natural elements: nothing otherworldly about that. I stopped and leant against a jut of cold rock. To the north, mountains and fells, like the scaly back of a giant beast, appeared sleepy in the sullen light. Before me was a clear stretch of hoar-frosted grass that narrowed off to a pathway that we'd never reached that day... that took you through the thick bushes and foliage and beyond to the higher fell. I looked into this space where Cali had disappeared. I looked so intently that the cold watered my eyes. I turned the cap of my flask and poured steaming tea into my cup, welcoming the token warmth. And I waited here, listening for whispers, searching for a way to resolve what was past.

∞∞∞∞∞∞∞∞∞

'Love is everything. Love is all.'

I emptied my cup and let the last drops of tea run out onto the white frost-feathered ground. I thought I'd stay here a while longer. Although it was bitterly cold, the sun was higher now and it was pleasant basking in the muted yellow light. I closed my eyes, and liberated stray thoughts until my mind settled. I didn't notice at first the shifting breeze, but then a low droning noise filled my ears, followed by a rush of air. Everything inside me turned over, ticking fast with realisation, but I was afraid to open my eyes. My breathing quickened. Could it be...? I sat there with gathering expectation, eyes tightly shut as if the action of opening them would make all that I wished for disappear. And then I heard her voice.

'Tom,' she said, gently. 'It's okay.'

My mouth trembled. And still I dared not open my eyes for fear that I was experiencing the ghost of her or some remnant of times gone by.

Then I felt the warmth of her hand touching my face and it was so real that I instantly opened my eyes. She was standing in front of me, eyes bright and empathic. She was dressed in a simple robe of what appeared to be silver satin. That river of dark hair cascaded over her shoulders and the air danced with the essence of her honeysuckle perfume. I shook my head, unsure. Were my senses deceiving me?

'I'm dreaming.'

'If you are, then so am I,' she replied, smiling.

I eased myself up. My eyes searched hers. I grabbed hold of her hands. She was here. She was actually here. I pulled her to me, embraced her, and she cradled her head against my chest and we held together like that for uncountable moments. My heart pounded against my chest. Tears filled our eyes.

'I'm sorry it took me so long to remember... to work out a way of coming back to you.'

'I always held on to hope,' I gasped.

I was shaking, not with cold but with emotion. We were here in the moment: past, present, and future. We kissed, and I knew for certain that I wasn't dreaming.

'You remembered what you'd forgotten.'

'Yes, I remembered,' she said. 'I remembered what grandmother told me. The ceremony came back to me as if I was there, as if I'd turned back a page in time, and I saw my child self and the knowledge that was lost to me. And it became clear I was being prepared to journey through other realms even then, that the guides had visited grandmother and that I was chosen, and that I accepted being chosen. It was the night that grandmother gave me her labradorite pendant, the night of a thousand meteors. And, yes, every word spoken that star-filled night came back to me.'

She paused to squeeze my hands, to keep reassuring me that she was really here.

'My grandmother had told me that I would have free passage between the stars. I was chosen to be a traveller between realms: to heal, to learn, to experience, to grow, so that I could spread the message of love, peace, and nurture throughout the universe. What she'd told me to remember was that I could travel at will. I had the ability to master the light. That once I'd acclimatised to the energy involved, I would be able to travel freely between dimensions, as easily as jumping in a car and driving away. All I had to do was focus my thoughts.'

'And you did... and you're here.'

She laughed, with that cheery singsong laugh I thought I would never hear again. 'It seems so simple now, so easy. Why did it take me so long to remember?'

'I guess everything happens in its own time,' I said, remembering again what my granddad had told me.

'It's been agonising to be so close to you and yet out of reach, so close that I have seen you at times, just a whisper away. Those times, I shouted so loud, I'm sure I made the veil between worlds shiver. And you had an inkling, more often than not, that I was there.'

'Aye, I did. There were times I felt you so close, but there was nothing I could do.'

Behind us, the portal was still shimmering brightly, like an earth-bound star, and questions filled my mouth.

'You're not staying?'

'No, I have to return. There is much work to do.'

My stomach lurched at the thought of losing her so soon, all over again.

'How long before you return? I'll wait forever, if I have to...'

'You don't have to wait. You can come with me... if you still wish?'

'Really? You mean now?'

'Yes,' she laughed, 'right now.'

It was as if I'd woken from a nightmare having spent the past six months apart. Of course I wanted to go with her. I felt no hesitation. I'd been ready to move on, only daring to imagine in those soaring moments before sleep that I'd be moving in terms of light years with my love by my side. All this time, I'd held on to the possibility. Now, it was happening. It was really happening.

And, so, I held her hand and we walked towards the trembling portal.

For a moment, I paused, in awe of the light glowing and weaving in front of us. 'What happens when we step into the light?'

She smiled, reassuring me. 'We wake up and start living our dreams.'

We stepped forwards and the light engulfed us. There was a moment of silence and intense brightness: a moment of complete stillness. And then *whoosh*, we were travelling, a kind of moving without actually moving. It was the weirdest sensation ever and it was so fast that the space around us distorted. I laughed. Was this really happening? We held on to each other, smiling, eyes meeting eyes, hearts beating one song, and we were safe in the knowing that love was everything.

∞∞∞∞∞∞∞∞

'In peace, we travel with you.'

PROFESSOR TRISTIAN NEEBLE'S DIARY

25 January

U pon being informed that Tom had gone missing, I knew he'd reunited with Cali. I knew this before they found his flask and empty cup on Silverthorn Howe, before I'd even had chance to read his journal, and before I received the envelope he'd left for me.

The note inside said:

'Tristian, if you're reading this, then you'll know Cali returned... and I'm with her.

Writing this now, my emotions still raw after losing her at summer solstice, it's hard to believe it will happen. Yet I live in hope. Sometimes, I think I hear her calling me. Often, I feel her near, as if she's only a breath away. So, I write this, daring to believe she'll find a way of coming back to me.

And, if you find me gone, be happy for me. I don't know if we'll return, whether we even can. All I know for certain is that I love her and I'll give anything to be with her. I know you'll understand. I've come to realise love is all. It might even be the secret holding the universe together. Imagine that!

It seems odd writing this and yet I think, in doing so, I'm writing the future, setting the intention, as Cali would say, manifesting the reality I've been dreaming of. Perhaps we really are creating reality with each passing thought. Now, how would that change physics?

I'll miss you, Tristian. Be brilliant, love deeply, and have a good life. I'm certain that we'll meet again, one day, perhaps as soon as you've locked down the physics. Until then, farewell, my friend.

Tom

PS. In the envelope, you'll find the crystal Cali brought back. You should have this, Tristian, because there are secrets within. Just watch the light inside the crystal flashing, and then think of me and Cali. Think real hard and, all being well, you will see what I mean.'

I examined the crystal. I focused on it for quite some time and thought of Tom and Cali. And, yes, after a while it seemed to do strange things. The light began to pulse. The colour changed from blue to silver to crystal-clear as I held it in the palm of my hand. It appeared to be emitting a signal. An image flickered into view, and I blinked. Two figures appeared and I realised it was Tom and Cali. It was like watching a tiny video screen. I'm not sure how the images were transmitted but I really could see them, smiling, waving to me, and behind them a blue crystalline mountain, and two moons hung low in the sky. After a few seconds, the light in the crystal stopped pulsating, and the images disappeared.

I laughed, marvelling at how I'd watched a video from another dimension in time and space. How extraordinary... or perhaps not. You see, it's only extraordinary until it's explained, and right now I'm working on that. I'm working on finding a way into these other dimensions. Tom's right. There are secrets locked within this crystal. In the wider physical world, there are hints that suggest some of the equations are wrong, and I must turn things upside down, work out how to decipher them to find a way through to the other side. A new theory is waiting its conception, a new theory of everything and, with it, a bold awakening for science and humanity. And so, it begins.

'The conduit is closing.'

Author's Extras

"My aim, with all my writing, is to take the reader on an extraordinary journey and leave them believing that all things are possible." - Carol Anne Strange

www.CarolAnneStrange.com

Acknowledgements

I am grateful for everyone who's been present with me over the years of bringing this work to fruition. I dare not try to name you all individually as I'm conscious of inadvertently leaving someone out, and that just wouldn't do. So, I give thanks to my soul kin, family, and friends, particularly for understanding my long absences when visiting other realms. I give thanks to all the amazing kindred spirits I've met or communicated with, including all the shining ones communing through my website, Facebook, Spiritual Network, and email. You know who you are and I am truly grateful for being in the presence of such sparkling individuals.

If we have exchanged words or blissful silent togetherness, if we have spent time together on the shores of this or other worlds, then you have my heart gratitude for sharing the journey.

I love you all.

Production Acknowledgements

Where bringing Light Weaver into the physical realm is concerned, I would like to give special thanks to ...

Mark Fenwick for his belief in me and for sharing the journey from the start by accompanying me on research trips and providing his services as a publisher.

Andrew Wille for intuitive guidance, enlightening expertise, and for giving me courage to make necessary leaps.

Richard Crookes for cover design and map illustration and Robert Clark for editing services.

Kindred writers, graduates, and tutors at University College Falmouth MA Professional Writing for guidance, inspiration, encouragement and support.

I would also like to thank Goldfrapp and Franz Ferdinand for musical inspiration; Professor Brian Cox and Professor Jeff Forshaw for physics inspiration; Kendal Library and their mobile library service; the magnificent muses and my SGs for creative inspiration and guidance; and kin light weavers (in this realm and others) for their loving presence.

About the Author

I was born in Lancashire, England in 1964 and brought up in a former blacksmith's cottage by the river. This was the beginning of my Starsong Journey. My childhood was filled with curiosity, nature, magic, and mystery. I recall timeless moments sat on the riverbank; long sweet summers cantering through tall oat grass; copies of *The Unexplained* magazine appearing from who-knows-where; a living room full of antique clocks all ticking away to their own time; obtaining spooky results from using the Zener cards; and building spaceships so I could return to the stars.

At the age of ten, a magazine published my letter about the moon and my telescope. The idea of being able to communicate widely through my writing enthralled me and this first little achievement provided a glimpse of my future. Star-gazing, and dreaming of worlds beyond, teased my imagination, as did my interest in life's mysteries and the unexplained, and thus began a journey fuelled by fascination.

Growing up, I didn't much care for many of life's conventions. I walked the human road and, for a time, I struggled against everything that was expected of me or considered 'normal'. Somehow, I made it through school only to find even more curious expectations, ways, and conventions that seemed just as alien and often illogical. I was now, however, free to walk my own path and explore.

In 1985, I started freelance writing, often drawing upon my knowledge and experience in holistic health, well-being, fitness, and personal growth. My articles appeared in print and digital format worldwide. Over the years, I added to my skills and experience of living a creative life.

After authoring non-fiction books and ghost-writing many self-development publications, I embarked on a rich variety of creative projects involving poetry, prose, art, film and fiction. I also mentored other writers and partnered a small online publishing company. During this time, my relationship with nature, love for the arts, and insatiable interest in science and the spiritual and mysterious realms deepened, inspiring my journey as a creative writer.

In 2009, I gained a place on the MA Professional Writing course with University College Falmouth. My aim was to focus on writing fiction. I completed the MA in January 2011 and passed with Distinction. Although the journey was challenging, I left with a solid draft of Light Weaver and a better understanding of the fiction writing process.

Light Weaver is the first of many contemporary novels with a reality-questioning theme. Today, I continue to be strangely fascinated with life and its possibilities and divide my time between writing fiction, living creatively, and travelling between realms. Right now, I'm on my Starsong journey, doing the work I came here to do and tuning into the vast wisdom of the cosmos. Like some of the characters in my novel, I'm receiving downloads. I know my true path. It is my hope that through my words, I can share sparks of wisdom and inspiration, and leave my readers with a preview of their own potential and a glimpse of what might be.

A Conversation with the Author

What drives you to write?

I'm motivated and fuelled by the question, 'what if?' I've always had an insatiable curiosity. Anything that challenges the standard model of reality is a concept I love to explore and feeds my writing. Apart from aiming to tell a good story, driven by its characters' journeys, I hope to inspire my readers to question the nature of reality and perhaps see the world from a new perspective. I aim to show the ordinary in the extraordinary and the extraordinary in the ordinary, creating believable stories that evoke thought or spark an emotional response. Equally, I'm driven to write through wanting to share my stories and ideas with others of like-mind.

What inspired you to write Light Weaver?

I've always been fascinated with the idea of other realms existing beyond our own. Equally, I'm intrigued by being able to travel between such realms or other dimensions crossing into ours. One day I began thinking: what if a guy fell in love with a girl who was travelling into other dimensions? Lots of thoughts leapt out from that question, turning sparks into fireworks.

How did you come up with the novel's title?

In 2007, I moved to a little house on the edge of a country valley park in Lancashire. One morning, a mobile library rolled up the road and parked across from my writer's nest. In that instance, The Mobile Librarian was born, and that was my working title right up until the cover was being designed.

It was at this point that Richard Crookes, the cover designer, tentatively suggested that the cover illustration didn't fit with the Mobile Librarian title. So, I spent a few days with the magnificent muses birthing the new title and, in the end, it wasn't so difficult to realise. Light Weaver had already been mentioned in the novel, and it felt like it should have always been called this.

When did you begin and complete the writing of Light Weaver?

Although I'd been gathering ideas for a while, I actually began officially researching and writing the novel in the summer of 2009 when I was six months' into my MA Professional Writing with University College Falmouth. I completed a rough first draft by the end of that year and a more substantial draft by the end of the course in 2011. The manuscript spanned five drafts in total before I felt the work was suitably finished.

Did you encounter any difficulties in the writing?

As it was my debut novel, the process was particularly challenging. It was a curious learning journey and one that was often experimental in terms of finding what worked best when it came to weaving those words in the most effective way. As I was writing the novel as part of my MA, I had a tremendous amount of feedback from tutors and peers. This was fantastic and greatly appreciated but I had to learn to be discerning and take only what I felt was needed to do the work. The novel went through much change through each draft. It was only during work on a late draft, while working under the supervision of Andrew Wille, I decided upon a radical change of direction. After some gentle prompting from Andrew, I made the decision to drop the dual first-person narrative (originally the story would have been told through both Cali and Tom) and I changed from writing in present tense to past tense. The shift was a dramatic one but, ultimately, felt right. Sometimes, you just have to run with your instincts and, as a result, any niggling doubts are overcome in the process.

Do you have a particular process for writing novels?
It's very much like a journey. You start with an itch to travel, you begin making plans and then you immerse yourself in the voyage. For me, the novel begins with a spark ... a single thought, feeling, situation or scenario. Often, these come as instant downloads, dropped into my head like an email from an unknown sender. In these moments, I'm tuned into a vast field of creative consciousness. I breathe air into the spark and ask, 'what if?' I then begin to visualise characters, story and plot in terms of scenes rather than chapters, and continually add layers to create depth. My writing process is visual in a filmic way. Usually, a scene plays out in my head and then I write. The whole process is aided by research on an informational, experiential, and sensory basis. I visit locations and immerse myself in the mood of a place. Sometimes, strange or curious things happen around me that provide fruitful inspiration. Music is crucial to the process, too. It helps to evoke mood – not just my own but the mood of the characters and setting. As I embark on the journey of writing, I continue receiving inspired downloads until the final draft. It's an enlightening but all-consuming journey.

What part of the writing process do you enjoy the most?
It has to be when the writing is flowing as if directed from some invisible force. It's also the point when I see the story and characters come to life. During this time, the world I've created is as real to me as life around me. It's as if the story is playing out in another dimension, as if the characters actually exist. Once I finish, the characters remain with me, like friends in a distant place. So, I guess the most enjoyable aspect of the writing process is aiming to create a story and characters that come alive in my readers' hearts and remain in their memories.

How important is the connection with nature in your writing?
It is hugely important in that it inspires and nurtures my writing. Since childhood, I recognised nature's magic and our ability to heal through being in tune and in balance with mother Earth. Spending forever moments on the riverbank, running and skipping through tall oat grass, and dreaming skywards while sitting in the rooted lap of an oak tree opened up a channel to something precious and often unseen. Not only did this connection instil a profound reverence for all life, it made me acutely aware of worlds that exist between worlds. I realised how privileged we are in nature's abundance.

Light Weaver is, fundamentally, a love story. Did you have that in mind when you started writing it?
Absolutely! Love is usually at the core of my writing and especially so in this novel. As I've come to know, even the forces of love can change the nature of one's reality.

Do you feel guided in your writing, as if it's being channelled or coming from a muse?

I receive what I call 'downloads' and this applies to my writing and to my life's journey as a whole. From a writing perspective, I usually receive guidance in terms of ideas and prompts, which often arrive in words and images. Assistance and inspiration also comes in other ways. For example, I'm always where I need to be at any particular time to experience or observe something that will inform my writing. This has always been the case. Some would consider these 'downloads' to be channelled messages, flashes of inspiration, guidance from source, or a direct link to a creative muse. On reflection, they are all of these at different times.

Are your locations real or imagined?

They are both. Light Weaver is primarily set in the English Lake District. You'll perhaps recognise some of the 'real' places, such as Coniston, Rydal, Grasmere, Kendal, Ulpha, and Silverdale (which is actually on the Lancashire / Cumbria border). I have, however, taken the liberty of stretching Cumbria's geological fabric to drop in a few new villages and towns. Maybe you'll stumble across them one day when exploring another dimension of Lakeland.

What would you like your readers to take from Light Weaver?

I hope they'll look at the world around them with a different perspective. I hope they'll find a subtle message somewhere within the story (or between the words) that resonates in an inspirational way. Mostly, I hope they'll enjoy the story and find whatever they need to enrich life's journey.

Some of your readers admit to being intuitively drawn towards your work. Why do you think this is happening?

I greatly believe we are guided towards what our spirit needs at any given time. Even though Light Weaver is a novel, the imagination blurs the edges between fact and fiction. There are plenty of very real possibilities and emotions running through the story and, while writing, I was mindful that the work itself was already weaving its light into the sub-conscious minds and hearts of kindred spirits. The work isn't me. It's part of something far more significant. And that's why I'm sure Light Weaver will find its readers and vice versa.

Did anything strange happen, such as unusual coincidences, while you were writing the novel?

During the writing of Light Weaver, I felt constantly tuned in to 'radio cosmos' and, as a result, I was certainly more aware of energetic presences, gifts from nature, whispers on the breeze, more active dream-time, vibrational tones, flashes of light, visual prompts, and information downloads. On many occasions, when I felt the most inspired, I experienced an awareness of invisible others in the room with me. Oh but strange things happen around me all the time. It's no coincidence that I am strange by name, and attract strange happenings by nature.

What are you working on next?

At the time of writing this in 2012, I'm working on my second novel, which is set in Scotland. It's about an astronomer whose beliefs are challenged. I also have other novels in development, which will likely have me travelling between realms for the foreseeable.

If you weren't a writer, what would you be?
A wandering spirit, probably.

Thank you to Joanne May, Roy Hale, Louise McCully, David Cook, Clare Whittam, Jackie Devereaux, and Philip Hilton for their questions.

Light Weaver

Signs, Secrets, and Symbolism

If you look between the seams of a page and the space between the lines, you will often find stories within stories. Light Weaver is no exception. It is full of little signs, secrets, and symbolism, which I feel is in keeping with my curious nature and the abiding question that drives me: what if?

Allow me to share just a few of the story's signs and symbolism, including some of the more obvious little curiosities as well as clues for further investigation.

Some of my characters' names are anagrams. You may have already guessed that my dear Professor - Tristian Neeble - is an anagram of Albert Einstein. Some of the other characters' names are also anagrams with physics or astronomical references: Matt Darker (Dark Matter); Mea Drodan (Andromeda); Verity Lait (Relativity) and Henry Ligget (Light Energy). There may be other anagrams I'm not consciously aware of. Perhaps you'll find those.

As for Tom Philips and Cali Silverthorn, you may be able to create some anagram from their names but they weren't chosen with that purpose. Their story is a secret.

There are certain key words and numbers mentioned often throughout the novel. You may have noticed them. The ones I'm aware of include Silver, Seven and Eleven. You'll find there are others. These mentions are by no means accidental but I can't tell you why they are so prominent. Perhaps you can make sense of it.

Water is also particularly relevant. We all know how important water is to life but this secret that is water will surprise us yet. I dare say that Professor Neeble, or someone like him, will be looking into the deeper connection we have with water. Perhaps then, the conduit will fully open.

Nature is the lyrical rhythm of the story, the constant song. The evolving and enduring landscape, shaped over millions of years, has a magical omnipotence connecting Tom and Cali. Of course, our Earth mother is what connects us all.

Birds fly freely through these pages. They are of land and sky, messengers from worlds beyond, and symbolic of the connection between this realm and others.

As for Light Weaver's secrets, well, they just wouldn't be secrets if I told you what they are. They are for the seekers to find. In time, someone may make a discovery as a result of some essence derived from reading between the pages and lines of this work: someone with a busy mind and pure heart. There will, however, be secrets that remain forever hidden. Oh but who knows what will come to light when someone with a curious mind starts to explore?

Reality is questionable and, in many ways, deeply subjective. The truth isn't out there; the truth is within you. Read between the lines, dear readers. Look beyond. Other worlds are there to be explored.

Love Light, Star-kin ...

Carol Anne Strange

THE STAR BEINGS' MESSAGE TO HUMANITY

The conduit is open ...

Question your eyes; there are other worlds within yours that you do not see.

Life is an illusion. You are the dreamer and the dream.

The weft of the universe is so finely woven.

There is always light in the darkness. There is always darkness in the light.

Everything is connected to the same source.

Look beyond the equations for the answer.

Do not be confused by conflicting voices. Listen to the ancient ones. Wait for their signs. They walk upon the Earth with you.

The ancient ones are kindred. Listen to their song. They speak in symbols and whispers.

The time has come to awaken.

Thought is energy.

Be settled in your heart. You will know.

Thought moves through dimensions without limits.

Time is immaterial. What you see in the physical realm is temporary.

Your world has many doorways into other dimensions. Open your mind and you will see.

We are one of many walking beside you. We are one of many just a breath away.

We are all energy, resonating at different rates.

Do you hear the rhythm in your veins? Listen! We are all one song.

Why seek what you already have?

Work with the elements and symbols. In nature, everything is as it's supposed to be.

Light is more than what it seems. Thought is the light. Thought directs light.

Past, present, and future co-exist. Other realities co-exist.

The world is as you dream it.

Everything is energy. Everything exists because of energy.

Move without moving to reach your destination.

It begins with consciousness.

What you think expands the universe.

What you know is not constant.

You are more than your physical journey. You are more than your earthly experience.

You are of the stars.

When you shift your perception, other dimensions become visible.

Life is a magical manifestation.

Embrace the moment; it is where all things begin and end.

What you see is of your own creation. There is no beginning or end: just motion.

The ultimate truth is within you.

So begins the silent counting.

Love is everything. Love is all.

In peace, we travel with you.

... The conduit is closing.

An Ending

Lightning Source UK Ltd.
Milton Keynes UK
UKHW041333280222
399337UK00005B/1353